D1707024

Marfa
for the
Perplexed

Lonn Taylor

MARFA
FOR THE PERPLEXED

LONN TAYLOR

Illustrations by Avram Dumitrescu
Foreword by Sterry Butcher

MARFA BOOK COMPANY
Marfa, Texas

Marfa Book Company
105 S Highland
Marfa, Texas

ISBN-13: 978-0-692-07611-8

for Gene West
who taught me about Marfa

CONTENTS

MARFA PAST AND PRESENT

MARFA PEOPLE

DOWN ON THE RIVER

SCENES OF A TOWN: THE WHY OF MARFA

WELCOME TO MARFA. People who visit or read about our town invariably have a lot of questions about the place. Are the Marfa Lights real? (Yes.) Are you an artist? (No.) Why do the shops and restaurants have unpredictable hours? (They just do.) What was Don Judd like? (Complicated, like the rest of us.) I've never been the tinkerer who takes apart the toaster or the vacuum to see how it works and therefore the questions about what Marfa is or what it isn't sometimes baffle me. I can appreciate, however, that other people want to see the ghost in the machine; they want to know how the place works. Thank goodness for Lonn Taylor. For all those who want to know the "why" of Marfa, Lonn's terrific, thoughtful and comprehensive range of essays will be a big help.

A certain suspension of disbelief by the reader, or at least a willingness to be open to elements that are unseen or unarticulated, will also be useful. Here's what I mean. A visiting Lannan Foundation writer some years ago was intrigued by Marfa's name. The old story is that railroad surveyors needed a name for a water stop along the line. One of the surveyors had his wife on board and she volunteered the name Marfa, plucked handily from the

11

Brothers Karamazov, which she was reading. The Lannan writer became convinced this story was patently false. The novel's date of publication and its appearance in this country apparently didn't jibe with the town's 1880s formation. He tried vigorously to convince people that the name was actually related to the Marfa Lights and had to do with a phosphorescent sea phenomenon called "mar-fire," that was later conjugated to Marfa. He published his findings in the newspaper, hoping for a lively debate, as happens sometimes on the local editorial page. No one, however, wrote in. No one cared. The story we already had suited Marfa just fine.

Marfans have something of a history of believing what they want to believe, regardless of whether it flies in the face of sense or fact. Take Don Judd, for instance. In the pre-internet, pre-cell phone, pre-Instagram days of the 1970s, Don Judd arrived in Marfa to remake a former military base into a synthesis of architecture and landscape that would work in seamless concert with the artwork he installed there, and he did so with the audacious notion that the work would be permanent. He knew his ideas about art placement, permanence and location were great, even if hardly anyone else initially agreed. He was right, of course. Judd's milled aluminum pieces never move but always change, their silvery forms shifting, floating and disappearing as sunlight slips over them. The concrete pieces in the field are purposeful and powerful but they also present a mystery in their sets of variations. How many iterations are there? What will this material do? How much do the sun and clouds and grassland matter? What else is possible?

And that's the crux of Marfa: plumbing the question of what is possible. It's a generous thing, to point out the limitlessness of the universe. Judd put an art museum of permanent work in an isolated, poverty-stricken, hard-to-access town set in a landscape of tremendous, austere and untamable beauty. If that perversity and its genius float your boat, you're probably inclined to be a doer yourself. Maybe you'd put on a play, start a band, coach soccer, write poetry, organize a health clinic, open a restaurant, learn Chinese, paint, drive a Meals-On-Wheels route, make boots, or all of the above. In Marfa, there is freedom to pursue dreams of all stripes and the tolerance of others to support that. The sparse population demands participation—we're all we've got, after all—and because we're a small town, we end up in friendships and relationships that we may never have had in a more citified, rarified, populated place. Judd sought an existence in which art intersected daily life and, in a way, that's how we ended up, in a place informed by creative energy but also deeply committed to one another as neighbors and friends. When you know everyone, everyone matters, and if they're doing something they believe is serious or important, then it's serious and important. Living in a small town tends to emphasize and escalate what we're supposed to know about the wide world: you need to be kind; you need to help; you need to contribute.

Judd didn't invent this generosity of spirit—it was already here and ingrained in the community by the generations of people who have lived here since the town was founded in the 1880s, many of whom are chronicled in Lonn's pages. My theory is that Marfa's remoteness and its lack of people or resources forced its people to be open to the eccentricities of whoever came along. When there are just a few people to make a community work, you have to take people as they come, whether they're a homemaker, a cowboy or a kilt-wearing artist from New York. You never know who you might need.

I moved to Marfa in the early 1990s, when it was a little dying cowtown. There wasn't much to do and no one had money to do anything anyway. Often nights were quiet, since there wasn't any place to go. The hoots of the great horned owls at the courthouse floated down the street. In winter, you could hear the stars blink on and off. Sometimes a few folks would congregate on the tailgates of pickups parked on Highland Avenue, Marfa's main drag. We counted the cars that passed; we waited for something to happen. Stories about Marfa unfurled on those nights and some of them explained a lot about the place.

Long ago, the people of Marfa became upset with the priest, whom they felt was not doing a good job. He was impatient, he was lazy, but the diocese would not send another to replace him. One Sunday, the congregation had more than they could take. The men packed up the priest and marched him off to the railroad tracks, where they allegedly stopped a train, hustled the priest on board and told the engineer to put him off in El Paso. For this, I was told, God will never bless Marfa.

Three or four cottonwoods grow in the creek that winds through Pinto Canyon, southwest of Marfa. These are strong, old trees that grow close together. Their leaves clap together like applause. Long ago, a family was traveling through the desolate, rugged canyon and they ran short of provisions. They stopped at a ford in the creek. The father left his wife, Eleanor, and their children at the ford and said he'd return with help, but he never came back. Eleanor and her children died at that spot and the cottonwoods grew where they expired. It's called the Trees of Eleanor, and the place, despite its beauty, is cursed.

And, long ago, a young lady from a decent family defied her

parents' wishes and snuck out the window to go to a dance at the venue that's now called Liberty Hall. She danced all night with a charming stranger, a well-dressed dandy with a bespoke suit, bewitching dark eyes and a courtly manner. At the end of the night, when the lights came up and the enchantment of the dance began to dissolve, the couples parted and everyone noticed, with horror, that the charming stranger had the feet of a chicken. The girl had danced with the devil and that, I was told, is why Marfa will never prosper.

Sitting on the cold steel of the tailgate and swatting at mosquitos, these tales were imparted with sadness and gravity and that is how I received them. The storytellers believed them very deeply. If they think it happened, I am not the one to say it didn't.

Marfa balances between permanence and impermanence. I suppose every place exists similarly, but here that balancing act seems much more fraught and fragile and obvious due to the landscape: the broad, unpeopled ocean of grass, the bald old mountains and the constant conversation of the wind. The sky is inescapable; the rocks do not change. It makes you feel small, because you are small. Despite our insignificance, people young, old and in-between are finding each other in Marfa. They're teaching school, opening shops, staking a claim, taking chances, having kids, volunteering like crazy, trying things out. Marfa's successes and its slow evolution aren't due to the single accomplishments of a few folks who just swooped in, but rather the long-term, careful and deliberate commitment of a wide range of people—recent arrivals and native Marfans alike—who choose to be here and choose to make this a vibrant community, for better or worse. It's an act of faith to be here, faith that it'll all work out, faith that people will look out for you, that you won't go broke, that you'll find contentment amid the loneliness. There ain't no guarantees.

There is an unexpected development lately: people now sometimes visit Marfa with art and Judd as afterthoughts, here because they've heard it's a place abuzz with hipsters and cool stuff to do or see. Theirs is an incomplete version of Marfa, and I tend to think those folks are missing out, but they don't usually stick around anyway. We'll continue to do what we're doing. Marfa's perplexing mysteries linger and its future won't untangle until we get there. Cottonwoods grew where Eleanor died. The devil danced in Marfa. Judd's concrete works loom stolid and solemn in the pasture. Some things are not meant to be understood fully.

— Sterry Butcher

INTRODUCTION

FIRST, A DISCLAIMER. I do not live in Marfa. I live in Fort Davis, 22 miles north of Marfa. But I have observed Marfa for the better part of 15 years and have occasionally recorded my observations in the column, "The Rambling Boy," that I write for the Marfa weekly newspaper, the *Big Bend Sentinel*. Those columns have provided the kernels for the essays in this book.

In those 15 years I have watched Marfa change from an artists' retreat grafted onto a small West Texas town to a mecca for tourists, corporate retreats, and destination weddings. Chartered jets arrive more frequently at Marfa's airport now than they did 15 years ago. The local Chamber of Commerce recently hired a team of consultants to show them how to bring more large groups to Marfa, which may or may not be a good idea. It is getting harder and harder to get a cup of coffee on a Saturday morning, although the number of places to get one and the price of the coffee have both increased.

Even though the publicity about Marfa in national newspapers has brought increasing numbers of visitors to Marfa each year, one thing has not changed. Most visitors come here to see the art and experience the lifestyle but have absolutely no knowledge of the history of Marfa and the Big Bend or of the multiple cultures that flourish here, and are consequently puzzled by what they find. If you are one of those people who wonder what a carne asada burrito or a calf-roping is and why you can buy one at the other, this book is for you.

I sometimes tell people that the entire history of the Big Bend can be summed up in the lives of four people: Juan Sabeata, Martha Pruett, Don Luis Mendias, and Donald Judd. Like most of written history this is a gross simplification, but a look at those four lives can be instructive.

Juan Sabeata is the first inhabitant of the Big Bend whose name we know. He was probably born about 1650, in one of the Indian villages at the junction of the Rio Grande and the Rio Conchos, about 60 miles south of Marfa, where the twin cities of Presidio, Texas and Ojinaga, Chihuahua are now. We know his name because it appears in both Spanish and French records. It is in those records because Juan Sabeata tried to manipulate these two world empires, rivals for dominance in North America, to save his people. He failed but his story is still worth telling because it shows that the Indian people of the Big Bend were active participants in its history, rather than passive victims of European aggression.

Juan Sabeata's ancestors probably settled at the junction of the two rivers about 1200 CE, and over several hundred years they developed a complex economy that combined irrigated farming in their villages with buffalo hunting on the plains east of Marfa and then trading the buffalo hides for pottery with the Hasinai people

18

of East Texas, making an annual round trip on foot of about a thousand miles.

Juan Sabeata first appears in Spanish records in 1683, when he led a delegation of his people, who the Spanish called Jumanos, to see the Spanish governor of New Mexico in El Paso. The Jumanos wanted Spanish troops to come to their villages to help them defeat the Apaches, aggressive warriors who were encroaching on the Jumanos' buffalo-hunting grounds. Juan Sabeata told the Spanish governor three things. He told him that he and his people were Christians but had no priests to comfort them. He told him that there were 10,000 souls in his villages waiting to be saved. And he told him that on his trips to East Texas he had seen people like the Spanish who came in floating houses but did not speak Spanish.

The governor assumed, as Juan Sabeata hoped he would, that the Europeans in floating houses were from France, Spain's great rival in the New World, and so he sent missionaries and soldiers to the Jumanos, hoping to create a buffer of loyal Indians between himself and the French. But instead of joining the Jumanos in their campaign against the Apaches the soldiers went on a five-month buffalo hunt and returned to El Paso with 5,000 buffalo hides, a very profitable venture.

Juan Sabeata was disgusted and decided that the Spanish were not going to be reliable allies, and so the next year, on his annual trip to East Texas, he met with the French, who under the leadership of the Sieur de la Salle had built a fortified settlement near the Texas coast. The French records of the meeting say that Sabeata told them that he was an enemy of the Spanish and asked them to send him troops or at least give him muskets, intending, of course, to use the troops and guns against the Apaches. The French politely refused, saying that they were traders and not soldiers, and shortly after that Juan Sabeata disappears from history. But the Spanish and French records give us a glimpse of one resourceful resident of the Big Bend who tried to manipulate two empires to benefit his people. As I said, he was unsuccessful. By 1720 the Jumanos themselves had disappeared. They were absorbed by the Apaches. The Apaches were such fierce warriors that they kept settlers out of the Big Bend for the next century. The Spanish called the Big Bend the *despoblado,* the unpopulated land.

Now, let's fast forward to the summer of 1880, when Philip and Martha Pruett and their eleven children drove a herd of 280 cattle west from San Angelo, Texas and settled in the Davis Mountains, thirty miles north of Marfa. Marfa did not yet exist; the only thing between the New Mexico line and the Mexican border was the military post at Fort Davis, established in 1854 to quell the Apaches. The Pruetts rented a one-room adobe house with a dirt floor in Limpia Canyon, just north of the fort, and turned their cattle out on what was euphemistically called the open range, meaning land that belonged to someone else—an absentee owner—who did not know that the Pruetts were using it. They had about 50 milk cows and the children milked those cows while Martha Pruett churned butter three times a day. She sold that butter to the fort for 75 cents a pound. In 1880 land here sold for 25 cents an acre, so every pound of butter Martha Pruett churned would buy three acres of land. Martha put in a vegetable garden and sold vegetables to the fort, and within a year the Pruetts had accumulated $1,800 from government contracting, so to speak.

They used that money to buy some land in Musquiz Canyon, just south of Fort Davis, where in 1883 Philip Pruett built an adobe house and planted some cottonwood trees. Those cottonwood trees are still there, marking the roadside park on the highway between Fort Davis and Alpine. The railroad came to Alpine that year, and Philip was able to get milled lumber, so that house was the first house Martha had ever lived in that had a floor and a ceiling. The railroad also made it possible for her to have her first cookstove and her first sewing machine. She had her twelfth child in that house.

She put in an orchard and a 150-acre irrigated farm and continued to sell milk, butter, and produce to the fort, and, as the country settled up, Philip started pasturing other people's cattle at 25 cents per head per month. They continued to buy more land, and by 1900 they had an 80,000-acre ranch, all from churning butter three times a day. In 1913 they sold that ranch to H.L. Kokernot, and it became the foundation for the 130,000-acre Kokernot 06 Ranch, today one of the 10 largest ranches in Texas.

The third story is about a man named Don Luis Mendias. By 1913, when the Pruetts sold their ranch, the Big Bend had been settled with ranches, the cattle industry here was booming, and Marfa, which had been founded when the railroad arrived in 1883, was a prosperous ranching town. But a revolution had started in Mexico in 1910 that would change Marfa forever, and Don Luis Mendias was part of that change. In 1913 Mendias was a prominent businessman in Ojinaga, part of the town's governing class. He owned a store, a restaurant, and a theatre on the plaza, and held a municipal office. He was in his 60s and was the father of 15 children. On Christmas Day, 1913, Pancho Villa's revolutionary army attacked Ojinaga, and not only the entire Federal army that was supposed to defend the city but about 2,000 civilian refugees fled across the

Rio Grande to Presidio, Texas. Don Luis Mendias was one of those refugees. He loaded several wagons with his household goods and his gold, but he was told that he could take no money and only one vehicle into the United States, so he unpacked his wagons and buried his gold under the porch of his house, and he joined the flow of refugees across the river in a buggy with his wife and younger children, with some money hidden in the baby's blankets. Once on the Texas side of the river, the Mendias family became part of a 12-mile long column of 4,000 refugees, soldiers and civilians, who walked or rode horseback the 67 miles from Presidio to Marfa under U.S. military escort. The column included three Mexican generals. It took them four days to make the trip. They camped out at night beside the road and the army fed them with rations of beans, tortillas, and coffee. When they got to Marfa the soldiers were confined in a pen at Fort D.A. Russell, and were eventually sent by train to El Paso and returned to Mexico, but many of the civilians, including Don Luis Mendias and his family, stayed in Marfa and became the foundation of Marfa's middle class Hispanic community. The census records tell the story. In 1910 30% of the population of Marfa were born in Mexico; in 1920 the figure was 74%. Today Marfa is 68% Hispanic.

Don Luis Mendias, who was 64 when he arrived in Marfa, started life over again. He opened a small store, where he sold tobacco and candy that his wife made in their kitchen. Several of his adult sons joined him and they expanded the store under the name Mendias Hermanos, and eventually opened a theatre next door, the Teatro Libertad. The Mendias family was active in the Hispanic cultural life of Marfa, belonging to the Mutualista Society, the Violeta Club, and the League of United Latin American

Citizens. Their store was in the building that now houses the Get Go Grocery Store.

After the Revolution was over, sometime in the 1930s, some of Don Luis's sons went back to Ojinaga to try to recover the gold their father had hidden, and they heard this story. A drunk had fallen through the rotten floorboards of the porch under which the gold was hidden and had found it. A man who was passing by saw what had happened and tricked the drunk out of the gold. That man used the gold to build a hotel in Ojinaga. A hundred years after Don Luis's arrival here there are still Mendiases in Marfa, and they all know the name of the man who built that hotel.

The final story begins in 1946, when an 18-year old army recruit named Donald Judd passed through Marfa on a bus on his way from basic training in Alabama to his assignment in Korea. He was so impressed with the spacious landscape of the Big Bend that he got off the bus at the next stop, Van Horn, and sent a telegram to his mother in New Jersey. It said, "Dear Mom, Nice town, beautiful country, mountains. Love, Don." After Judd got out of the army he went to art school, and by the 1960s he had developed a reputation in New York as an innovative artist and an insightful art reviewer. He had moved through painting on canvas and was focusing on sculpture, and he had developed a philosophy of art that was shaped around the concept of integration. He felt that art should not be confined by frames or pedestals in museum and gallery exhibits, but should be permanently installed in such a way that it is integrated into the surrounding landscape.

In 1970 Judd began a search for the ideal landscape for his art, and he remembered his bus trip through Marfa. He started coming here in 1971, when Marfa was dying on the vine, the ranching industry ruined by the great drought of 1949–1956. He bought the old army quartermaster depot by the railroad tracks and converted it into a residence for his family and a studio for his work, and in 1979, with the help of the Dia Foundation he purchased most of Fort D.A. Russell, the defunct cavalry post that the quartermaster depot had been established to serve. Judd spent the last 20 years of his life making art here in Marfa—he died in 1994. He eventually acquired 15 downtown properties and 40,000 acres of ranchland south of town, and he created 30 to 50 permanent jobs here.

He invited other artist friends to come here and work and install their works, and the result is that Marfa is now an international art center and people come from all over the world to see the art installations, which are administered by the Chinati Foundation and the Judd Foundation. You can hear at least three languages besides English and Spanish spoken on Highland Avenue any day of the week.

Donald Judd was an individualist and an eccentric. He liked to dress up in a kilt and play the bagpipes, and did not always get along well with his neighbors. He was a precisionist and could not have been an easy person to live with. I think one key to understanding his character, and perhaps his genius, is that, like many proud parents, he recorded his children's growth by measuring their height and making pencil marks on a wall. But he recorded not only their height and the date but the hour and minute that he made the measurements. You can see them today if you tour his residence, marks on the posts that support the loft. Beside them are written the words, "FJ 3/3/83 6:32 PM" and "RJ 3/3/83 6:35 PM."

Donald Judd may have been a little peculiar, but he single-handedly revived the economy of Marfa. He exemplified the individualism that characterized all four of the people in these stories, and that I think characterizes Marfa. One reason that the art community has taken root and flourished here is that Marfans have always respected individualism.

The town of Marfa itself was established as a water stop and shipping point when the Galveston, Harrisburg, and San Antonio Railroad was extended across West Texas to join the Southern Pacific Railroad in 1883. For many years the story was circulated, and even appeared in print in such usually unimpeachable sources as the Texas State Historical Association's *Handbook of Texas*, that the town was named by the wife of a railroad executive for a minor character in Fyodor Dostoevsky's novel *The Brothers Karamazov*. However, in 2008 research by Barry Popik, an etymologist who specializes in slang terms and town names, uncovered an article in the December 17, 1882 *Galveston Daily News*, describing the founding of Marfa and saying that the town was named after one of the characters in Jules Verne's novel *Michael Strogoff, Courier of the Czar*, which was published in 1876 and was immediately translated into English and adapted into a popular play. The fact that *The Brothers Karamazov* was not translated into English until 1912 adds weight to Popik's discovery, but old stories die hard and Marfa is full of people who will insist that their town was named after someone in *The Brothers Karamazov*.

Marfa was a cattle town from the start. The original loading pens were on the south side of the railroad tracks just east of the Godbold Mill; they were later moved to a point east of town near the golf course and can still be seen there. Ranchers from Central and South Texas, people like Philip and Martha Pruett, began bringing their herds into the area in the early 1880s, attracted by the abundance of nutritious grasses and cheap land and by the presence of the railroad, which allowed them to ship cattle directly to eastern markets. In 1918 the Highland Hereford Breeders Association was organized in Marfa by 50 of the most prominent ranchers in the Big Bend, and its annual banquets were the premier social event in Marfa for the next 50 years. Sheep and goats, raised for their wool, were also an important part of the Big Bend's livestock industry, especially during World Wars I and II, when the demand for wool for military uniforms was high. The Chinati Foundation's building in downtown Marfa that houses the John Chamberlain sculptures was built as a wool and mohair warehouse. The livestock industry in the Big Bend prospered during the 1920s, 30s, and 40s and that prosperity is reflected in the large houses that cattle and sheep ranchers built north of the railroad tracks in Marfa, the largest of which is the home built by cattle rancher Lucas Brite in 1914 at 601 North Ridge Street. Brite was also responsible for the First Christian Church on the west side of the courthouse square and the Brite Building at 103 North Highland Avenue.

The Mexican Revolution of 1910–1920 had a profound effect on Marfa. The outbreak of the fighting in Mexico stimulated a brisk illegal arms trade on this side of the border, with most Big Bend merchants on the Texas side of the Rio Grande becoming involved in smuggling guns and ammunition to revolutionaries on the other side. In 1911 a cavalry post was established at Marfa to try to control the smuggling. By 1922 Camp Marfa, as it was called, had grown into a full-fledged military post, with 184 permanent buildings and a complement of 92 officers and 2,826 enlisted men. In 1930 its name was changed to Fort D.A. Russell. It was the last large cavalry post built by the U.S. Army, and it made Marfa unequivocally an army town. There were polo matches, band concerts, regimental dances at the officers' club and the Paisano Hotel, summer maneuvers on adjacent ranches, and, of course, romances between ranchers' daughters and cavalry officers. In one year, 1923, there were eight marriages between officers and local girls, and that was about average through the 1920s and 30s. An astonishing number of men who rose to the rank of general in World War II were married to Marfa women. The army continued to be a factor in Marfa life, with a two-year hiatus between 1933 and 1935, until the fort was closed at the end of World War II. One of the post commanders during the 1940s had the remarkably bellicose name of Colonel Napoleon Rainbolt.

The Revolution also injected elements of fear and hostility into relations between Anglos and Hispanics in Marfa. Some of the oldest Hispanic families in the area, such as the Russells, the Leatons, the Favers, the Burgesses, the Spencers, and the Landrums, were the results of intermarriage between Anglo-Americans who settled along the Rio Grande in the 1850s and Hispanic women, but by 1900 the two cultures led largely segregated but reasonably harmonious lives in Marfa, living in separate neighborhoods and attending separate elementary schools and churches. The influx of refugees from Mexico, combined with raids by Mexican revolutionaries on ranches south of Marfa and a retaliatory raid by Texas Rangers on the Presidio County community of Porvenir, in which 15 Hispanic men and boys between the ages of 16 and 72 were lined up and executed while their wives and mothers watched, created tensions that embittered both groups. When the first refugees arrived in January 1914 a committee of Marfa's leading Anglo citizens telegraphed Governor O.B. Colquitt, asking that steps be taken to protect the town from "indigent refugees." In December 1917, following the raid on the Brite Ranch, 200 Marfans gathered at the Stockmans' Club and formed a vigilance committee to register and disarm all Hispanic males in the Big Bend. A telegram was sent to the adjutant general of Texas, requesting a cavalry regiment of state troops to aid the committee in its work. In November 1918 an editorial in the Marfa *New Era* called Hispanic voters "illiterate and dangerous" and urged the women of Marfa to use their newly-obtained voting rights to strike a blow for "clean American politics."

This rift between cultures lasted for many years. Marfa's elementary schools remained segregated until 1965; the first Hispanic sheriff was not elected until 1978, and that election was reversed by a court order; the first Hispanic majority took control of the Marfa city council in 1987. In 2010, Hispanics made up 66.3 % of Marfa's total population. Marfa's median household income that year was less than half of the median household income for all of Texas and 23% of Marfa's families lived below the poverty line.

Texas weather has always been a cycle of drought and recovery, and the livestock industry in the Big Bend was occasionally affected by two- or three-year droughts from the very beginning, but the drought of 1949–1956 was the most drastic of the 20th century and brought about the failure of many Big Bend ranches, with a disastrous effect on the economy of Marfa. The town went into a decline that was only partially arrested by the filming of the movie *Giant* on the nearby Worth Evans Ranch in the summer of 1955. Locally recruited extras were paid $5.00 a day, $10.00 if they had a speaking part, even if they only said a few words, and this, plus the spending of the 50-person cast and crew provided a temporary economic stimulus. Billy Lee Brammer, author of the Texas classic political novel, *The Gay Place,* came to Marfa from Austin to cover the filming for the *Texas Observer* and later incorporated some of his observations into *The Gay Place.* In one of his *Observer* articles he described Marfa as "this bleak and blissful and altogether unworldly little town." The filming brought tourists from all over the Southwest, who planned their vacations around a chance to see Elizabeth Taylor, Rock Hudson, and James Dean. But the economic boom only lasted a month, and when the movie people went away Marfa's economic decline continued. The filming of *Giant* left in its wake a play by Midland, Texas Theatre Guild director Ed Graczyk, *Come Back to the Five and Dime, Jimmy Dean, Jimmy Dean,* which Graczyk first produced on stage in 1976 and which was turned into a film by Robert Altman. A later manifestation of that memorable Marfa summer was a documentary produced by Hector Galan in 2015, *Children of Giant,* which dealt with the segregation of Hispanics in Marfa in the 1950s.

Although it started raining again in the summer of 1956, Marfa struggled through the 1960s with yearly declines in population, bank deposits, and sales receipts. Many of the old ranches had been sold during the drought to outsiders who used them as hunting preserves, and some Marfans felt that a century-old way of life had disappeared when the ranches were sold. Marfa historian Cecilia Thompson, remembering those years, wrote, "When the ranchers had to sell and move off their ranches they left their homeland... It was not so much about loss of money than loss of 'heart country'. The loss did not come from mismanagement but from misfortune and the vagaries of nature. The pain of that loss was terrible." A photographic history of Marfa written by two local women in 2009 describes life in Marfa in the 1960s as "abysmal."

Art saved Marfa from oblivion. Donald Judd's work here was supported by the Houston-based Dia Foundation, a non-profit entity formed in 1974 by art dealer Heiner Friedrich, his wife, the former Philippa de Menil, who was an heiress to the Schlumberger oil exploration fortune, and art historian Helen Winkler. By 1979 the Dia Foundation had purchased about 40 buildings in Marfa, including a large part of Fort D.A. Russell, and 240 acres of land, and had entered into a contract with Judd to pay him a monthly stipend of $5,000 for five years. But in 1983 the price of crude oil began its three-year decline, accompanied by a decline in Schlumberger dividends, which were the principal source of Dia's income. The Dia Foundation was forced to shed some of its responsibilities, and Judd's Marfa projects were briefly reorganized as the Art Museum of the Pecos and then, in 1987, as the Chinati Foundation, with the Dia Foundation transferring its Marfa properties to the Chinati Foundation and Judd himself providing most of Chinati's working capital from the sale of his works. The Chinati Foundation was inaugurated with a huge party in Marfa in October 1987 and that anniversary is still celebrated every year with Chinati Weekend, a three-day artistic blowout that brings the international art world to Marfa. Thirty years later the Chinati Foundation still dominates creative life in Marfa, holding exhibitions, sponsoring educational programs, and bringing in artists-in-residence. It was joined in 1994 by the Judd Foundation, which maintains Donald Judd's home, library, and archive, and in 1998 by the Lannan Foundation, a Santa Fe-based foundation which operates a residency program in Marfa for writers, bringing 24 to 26 writers a year to town for three to six week stays. Foundations are so much a part of Marfa life that when two young entrepreneurs opened a pizza restaurant here several years ago they named it the Pizza Foundation.

Part of this book is about the country south of Marfa, the country between Marfa and the Rio Grande, the country that Juan Sabeata knew. Ted Gray, a Big Bend rancher who lived in Alpine in his old age, once said to me, "There is a line that runs east to west from Marathon through Alpine and Marfa to Van Horn. South of that line the country is so poor that everyone who lives there has had to do something wrong at least once in their life just to get by." This country includes the Chinati Mountains, the Sierra Vieja, Big Bend National Park, and Big Bend Ranch State Park. The best way to appreciate its vastness and isolation is to drive south from Marfa to Presidio on U.S. 67, turn east at Presidio on FM 170 and drive along the Rio Grande to Study Butte (pronounced "Stoody Bewt"), turn right at Study Butte and enter Big Bend National Park, and then explore the park and exit on U.S. 385 at Panther Junction and follow that highway north to Marathon, then turn west and take U.S. 90 back to Marfa.

That drive takes you through the ghost town of Shafter, a silver-mining town that made an important contribution to the economy of the Big Bend from the 1880s until the mine closed in 1941, and Terlingua, another mining ghost town (mercury) which became a haven for counterculture refugees in the 1960s and still maintains that atmosphere. Blair Pittman, who lived in Terlingua at Villa de Mina and liked to give parties at the bottom of the mine shaft, enjoyed telling about the time in 1985 that Governor Mark White paid a visit to Terlingua. At that time there was a cattle guard on State Highway 118 at Bee Mountain that was regarded as the gateway to Terlingua, and just across the cattle guard was a café run by a character called Uncle Joe, a retired wrestler, a big man with a full white beard. The governor had been at a meeting in Alpine, and he and his entourage pulled up to Uncle Joe's in several cars. It was a very hot day and Uncle Joe was sitting in a recliner on the porch, swatting flies. He called to them to get whatever beer and cold drinks they wanted out of the cooler, mark it down on the blackboard, pick out some tables, and pay him when they left. The governor, thinking he should do a little politicking, walked over to Uncle Joe, put out his hand, and said, "Excuse me, sir. I'm Mark White. I'm the governor of Texas." Uncle Joe looked up at him and said, "Son, when you cross that cattle guard, you can be anybody you want to be."

An alternate route to the south country is to take Farm-to-Market Road 2810, known as the Pinto Canyon Road, south from Marfa and follow it to the community of Ruidosa on the Rio Grande where FM 170 will take you east down the river to Presidio. The Pinto Canyon Road requires a high-clearance vehicle because 20 miles south of Marfa FM 2810 turns into a dirt road with some serious ruts and potholes, especially after a rain. If you stop on the dirt road you may have to explain yourself to the Border Patrol, as it is a favorite route for *narcotraficantes,* especially after dark.

This is the country where some of the big ranches were located in the 1880s and 90s, country so devoid of nutrients that ranchers estimate that it takes 50 to 100 acres to feed one cow and her calf, which is why the ranches in the Big Bend are so big and so isolated from each other. Living on these ranches encouraged individualism and self-reliance, and southern Presidio and Brewster counties produced some memorable characters. They came to town once a month, or sometimes once a year, to get supplies, and Marfa was the town they came to. From the 1880s until the Depression, a Marfa mercantile store called Murphy and Walker supplied ranchers all over the Big Bend and down into Chihuahua with groceries, dry goods, tools, barbed wire, household utensils, feed, mail, and newspapers, as well as advancing cash for operating expenses.

A third route south, and the most historic one, is to follow the old Chihuahua Trail down Alamito Creek to Fort Leaton on the Rio Grande. You can do this by heading south on SH 67 and then, just past the Border Patrol checkpoint south of Marfa, turning left on FM 169, called the Casa Piedra Road. This road is the original Chihuahua Trail, laid out in 1839 by Chihuahua City merchant Henry Connelley to facilitate the movement of goods from Chihuahua City to San Antonio, Texas. Numerous springs along Alamito Creek made ideal camping places for wagon trains, and in fact the route had been used by Native American traders for several thousand years before Connelley turned it into a road. In the 1860s a Kentuckian named John Davis and his wife, Francisca Herrera, established a ranch at one of those springs called El Alamito, and the community of Casa Piedra grew up around it. The ruins of the Davis ranch house are still visible. In 1930 the Kansas City, Mexico, and Orient Railroad laid tracks down Alamito Creek in order to connect Presidio with Alpine, and a water tower was built near Casa Piedra at a stop named Plata.

I once interviewed a tough and charming woman in Alpine named Mojella Moore, who grew up in a one-room adobe house on a goat ranch below the Candelaria Rim, one of the most isolated parts of the Big Bend. When they went to town they went to Marfa, an all-day trip in a Model T Ford. She always looked forward to the trips because the storekeepers gave her candy when her father paid the bills. Once, in the depths of the Depression, an entire year passed without a trip to town. She asked her mother if they were not able to go to town because they were poor, and her mother said, "No, we're not poor. We just don't have any money."

Dora Amelia Wilson Dowe moved into Pinto Canyon with her family in 1907, when she was 10 years old. At that time there was no road into the canyon, only a horse and mule trail. Their one-room rock house was only 35 miles from Marfa, but the nearest store was at Ruidosa, 16 miles down the canyon on the Rio Grande. That was where they did their grocery shopping. Their father would ride horseback down the canyon leading a pack horse, leaving at dawn and returning at sunset with a week's groceries on the pack horse. Hers was the first family to settle in the canyon, but as other families moved in the county finally built a road through the canyon and a one-room schoolhouse on Horse Creek, and hired a schoolteacher. Dora's father hitched up his wagon and used the new road to drive to Marfa to pick the teacher and her luggage up at the railroad station, and Dora went along. It was a three-day trip, as it took all day to drive to Marfa and all day to drive back. Dora wrote in her memoirs that that trip to town was the first time she had been out of Pinto Canyon in three years.

One morning in the mid-1960s Evan Davies, the young vicar of St. Paul's Episcopal Church in Marfa, was walking down Highland Avenue to the post office when he saw Marian Walker, who ran the store at Candelaria, a tiny place on the Rio Grande 50 miles southwest of Marfa, coming toward him looking distraught. "Good morning, Mrs. Walker," he said. "You look troubled. Can I do anything for you?" "It's my husband, Jimmy. He's dead," she said. Davies made appropriate sympathetic noises and offered to have the Marfa undertaker send a hearse to Candelaria. "No need to do that," Walker said. "He's in the car. I put him in the front seat and brought him to town."

Today Marfa's universe has expanded far beyond the Big Bend, and people are coming to town from Europe, Asia, and Africa as well as New York, Chicago, and Los Angeles. Marfa may still be bleak and blissful but it is no longer unworldly. I hope that the short essays in this book will expand those visitors' universes in time as well as space, and that reading them will add new dimensions to their visit here.

TIPS FOR NEWCOMERS

I WROTE THESE several years ago, after listening to one of my favorite Marfa Public Radio programs, the Anderson brothers' "Literary Hour," on KRTS. Steve Anderson had just finished giving his weekly traffic report—he had seen 33 cars between Alpine and Marfa, or approximately one and one-half cars per mile, but no wild animals—and then he said he was going to add a new feature to his program, tips for newcomers. I have now forgotten what his tips were, but mine are still good advice. Here they are:

1. The months of July and August are our rainy season. Do not ever complain about the rain. We live in the middle of the Chihuahuan desert and we get an average of 14 inches of rain a year. We need every drop we get. This is ranching country. You may have noticed that there are fenced pastures on either side of all the roads leading to Marfa. Those pastures are for cows. Cows eat grass, and rain makes grass grow. The prosperity of everyone who lives here depends on our annual rainfall. This may be the only place you will ever live where people gather in churches and pray for rain. We welcome it.

In 1941 Presidio County got 42 inches of rain. No one

complained. The bridge between Ojinaga and Presidio was closed for a month due to high water. Not one voice was raised in protest. R.D. Harper, a rancher on Alamito Creek, got 6 inches of rain in 3 hours. His only comment was that he had never seen so much water in his life.

A few summers back we got almost enough rain to equal the 1941 record. It seemed as though it rained every day for a month. I asked Gene West of Marfa, who ranched here all of his life, if he thought that people would be saying that we had too much rain. "You will NEVER hear me say that! NEVER!" was his emphatic reply.

2. Speaking of ranchers, do not ask a rancher how much land they own or how many cattle they have. That is tantamount to asking someone how much money they have in their bank account. It is bad form. Since it can take up to 100 acres of arid Big Bend land to support a cow and her calf, some of our ranches encompass quite a few acres. Most people here are too polite to reply, "It's none of your business" to the how much and how many questions. The standard answer is "enough."

3. Do not under any circumstances drive your expensive sedan down the Pinto Canyon Road, or any dirt road in the Big Bend, after a rain. Dirt road surfaces here have a high clay content and are slick as bacon grease when they are wet. A second of inattention can put you in the ditch or, on the Pinto Canyon road, over a hundred-foot drop. An additional hazard is washes, which occur when water flows across the road and cuts a ditch a foot or so deep that will ruin your oil pan or break an axle. Those picturesque low-water crossings are subject to flash floods, when a wall of water four feet high will sweep down an arroyo pushing two-foot

boulders in front of it. You don't want to be sitting there admiring the scenery when that happens.

A few years ago the Chinati Foundation threw a big barbecue at Donald Judd's ranch in Pinto Canyon during Chinati weekend. Abandoned Audis and Mercedes-Benzes, all with out-of-state license plates, lined the shoulders of the Pinto Canyon road for miles. Little clumps of people stood in the center of the road trying to hitch rides. The secret here is not necessarily four-wheel drive, although that helps, but high clearance. A Toyota Tacoma pickup truck is preferable to a Saab.

4. Do not try to pick the beautiful prickly pear or cholla blossoms or the delectable-looking fruit of the prickly pear called *tuna*. Everything that grows in the desert has thorns on it and that goes double for prickly pear and cholla. Several years ago my wife and I were entertaining a couple who were visiting us from Washington, D.C. They were intelligent, sophisticated adults but they were also the ultimate Easterners, raised respectively in Boston and the Bronx and seldom venturing west of the Appalachians. We drove them from Fort Davis to Presidio and then started down the River Road, stopping at Fort Leaton. When we got out of the car in the parking lot there, Ms. Easterner stopped to admire a prickly pear that was covered with big purple *tunas*. Before we could stop her she reached down and plucked one of the *tunas*. My wife and I spent the rest of the day taking turns pulling spines out of her hand with the tweezers from my Swiss Army knife.

5. Do not become impatient while standing in line at a store counter if the cashier is chatting with the customer in front of you. Exchanging gossip is one of the main purposes of shopping in the Big Bend. How else are you going to know who has had a baby,

who is in the hospital, who has their ranch up for sale? If you keep your ears open you will learn all you need to know about your new neighbors. And, when the clerk and the customers stop gossiping about you and start gossiping with you, you will know that you are no longer a newcomer.

6. Finally, keep a smile on your face, and greet strangers with a cheerful "hello" or "howdy." West Texans are brought up to believe that it is part of their job in life to make other people feel good, and that is a pretty good rule to live by. If you are male, stand up when ladies or older men enter the room. And above all, wave at passing cars, even if you can't see whether their drivers are waving back. Not long ago someone was telling me about a man who was considered a bad neighbor. He didn't pay his bills promptly, he didn't keep his fences up, he let his livestock wander, but worst of all, my informant said, "He never waved at anybody. Just drove right by with his windows rolled up." You don't want people saying that about you.

July 15, 2010

MARFA
PAST AND PRESENT

WHY MARFA WILL NEVER BE LIKE SANTA FE

EVERY ONCE IN a while I hear someone wonder if Marfa will become the next Santa Fe. I don't think that will ever happen. I lived in Santa Fe in the early 1980s and I learned a lot about the City Different, as its promoters used to call it, and I can tell you that it is very different indeed from Marfa.

I moved there to write a book, and when the book was finished I was offered a job at the Museum of New Mexico, a state agency, which I accepted. A month after I took the job a new governor took office and decided that he wanted to reward some of his supporters with the top six jobs at the museum, including mine.

He ordered the museum's board of regents to fire us, and the board refused, and for the next year working at the museum was like being in the trenches with a lot of heavy artillery passing overhead as the regents and the governor went at it hammer and tongs. At one point, the governor managed to get himself quoted in the Santa Fe paper as saying there were too many Texans working at the Museum of New Mexico (there were three of us). A Jewish friend, who had just been fired from the state archives by the governor, sent me a framed motto that said, "In A Holocaust We Are

All Texans." I got myself quoted in the paper as saying that Santa Fe was a cross between Disneyland and Paraguay and then I moved on. Now, none of that would have ever happened in Marfa.

I was back in Santa Fe not long ago, and I realized that God endowed Santa Fe with several important resources that He denied Marfa. Mountains, for instance. The Sangre de Cristo range rises to 12,000 feet right behind town and includes a ski basin that attracts 175,000 visitors a year. The nearest ski basin to Marfa is in New Mexico. Santa Fe has a beautiful little river running through town, its banks lined with cottonwoods. The nearest river to Marfa is 60 miles away and it seldom has water in it. Then there are the Indians. About 10,000 Native Americans live on pueblos within an hour's drive of Santa Fe. Many are fine craftspeople and make beautiful pottery and jewelry which they sell to tourists. The last Indians seen around Marfa were Victorio and his Apaches, who passed through in 1880 on their way to Mexico. Marfans might work something out with the Tiguas over in El Paso, but somehow I don't think it would be the same thing as driving up to San Ildefonso to buy pots from Maria Martinez's grandchildren.

Santa Feans have made good use of these resources to attract 1.2 million tourists per year. This means that on any given day of the year there are 33,000 tourists in Santa Fe, a city of 84,000 people. If tourists came to Marfa in that same proportion to its population there would be 1,000 visitors there every day. They would have a hard time finding a place to eat lunch. There are 105 art galleries in Santa Fe, of which five have anything in them that people of taste and sensibility would want in their house. Marfa has five art galleries, all full of very high quality stuff. Santa Fe has a plethora of pueblo-style buildings, most of them built between

1920 and 1950 by an Anglo architect named John Gaw Meem as part of a civic program to make the City Different, well, different. Marfa has no pueblo-style buildings but the buildings it does have are real. Santa Fe has rich Californians. In the 1990s everyone in California who had more than a million dollars—and there were a lot of them—bought a house in Santa Fe and then doubled its size. The nearest thing Marfa has to Californians is Houstonians, but at least they are Texans and most of them are pretty nice folks, just trying to reconnect with their small-town roots.

Finally, there are the costumes. People get duded up in silver concho belts and big hats to visit Santa Fe. Several years ago, my friend Rayna Green and I were sitting on the porch of the St. Francis Hotel there watching women in fringed buckskin jackets, pink cowboy hats, and strings of turquoise, and men in ankle-length dusters and knee-high boots walk by. "I swear," Rayna said, "There has to be a changing room in the Albuquerque airport for these people." Most visitors to Marfa wear blue jeans and tee-shirts. The city council here needs to get cracking on a dress code if they are going to emulate this aspect of Santa Fe.

Marfa the next Santa Fe? I sure hope not. Marfa right now is what Santa Fe was about 1920, a small western town full of individualists, some of whom are artists. Somewhere along the way Santa Fe lost its innocence and sold its soul. Folks in Marfa have too much good sense to let that happen here.

August 5, 2004

THE MARFA LIGHTS

I HAVE NEVER seen the Marfa Lights. I have been told that the best time to see them is in the winter a couple of hours after sundown or a couple of hours before sunrise. A couple of hours after sundown in the winter is my supper time and a couple of hours before sunrise is my sleeping time, and besides that, it is cold out there at the viewing station in the wintertime. But I believe they are there. At least I believe something is there, because I know a lot of reliable people who have seen some sort of lights on Mitchell Flat.

Scoffers will tell you that the Marfa Lights are the lights of automobiles traveling north from Presidio on Highway 67, or the lights on ranches on Mitchell Flat, or the lights on airplanes or Border Patrol helicopters. My friend Aurie West, a totally dependable woman in her 70s whose family has ranched on Mitchell Flat since the 1880s, has seen a light out there since she was a little girl. She describes it as a ball of pulsating light that glows for 30 seconds or so and then disappears, only to reappear a minute or so later. Her father saw it, her grandfather saw it, and her great-grandfather saw it in the 1880s. Robert Ellison, who drove a herd of cattle to Marfa in 1883, saw lights glowing in that direction as he brought his cows over Paisano Pass. He did not write about them in his memoir, as a lot of journalists have alleged, but he told plenty of people about having seen them. So did O.W. Williams, who heard about them while surveying around Marfa in 1901 and 1902 and told his grandson, rancher and oil man Clayton Williams, about them. Many people who think they are seeing the Marfa Lights are undoubtedly looking at automobile headlights or ranch lights, but it is clear that there were other lights out there before there were either automobiles or electricity in the Big Bend, and they are still out there.

Marfa people tended to consider the lights just part of the landscape until World War II, when cadet pilots from all over the country were being trained at the Marfa Army Air Field on Mitchell Flat. The young pilots chased the lights in jeeps and in airplanes. They never caught them, but when they completed their training they spread word about them all over the world. People started turning up who wanted to see them, and eventually the State Highway Department developed a roadside park on U.S. 90 east of town to accommodate the people who were parking on the shoulder at night to watch for them. Armando Vasquez, now in his 90s, remembers that in the 1970s he started taking people from motels out to see them. "I saw it could help our economy," he told *Texas Monthly* writer Michael Hall, who did a story on the lights in 2006. The Chamber of Commerce, at Vasquez's urging, put up signs on U.S. 90 that said "See Marfa's Mystery Lights." Allison Scott recalls that in 1995 County Judge Jake Brisbin persuaded the Presidio County commissioners to replace the signs with big billboards because people kept stealing the signs. Finally, in 2001, as the result of an eighth-grade school project to improve Marfa, the state spent $720,000 to turn the roadside park into an official Marfa Lights Viewing Area, with covered seating, mounted binoculars, and restrooms. Clayton Williams, whose grandfather had told him about the lights when he was a boy, donated the additional land needed for the expansion.

The guru of the Marfa Lights is James Bunnell, a retired NASA engineer who started observing the lights systematically in 2000 and has published four books about them. The books are combinations of detailed guidebooks for watching the lights, with maps and charts telling observers what direction to look in and what not to confuse with the lights (automobile lights, ranch lights, radio tower lights), and expositions of Bunnell's hypotheses about what might be causing them, hypotheses that have evolved over time. Bunnell found that the main impediment to scientific observation of the lights was the infrequency and unpredictability of their appearance. He got around this by persuading ranchers on Mitchell Flat to allow him to place 10 automated video camera systems on their property, and by 2015, when he published his most recent book, *Strange Lights in West Texas* (Benbrook, Texas: Lacey Publishing Company), he had the most complete photographic record of the Marfa Lights ever made.

The videos allowed Bunnell to study not only the paths and varying brightness of the mysterious lights but to analyze their combustive processes. In *Strange Lights in West Texas* he sets out the hypothesis that the lights are the result of electrical charges that build up in the layers of igneous rock that underlie Mitchell Flat and then discharge as what Bunnell calls "underground lightning." The electrical charges, Bunnell says, are the result of high tectonic stress along the line where the South American—African plate pushes against the North American plate, a line known to geologists as the Ouachita Trend, which runs near Marfa. The charges percolate upwards through the ground and emerge as what Bunnell describes as "dusty plasma structures"—Marfa Lights.

What makes Bunnell's hypothesis compelling is that he describes other places in the world where similar geologic conditions exist and similar mysterious lights appear: Hessdalen, Norway; the Taro River Valley in Italy; Min Min, Australia; and Brown Mountain, North Carolina. Bunnell has become part of an international group of scientists who study this worldwide phenomenon.

There are, of course, alternate explanations for the lights, some of which Bunnell lists in his books. My favorite is that they are caused by the glowing fur of jackrabbits which have encountered radioactive material left over from secret World War II experiments carried out at the air force base.

Just the other day I was in the lobby of the Paisano Hotel when a tourist walked up to the desk and said, "We want to see the Marfa Lights." A cowboy who had been chatting up the woman behind the desk turned to her and said, "We don't turn them on until after dark."

May 18, 2017

WHAT IS THAT BIG
WHITE BUILDING NEXT TO THE COURTHOUSE?

VISITORS TO MARFA always comment on the four particularly handsome buildings along the west side of Highland Avenue—the First Christian Church, the Paisano Hotel, the Brite Building, and the Marfa National Bank. The Paisano was designed by the well-known El Paso firm of Trost and Trost, but the other three buildings are the work of a much more obscure architect, Leighton Green Knipe. They are built in a style that is a combination of Spanish-Pueblo Revival and Art Deco, and they are very fine buildings indeed.

Knipe came to the Big Bend in the mid-1920s and worked in Marfa under the patronage of rancher Lucas Brite for 15 years, but he has proved to be an elusive fellow to learn anything about. Lee Bennett remembers him as a diminutive man with a little goatee who lived by himself in an apartment that he rented from her mother, and Jane Brite White recalls that he smoked little Between the Acts cigars, that she and her sister called him Uncle Billy, and that he had a scientific bent and helped her grandfather drill some oil wells on the Brite Ranch that turned out to be dry holes, but beyond that he did not make much impression on Marfa's collective memory. Both Bennett and White have small pewter statues that he made of them when they were little girls. He died in Marfa in 1941, and his body was shipped to California for burial.

The odd thing is that when I started looking into his career I discovered that he is something of a cult figure to architectural enthusiasts in Arizona and California, where he designed some important buildings, but no one that I talked to there knew that he had left an architectural legacy in Marfa. It is as though he had two separate careers.

Dr. Beverly Brandt, professor of architectural history at Arizona State University, has told me that Knipe designed some of the earliest campus buildings there, one of which, Matthews Hall, built in 1918, is on the National Register of Historic Places. Brandt also told me that in 1918 Knipe played a major role in the design of the Southern Cotton Company's model company town, Litchfield Village, outside of Phoenix. The hotel he built there is now a popular golf resort, The Wigwam.

John Akers, curator of history at the Tempe Historical Society and another Knipe fan, filled in some biographical details for me. Knipe was born in Texas in 1878, went to Lafayette College in Pennsylvania, and called himself a structural engineer, rather than an architect. He built the Egyptian Revival First National Bank of Tempe, now being restored, in 1912; and became City Engineer of Tempe in 1913. Before coming to Arizona Knipe worked for A. Prescott Folwell, one of the country's leading urban sanitary engineers.

Another Knipe enthusiast is Gwilym McGrew of Los Angeles, who with his wife, Peggy, is restoring a 6,000 square foot Spanish Colonial Revival ranch house in Woodland Park that Knipe designed in 1928 for millionaire John Show. The McGrews (whose e-mail address is "ProudCelts") and I have entered into a spirited correspondence about Knipe, and they have identified the tile he used on the façade of the Brite Building as being from the Claycroft Potteries in Los Angeles, an important art tile pottery in the 1920s. They also called my attention to a second large Spanish-style Knipe house in Los Angeles, the Orcutt Ranch House, built in 1926 for W.W. Orcutt, a pioneer California geologist and oilman. The Orcutt House is now a Los Angeles Historical Monument, owned by the city and open to the public.

The Orcutt House was built the same year that Knipe completed the First Christian Church in Marfa for Lucas Brite. Jane Brite White thinks that perhaps Knipe met her grandfather in Phoenix, because Brite owned a ranch near Phoenix and went there a good deal in the 1920s. However they met, Knipe's design for the First Christian Church was an eccentric expression of his own peculiar genius. It is the only church I have ever seen in which the sanctuary is not the most important room in the building. Knipe designed the church around an enormous octagonal community room with a stage on one of its sides and doors opening into the other spaces, including the sanctuary, on the other seven sides. The sanctuary is big—it will seat 500 people—but the community room is clearly the most important room in the building. Perhaps it says something about the architect's feelings about the importance of community.

For some reason, Knipe gave up a promising career with wealthy patrons in Los Angeles to move to Marfa. Perhaps Brite promised him a steady string of commissions, and indeed he did build not only the Brite Building and the Marfa National Bank but also the little building that is now the Marfa Health Clinic. Or perhaps he was the first in an increasingly large crowd of cosmopolitan urbanites to reject big city life and settle in Marfa. Whatever the reason, he gave Marfa a wonderful gift of distinguished buildings, and Marfans should be grateful to him.

January 19, 2006

THE GREAT MARFA PAYROLL ROBBERY

 EVERYONE IN TEXAS knows stories about the way that the Mexican Revolution of 1910–1920 spilled over the border. These stories are usually about raids across the river that resulted in bloodshed on this side, such as the Glenn Springs raid in 1916 and the Brite Ranch raid in 1917. My own mother lived in Kingsville, Texas as a girl and vividly remembered her terror when news came one Sunday morning in 1915 that Aniceto Pizaña and his men had derailed the train between Kingsville and Brownsville and murdered the engineer. The engineer's daughter was her best friend.

But what does not find its way into the stories is that the violence flowed both ways across the permeable border. There was the Great Marfa Payroll Robbery, for instance. In July, 1919, a Captain Palma, a Mexican Army paymaster, got off the train at Marfa with a briefcase containing $22,600, the payroll for the Mexican Army garrison at Ojinaga. Because of the difficulty of reaching Ojinaga from Ciudad Juarez, Palma and his escort of four soldiers had crossed the border and taken the train east from El

Paso. At Marfa they arranged for a local man, Andy Barker, to drive them to Presidio, where they intended to cross the border again, pay off the garrison, and return to El Paso. They started off from Marfa after dark, but about two miles south of town they found the road blocked by a Ford automobile parked across it. Several men with guns jumped out of it, grabbed the briefcase from Captain Palma, got back in their car and took off into the darkness. Because of its international implications the F.B.I. investigated the case, as did the Texas Rangers. Both agencies gave the district attorney's office a list of suspects, which included Andy Barker and the sheriff's brother. After a brief period of indirection during which the sheriff tried to throw suspicion on a group of soldiers at Camp Marfa, the district attorney tried to bring indictments against the men on the list, but the grand jury refused to indict some of Marfa's best-known citizens and the robbery is still officially unsolved.

Then there was the killing of General Pascual Orozco on the Love Ranch in Hudspeth County. Orozco was one of the original leaders of the 1910 revolution against Porfirio Diaz, but after Diaz's fall Orozco parted ways with his fellow revolutionaries and threw his support behind Victoriano Huerta, a former general in Diaz's army who became president in a counter-revolutionary coup in 1913. Huerta was soon overthrown in turn and went into exile, but he tried to make a comeback. Orozco traveled around the United States buying guns for him and enlisted the support of many conservative Texas businessmen and ranchers. In June, 1915, both Orozco and Huerta were arrested by federal officers at Newman, New Mexico, taken to El Paso, and charged with violating the Neutrality Act. They made bond, and the mayor of El Paso offered to defend them in court, but a few days later Orozco jumped bail and disappeared into the Big Bend. A few weeks later he and three companions, all armed, rode up to the isolated Dick Love ranch house south of Sierra Blanca and asked the cook there to fix them breakfast. While they were eating it they saw a car coming up the road toward the house and, spooked, jumped on their horses and headed for the Eagle Mountains. The car contained Love and some of his cowboys, come to start the fall roundup. When the cook told Love that there were four strange armed Mexicans on the place, Love jumped to the conclusion that they were bandits and called the sheriff at Sierra Blanca to get a posse together. The posse tracked Orozco and his men through the Eagle Mountains for two days, finally pinned them down in a canyon, and killed all four of them. It was only when they found a watch with the initials "P.O." on one of the dead men that they realized whom they had killed.

The fluid nature of the border in those years is nowhere better illustrated than by the words used by Sheriff Amador Sanchez of Laredo in applying for a presidential pardon after he was convicted of smuggling guns across the river to assist an uprising planned by General Bernardo Reyes in 1911. In a tone of outrage he wrote to President Taft that "this custom of purchasing arms, horses, and munitions of war along the Rio Grande for revolutionaries in Mexico has prevailed ever since I was a boy, and no one has ever been prosecuted for it until now." People crossing the border for illegal purposes is nothing new in Texas. In fact, you might almost say it is a tradition.

October 20, 2005

MEMORIES OF GIANT

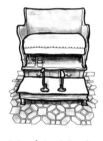 JUNE AND JULY 2015 marked the 60ᵀᴴ anniversary of the filming of *Giant* in Marfa. New interest in that episode in Marfa's history was sparked by the release of Hector Galán's documentary *Children of Giant* on PBS on April 17 of that year, a film about the memories that Marfa's Mexican-American community had of the filming. I thought it would be interesting to see what the bible of late 20ᵀᴴ-century Marfa history, Louise S. O'Connor's and Cecilia Thompson's *Marfa and Presidio County, Texas, 1937–2008*, had to say about those six weeks in the summer of 1955 when Hollywood came to Marfa.

Like all good historians, O'Connor and Thompson start at the beginning, which in the case of *Giant* was in 1947. The summer of that year Edna Ferber, the author of the novel *Giant* upon which the film was based, was doing research for the novel and came to the King Ranch to visit Robert and Helen Kleberg. Ferber, a New Yorker, was an established literary figure, famous for her novels *Show Boat, Cimarron,* and *So Big,* which had won a Pulitzer Prize in 1925. O'Connor and Thompson quote Helen Kleberg Groves, Robert and Helen Kleberg's daughter, concerning Ferber's visit to the Kleberg home.

Groves remembered that her mother was ill, and she served as her father's hostess the day that Ferber arrived at the ranch for lunch. Ferber told her father that she was going to write a novel based on him, his wife, and the King Ranch. Kleberg replied that someday he would see that an accurate history of the ranch would be written upon which she could base her novel, but until then he would prefer that nothing be written. Ferber replied that she was going to write her book anyway and, according to Groves, "became rude." Groves said that her father turned to her and asked her to go to the kitchen and call Ferber's driver, saying, "She wants to leave now and won't be coming back."

Ferber visited ranches all over Texas doing research for the novel, which was published in 1952. She left a bad taste in the mouths of most of the people she visited. When O'Connor and Thompson interviewed Susan Reynolds Hughes in 2008 she told them that when Ferber visited the Reynolds' X Ranch "we offered to introduce her to other people but she said, 'Oh, no, I don't want to know any more people like you.'" It is clear that Ferber's unkind words still stung 60 years later. O'Connor and Thompson add that several other local ranchers "had what was described as the 'misfortune' of meeting Ms. Ferber" while she was visiting the area.

Local folks did not transfer their antipathy for Ferber to director George Stevens and the 50-person cast and crew of the film, which included Elizabeth Taylor, Rock Hudson, and James Dean, when they arrived at the Marfa airport on June 1, 1955. In fact, people from all over the Big Bend turned out to welcome them, and the Pilot Ladies Club of Marfa put on what O'Connor and Thompson describe as "one of their famous outdoor barbecues" for them. The only member of the group who seemed to rub Marfa people the wrong way was Bob Hinkle, a former rodeo cowboy who was James Dean's roping coach. O'Connor and Thompson say that those who watched the filming remember Hinkle as "a blowhard and a jerk" and think that Dean learned a lot more about roping from the Mexican cowboys he befriended than from Hinkle.

Clay Evans, the son of Worth Evans, who owned the ranch west of town where the outdoor scenes were filmed, was 19 that summer. He told O'Connor and Thompson that "the cast were all friendly except for Elizabeth Taylor. She was not terribly friendly to teenage boys. Rock [Hudson] and Jimmy [Dean] were fun. Chill Wills was asleep most of the time. He was always hung over." Evans went on to say that director George Stevens "was a nice guy. He did not make a mess of the ranch; he was a gentleman and treated the ranch with respect." He added that he and his brother Bub (Worth Evans, Jr.) were on the film's payroll, riding bucking horses and moving a thousand head of cattle around for the shoots. Warner Brothers paid the Evanses $20,000 for the use of their ranch and livestock, which was a welcome windfall in the middle of the 1949–1956 drought.

James Dean seems to have been the friendliest of all the cast. He was a very young man, only 24, and he liked to drive fast. Ron Lewis, who worked at the SnoKream that summer, rode around with him as he cruised Marfa's streets and remembered that "he was a nice guy." Lewis also befriended Dennis Hopper, who at 19 was making his second film with Dean.

There was one local who had a part in the film who O'Connor and Thompson could not interview, because he died in 1972. Granison Chaney, one of the very few African Americans in Marfa, had a shoeshine stand in Hayes Hord's barber shop on Highland Avenue. George Stevens went into Hord's barber shop for a haircut the first Saturday that he was in Marfa, met Chaney, and was impressed by his dignified bearing and friendly smile. Stevens immediately signed him up to play the railroad porter who helps Rock Hudson and Elizabeth Taylor off the train when they arrive at Reata as the newly-married Benedicts. Chaney even had one line, "Thank you, Mr. Benedict," when Hudson hands him a tip. Chaney, who had often met the trains in Marfa in real life when he worked as a porter at the Crews Hotel, was extremely proud of his role in *Giant*. Robert Silva told O'Connor and Thompson that as a boy he wrote letters for Chaney, who was blind in his old age, to radio station KWKH in Shreveport, Louisiana, requesting songs to be played over the radio. Chaney would always ask Silva to sign them, "from the movie star in Marfa, Texas."

Long after Chaney died, Bob Wright was remodeling Hord's barber shop for his real estate office and found a handwritten note under the floorboards. It began, "To whoever finds this or whoever shines shoes here, I am a shoe shiner here at present at Hord's Barber shop. I hate the damn business but I keep at it..." Granison Chaney may have hated shining shoes, but he loved being in *Giant*.

April 30, 2015

BOB HINKLE AND JAMES DEAN IN MARFA

BOB HINKLE, JAMES DEAN'S roping coach, must have rubbed someone in Marfa the wrong way, and that person described Hinkle to Louise O'Connor and Cecilia Thompson as "a blowhard and a jerk." There is another side to the story, which Hinkle tells in his memoir, *Call Me Lucky* (University of Oklahoma Press, 2009), and I would like to tell that side here.

Bob Hinkle grew up in Brownfield, in the Texas Panhandle, and dropped out of high school to join the Air Force when he turned 18. When he got out of the Air Force he started rodeoing, and rodeoing took him into the movies. As he tells it, he was winning $50 or $60 prize money at rodeos while working as a $2-an-hour carpenter, and he happened to hit the Pendleton, Oregon rodeo while Budd Boetticher was filming *Bronco Buster* there. Boetticher hired Hinkle to double for John Lund in the riding shots for $300 a day, and Hinkle decided his future was in the films and not in carpentry. He moved to Hollywood and started working as an extra and stuntman. Three years later, when he was 24, George Stevens hired him as a dialogue coach for *Giant*. His job was to teach Rock Hudson and James Dean to be Texans.

Hinkle devotes five chapters of *Call Me Lucky* to his work on *Giant*, which he describes as the most fun he ever had. He tells some good stories about the filming which I don't think have been in print elsewhere. He shared a room at the Paisano Hotel with singing cowboy Monte Hale, who played Bale Clinch in the film. He and Hale liked to hang out in the Paisano lobby in the evenings, with Hale doing a little picking and singing. One night James Dean walked over from the rented house he shared with Rock Hudson and Chill Wills and joined them. Dean quickly became a regular fixture at the evening sing-alongs. Hinkle bought him a cheap guitar and taught him a few chords and he enjoyed playing along with them. One night Chill Wills walked in while they were taking a break, picked Dean's guitar up from the chair where Dean had laid it, took it by the neck, and smashed it across the back of the chair. Dean was outraged. "What the hell did you do that for?" he yelled. "That's my guitar!" "That's not a guitar," Wills said. Then he reached behind the chair and pulled out a guitar that he had hidden there earlier and handed it to Dean, saying, "Now, this is a guitar." Wills had driven to Ojinaga earlier in the day and bought Dean a really fine Mexican guitar. Dean hugged Wills right there in the lobby.

Hinkle says that the cast normally worked six days a week, taking Sundays off, but July 4 fell on a Monday in 1955 so they had two consecutive days off. Elizabeth Taylor wanted to use the extra day to go to Dallas and shop at Neiman-Marcus, which she had heard of but had never visited. Hinkle called Neiman's to arrange the trip and talked to Stanley Marcus, who told him that the store was not normally open on Sundays but he would be happy to open it for the *Giant* stars and would even send his private plane to Marfa to pick them up. Hinkle, Taylor, Dean, and several other cast members flew to Dallas on the Marcus plane after the day's shooting was over on Saturday, were entertained by the Marcuses that night at what Hinkle calls "a party with the two hundred richest people in Dallas," and were taken to the store for a private shopping trip the next day. Since Dallas had laws prohibiting Sunday sales no cash could change hands, but Marcus opened charge accounts with $10,000 credit limits for each of his guests. Hinkle, a small-town boy from Brownfield who had never spent more than $50 on a suit, was overwhelmed. He bought his wife a bottle of perfume, and Marcus gave him a tie.

Hinkle and Dean got to be close friends on the Marfa set. They were the same age, 24, and they both enjoyed the same things, including rabbit hunting. Hinkle explains that the filming took place in the middle of the 1949–1956 drought—"it was so dry the trees were bribing dogs," he says—and the rabbits were competing with the cattle for grass, so the county had placed a bounty of five cents for a pair of ears on them. He and Dean would take a studio car out on the highway at night and take turns shooting rabbits out of the windows, putting the ears in a tow sack and trading them in at Livingston's Hardware for ammunition. Eventually they brought in so many ears that Livingston's refused to take any more, and Hinkle decided to get rid of the surplus by boxing them up and mailing them to Jack Warner, head of Warner Brothers Studio. Warner had asked Hinkle to send him a pair of cowboy boots from Marfa, so Hinkle got an empty boot box from Livingston's, stuffed it full of ripe rabbit ears, and mailed it to Warner. He did not know that Warner had an explosive temper and an exaggerated sense of his own importance until several days later when Tom Andre, the *Giant* production manager, drove out to the set with a personal message from Warner to Hinkle: "Tell that S.O.B. Hinkle I'm going to kill him." Hinkle immediately went back to Livingston's and sent Warmer the best pair of black 9D cowboy boots they had. When the cast got back to Hollywood there was a big party for them at which Warner, all smiles, was showing off his new boots to everyone. Hinkle asked him, "Didn't that first pair fit you?"

In his book, Hinkle describes the people of Marfa as "the nicest people in the world." Perhaps O'Connor and Thompson heard about him from Jack Warner.

May 21, 2015

MURDER IN THE FAMILY

THE BIG BEND is full of old stories about killings that were the results of disputes over fence lines, water holes, and unbranded calves. Some of these stories have been told and retold, on porches and around campfires and in print, with a detail added here or altered there, until they are well-worn and widely-known. Some are still unpolished, kept in the closets of the families involved, details closely guarded and hard to ferret out.

The killing of Henry Harrison Powe at the Leoncita Ranch in Brewster County on January 20, 1891 over the ownership of a calf that was subsequently branded with the word "murder" is in the well-worn and widely-known category. It was apparently first published in the mid-1890s as an article in the *Galveston News* and then repeated in books about the Big Bend by Carlysle Graham Raht, Barry Scobee, and Virginia Madison, then picked up by J. Frank Dobie, and subsequently published as a feature story in newspapers and magazines all over the country, with a varying array of details.

The core of the story is this: Henry Harrison Powe was a one-armed Confederate veteran who had come to the Big Bend after the Civil War. At a roundup on the Leoncita Ranch in Brewster County he got into an argument with a man named Fine Gilliland over the ownership of an unbranded yearling bull, and Gilliland killed him, taking off for the Glass Mountains after the fatal shot was fired in front of a dozen witnesses. The shocked cowboys roped the bull, dragged him to the branding fire, and with a running iron burned the word "MURDER" and the date "1-20-91" on his flank and turned him loose to roam the Big Bend for the rest of his life. To see him was to incur certain bad luck. Henry Harrison Powe left a widow and 10 children behind him.

A far less well-known story is the one about the killing of Thomas M. Wilson on his ranch south of Marfa in 1938 by Wayne Cartledge and his son Eugene. Wilson was a pioneer Big Bend rancher who came to the Davis Mountains in 1886. He prospered and in 1902 he married an Alpine schoolteacher and moved to Marfa. When the Marfa State Bank was organized in 1910 he was named president. He served as president until September 1932, when he resigned and was replaced by a younger man. It was in the depths of the Great Depression, and he was too tenderhearted to foreclose on the ranchers that he had known most of his life. He moved to his 40,000-acre Peñitas Ranch south of Marfa, and that is where he was killed on December 3, 1938.

The exact circumstances are hard to get at after nearly 80 years, but it appears from the newspaper accounts of the Cartledges' trial that Wilson and the Cartledges had become involved in an escalating dispute over a fence line and a water trough. The water trough was on Wilson's side of the fence, and Cartledge claimed that his purchase of the adjoining ranch included access to it. The two antagonists had exchanged words and notes about the matter for several months. Matters came to a head on the morning of December 3 when someone came to the Wilson ranch house and told Wilson that the Cartledges were preparing to cut the disputed fence and drive a herd of cattle through the gap to water them. Wilson drove out to the water trough and was waiting when the Cartledges drove up in a car. According to Eugene Cartledge's testimony at the trial, Wilson fired a rifle shot at his father, who was seated in the front seat of the car, and Eugene jumped out of the car and fired his pistol twice at Wilson, killing him instantly.

The state's lawyers told a different story, saying that Eugene Cartledge had fired first and that Wilson had discharged his weapon after falling to the ground, the bullet going through the running board of his own car.

Wilson was buried in the Marfa cemetery the next day. He had 90 honorary pall bearers. The *Big Bend Sentinel* listed their names on its front page. They included every prominent rancher in the Big Bend. This not only indicated the high esteem in which Wilson was held by his fellow-ranchers, it constituted a public endorsement by them of his actions the day before. His widow and two daughters placed a memorial window to him in St. Paul's Episcopal Church.

Wayne Cartledge was also an important self-made man in the Big Bend. He was a native of San Angelo, and had come to Terlingua in 1910 to work as a clerk in Howard Perry's Chisos Mining Company store. He quickly advanced to bookkeeper and then manager and purchasing agent, and in 1918 he and Perry formed a partnership which became the La Harmonia Trading Company, with a store at Castolon. He invested his profits in ranch land and cattle, and by 1938 he was a wealthy man. After Wilson's killing he hired one of West Texas's most prominent lawyers, Tom Lea of El Paso, to defend him and his son from the murder charges that had been brought against them. At the Cartledges' trial in August 1939 it took a jury just four hours to find them not guilty on the grounds of self defense. Eugene Cartledge died in 1960; Wayne Cartledge in 1972.

The two murder tales about Henry Harrison Powe and Thomas Meade Wilson came together in a particularly poignant way for me a couple of weeks ago. It was a Sunday and we had just finished services at St. Paul's Episcopal Church in Marfa when a lady approached me and introduced herself as Mrs. Dorothy Bauer from Seguin, Texas. She said that she understood that I was interested in the history of the church's stained glass windows, and when I said that I was she identified herself as Thomas M. Wilson's granddaughter. We discussed his killing, and the stories about it that she had heard from her grandmother, Wilson's widow. I said that incidents like that had been fairly common in the early days of the Big Bend, in the 1880s and 90s, but that they were rare in the 1930s, and that was why her grandfather's death had been so shocking. She said, "Oh, I know all about those old murders. My grandmother Wilson was Henry Harrison Powe's daughter." I asked Mrs. Bauer what her grandmother did after losing both her father and husband to violence in the Big Bend and she replied, "She moved to San Antonio."

April 28, 2016

THE EATING EPISCOPALIANS

IN THE 1930S the Methodists in Marfa were known as the Shouting Methodists because of the enthusiasm of their worship services. The Baptists were called the Dunking Baptists because of their commitment to total immersion as a form of baptism. The Episcopalians were the Eating Episcopalians because of the frequency of their church suppers, which anyone in the community was welcome to attend for a dime. Those suppers were a godsend to some families during the hard times of the Great Depression.

St. Paul's Episcopal Church in Marfa still feeds the community once a year on Thanksgiving, when 200 or so people have their Thanksgiving dinner in the parish hall. My wife, Dedie, and I first learned about the St. Paul's Thanksgiving dinner when we moved to Fort Davis in the summer of 2002. We are Episcopalians, and since there is no Episcopal church in Fort Davis, we started going to St. Paul's. When November rolled around and we heard about the dinner, my wife suggested that we go, and I said absolutely not, that I had eaten Thanksgiving dinner at home all of my life and I was not about to change, and that was it. My wife acquiesced, but the next year she said that if I would agree to go to the church dinner she would fix a second Thanksgiving dinner at home the next day. That sounded fair, so I agreed, and we had such a good time that we have gone back every year and I have never felt the need for a second dinner at home. St. Paul's Thanksgiving has become our family Thanksgiving, as it is for dozens of other Big Bend residents.

The Thanksgiving dinner at St. Paul's started in the early 1970s when some of the church ladies realized that there were many widows in Marfa who had no place to go on Thanksgiving Day. The ladies prepared a turkey and ham dinner in the parish hall and served it free to all comers. It is still free, and it still features ham and turkey, although for the past couple of years Tom Rapp and Toshi Sakihara of Cochineal have contributed a delicious brisket. The best part, however, is the side dishes: sweet potatoes, mashed potatoes, casseroles, three kinds of cranberry sauce, five kinds of dressing. Evelyn Luciani made fifty pounds of mashed potatoes, and a lady from San Antonio showed up at our house one year the Wednesday afternoon before Thanksgiving to put together the dressing she had promised to bring after the previous year's dinner. I won't even try to write about the desserts. As I looked around the parish hall last Thursday I realized that the St. Paul's Thanksgiving Dinner is not just a Marfa community event, it has become a tourist destination. The same families from San Antonio and Fort Worth and Austin return each year.

St. Paul's has been woven into the fabric of life in Marfa for a long time. In 1884 Mary Walker Humphris started a non-denominational Sunday school in her home on San Antonio Street (now the Marfa-Presidio County Museum). Humphris was an Englishwoman, the wife of John Humphris of Humphris, Walker, and Murphy, Marfa's largest mercantile store. She was an Episcopalian and was concerned about the religious education of children in the wild frontier town that Marfa was then. In 1887 she and her husband persuaded several other Protestant families to join them in building an adobe Union Church, where visiting ministers preached sporadically. That building is now Camp Bosworth's and Buck Johnston's art studio.

Mary Humphris occasionally got a visiting Episcopal priest to hold services in the Union Church, but Episcopal priests were few and far between in the trans-Pecos in those days, and she used the Book of Common Prayer to conduct baptisms and funerals and lead prayers for the sick and dying herself. In fact she did everything an Episcopal priest could do except celebrate Eucharist and marry people. Finally, in 1898, the Missionary Bishop of New Mexico gave Marfa's Episcopalians permission to build their own church, with the peculiar (for Episcopalians) proviso that no entertainments be held to raise money for the construction costs. John and Mary Humphris paid for the building, which was on the lot where the Paisano Hotel now stands. That was the first St. Paul's.

That building was demolished in 1929, when the Paisano was built, but the stained glass windows were moved to the new St. Paul's on North Highland, just north of the courthouse. It was from those windows that I first started learning about the history of Marfa. One of them was given in 1924 in memory of Sarah Newton Bogel, the wife of Judge William Wordsworth Bogel. The Bogels came to Presidio County in 1884 and settled on Alamito Creek, where they developed one of the largest sheep ranches in the trans-Pecos. Part of St. Paul's folklore has to do with the time Judge Bogel presented the church's rector with a new car. The rector was so grateful that he drove all the way out to the ranch to personally thank the judge. A thunderstorm came up, and the judge invited the rector to remain at the ranch overnight. The rector somewhat brusquely declined, saying that he had to get back to town. On the way back he tried to drive across a flooded arroyo. The new car was washed away but the rector survived. Judge Bogel did not offer to replace the car.

Another window commemorates the death in World War II of Ephraim King, Jr., the son of a prominent Marfa insurance man. It depicts the young soldier as St. George in armor, a lance in his hand and a white horse beside him. He was killed when the B-17 in which he was a waist gunner was shot down over Italy. He was the only member of the crew who was unable to parachute to safety.

Ted and Frances Harper, who ranch near Casa Piedra, don't get in to church as often as they used to—Ted is 93 and it is 40 miles over a dirt road to their ranch —but when they do come it is a family affair. Their children and grandchildren and great-grand-children fill three pews. A couple of years ago, as we were all leaving the church after the Christmas Eve service, Frances said to me, "This is the 70ᵀᴴ Christmas Eve that Ted and I have come to this service." Two years ago their children gave a stained glass window in their honor, saying that they wanted their parents to see it while they were still living. It depicts the view from their ranch house, a landscape of blooming prickly pear and ocotillo with twin mountains on the horizon. Drop by and see it some-time—St. Paul's is always open.

December 3, 2009

THE 1970 WORLD SOARING CHAMPIONSHIP

THE FOURTH OF JULY, 1970, carried an extra punch for Marfa. The Fourth was the final day of the 12TH World Soaring Championships, 14 days of sailplane competitions among pilots from 25 countries, and a thousand people from all over the world had gathered in Marfa to watch them. The championship meet was held in Marfa because of something called the Marfa Dry Line, a meteorological phenomenon involving the collision of moist air from the Gulf of Mexico with dry air from the Western deserts. The collision produces thermal columns of rising air that have made Marfa a paradise for sailplane enthusiasts because sailplane pilots use those thermal columns to gain altitude and distance for their motorless gliders.

The columns were first discovered in the summer of 1960, when some sailplane pilots visited Marfa after the National Soaring Championships in Odessa. They brought back enthusiastic reports of the soaring opportunities on the Marfa Flats, and throughout the sixties soaring enthusiasts turned up in increasing numbers every summer. In 1962 George Moffat set some speed records here, and in 1963 Neil Armstrong, just beginning his career as a NASA astronaut, participated in the first organized Marfa Soaring Meet. Four years later Marfa hosted the 34ᵀᴴ National Soaring Contest, an event that was repeated in 1969, when some of the pilots used the new fiberglass sailplanes (the earlier ones were made of metal).

The two national meets at Marfa set the stage for the 1970 World Soaring Championships. It was the first time that the biennial contest had ever been held in the United States. Contestants and their crews and planes started arriving in Marfa the second week in June and practice flights started from the Presidio County Airport—the old Marfa Army Air Force Flying Field on U.S. 90—on June 16. Most teams shipped their planes to the States by freighter and then trailered them to Marfa (the New Zealanders plane got lost and they had to drive from San Francisco to Tacoma to retrieve it), but the Chilean team and their plane arrived at the Marfa airport in a Chilean Air Force DC-6. By opening day, June 22, teams had arrived from 25 countries, including the island of Guernsey in the English Channel, which under the rules of the International Aeronautical Institute qualified as an independent nation. The pilots and the team managers were housed in air-conditioned trailers at the airport; the crew members were in rows of tents. Meals were catered in a makeshift mess hall.

Sailplane pilots are a free-spirited bunch and the contest's mimeographed daily bulletin is full of accounts of parties. Local families adopted each team and entertained them. The Poles won all of the contests on the opening day and the Herman Ledbetters invited them home and fed them steaks. The Christophers gave a party for the Austrians at which "copious quantities of Lone Star beer were demolished," according to the bulletin. Bill and Mary Kay Meriwether gave a ranch party for all the pilots and officials, about 300 people, and served them barbecue and "baked head in the ground." The 400 crew members who were not invited to the Meriwethers that night had a party of their own at the Municipal Swimming Pool, where Mayor Clyde McFarland made a speech and a mariachi band played until midnight.

The contest rules divided the sailplanes into two categories: limited class, for planes with wingspans of under 15 meters; and open class, for planes with wider wingspans. Prizes were given in both categories. The "tasks," as the daily contests were called, involved "out and return" flights over set courses of several hundred miles—Marfa to Sierra Blanca and back, Marfa to Carlsbad and back, Marfa to Fort Stockton and back—and the pilots were scored on a combination of speed and distance. The planes usually took off about 11:00 A.M. and returned late in the afternoon. Sometimes a pilot did not have enough altitude to make it back to Marfa and would have to land his plane somewhere and have it trailered back. On the first contest day, June 22, Willi Deleurant of Canada came down in the desert north of Van Horn and walked 28 miles to a ranch with a telephone. That same day one of the Australian pilots put his plane down on U.S. 90 at Van Horn and was fined $100 for blocking the highway; a few hours later a South African pilot did the same thing; his fine was $150. Fritz Kahl, who served as contest director, and his assistant, Red Wright, were on the scene at the time of the second landing and passed a hat around, raising enough money from the crowd that had gathered to recompense both pilots. Even the arresting officers contributed.

The weather was not ideal. It rained every afternoon until July 1, but the pilots guided their planes around or above the thunderstorms. There were hazards on the ground, too. The Germans and the Austrians got into a contest to see which team could catch the biggest snake. The prize was the number of cans of beer that equaled the length of the snake, measured in the diameter of the beer can. A member of the Italian team, Piero Morelli, was bitten by a Brown Recluse spider and taken to the Alpine hospital to be treated. Morelli later said, "The only living creature in Texas that did not welcome me was a spider."

When the final scores were totted up on July 4ᵀᴴ, Helmut Reichmann of West Germany was the winner of the standard class and George Moffat of the United States of the open class. Reichmann, who had only 250 hours of glider flying under his belt, went on to win two more world soaring championships and became a professor of industrial design at the University of Saarbrucken. Moffat, who started flying gliders in 1959 and won a second world championship in 1974, has written two books and 85 articles on soaring. Neither man ever forgot Marfa, nor did any of the other thousand people who gathered here over those two weeks in 1970. One of them, Burt Compton, who was 19 at the time, returned to Marfa 30 years later and established a glider school. He is still here and will share the thrill of soaring with you any day you care to take a glider ride.

October 17, 2015

THE FOOD SHARK

TWENTY-FIVE YEARS ago the Irish novelist Roddy Doyle published a hilarious book called *The Van* about the misadventures of three working-class Dubliners who purchase an old van and try to sell fish and chips from it. In Doyle's novel everything goes wrong that possibly can, and the entrepreneurs end up driving the van into the Irish Sea and leaving it there. I doubt if this will be the fate of Marfa's first food van, the Food Shark. I spent an afternoon not long ago talking with the Food Shark's proprietors, Adam Bork and Krista Steinhauer, and they seem far more competent than Doyle's characters, who are lovable but seldom sober. Another major difference is that Doyle's trio started their mobile food business out of economic necessity, while Bork and Steinhauer started theirs because they bought a van and then had to figure out what to do with it.

The van is not exactly a thing of beauty or an example of classic automobile design. It consists of a bulky aluminum body built 30 or so years ago onto a 1974 Ford truck chassis by a now defunct outfit in San Angelo called Ford Brothers. Internal evidence shows that it was once a Rainbow Bread delivery truck, but when Bork and Steinhauer spotted it sitting behind a short-lived barbecue joint in Marfa last year it had been converted into a food service vehicle. "It had a lot of personality," Steinhauer told me, "a kind of cute grill and face." They decided that they couldn't live without it, and with the help of their friend Ginger Griffice they bought it (Griffice, who sometimes helps out with lunch at the Food Shark, describes herself as a "plankholder" in the enterprise, which must be something more substantial than a stakeholder).

When they bought the van in February 2006, neither Bork nor Steinhauer, who came to Marfa from Austin in 2004 to help open the Thunderbird Motel, had any previous experience in the food preparation business, although Bork was once a waiter and busboy in an Austin restaurant and Steinhauer had put in a brief stint as a cheese and chocolate buyer for a specialty food store in San Francisco. In fact Bork was a well-known musician in Austin, playing the electric guitar in venues like Antone's and the Continental Club under the name Earth Pig (he will be putting out an album soon, recorded at the Gory Smelley studio in Marfa).

Steinhauer, however, lived in Florence, Italy for four years and traveled a good deal in the Eastern Mediterranean, where she acquired a taste for what she describes as "Middle Eastern street food." Not only that, her father had once been in the food van business, and when she told him about the new vehicle he started sending her drawings showing how to install kitchen equipment in it (actually, when she first sent him a picture of the van, his response was, "Maybe you should have sent me a photo before you bought it," but then the drawings started arriving). "Things just jelled." Bork says. "It was just crazy enough to work."

They started serving lunch from the van in October 2006.

Steinhauer is in charge of the menus, which have a core of Middle Eastern falafel and hummus supplemented with daily specials that tend toward dishes that Steinhauer describes as "more instantly recognizable," such as barbecue sandwiches and tacos. She prepares most of the food, while Bork is in charge of mixing the hummus and taking care of the cold drinks. Their day starts about 7:00 AM, when Steinhauer starts making the day's supply of falafel in her catering kitchen and transferring it to the van for final assembly. Falafel, she explained, is a mixture of ground garbanzo beans, cilantro, Italian parsley, fresh mint, garlic, onions, "plus a couple of little secrets." The van is equipped with an ice box, a hot plate, and a deep-fryer, and the falafel balls that are the Food Shark's staple are formed from Steinhauer's pre-mixed supply and fried when the customer orders them. Hummus is also based on garbanzo beans, cooked and mixed with lemon juice and olive oil—"We go through buckets of olive oil," Steinhauer said. Bork and Steinhauer obtain their ingredients from a variety of sources. A wholesale food company provides the basics, but they make monthly runs to Austin and El Paso for cheese and olive oil, and they are making increasing use of locally-grown cucumbers, carrots, herbs, and greens. "The more we can get locally the better," Steinhauer says.

By 11:30 AM on most days the van is in place next to the railroad crossing on South Highland Avenue. They generally serve lunch four days a week but as Bork says, "like all Marfa businesses that is not an absolute." On open days between 50 and 80 people will have lunch at picnic tables under a metal canopy provided by Lynn and Tim Crowley, who own the land that the van parks on and have been major supporters of the enterprise. Diners are treated to classic country music—Ray Price and Tammy Wynette with an occasional sprinkling of rock bands like The Guess Who—played at a moderate volume from a pair of orange speakers mounted on top of the van. One of the first things Bork added after buying the vehicle was an 8-track tape sound system. After all, he is a musician. They usually serve their last meal about 2:30—"unless we run out of food," Bork cautions—and by 3:00 PM the van is buttoned down and ready to be driven back to the catering kitchen. Bork says that they put 1.2 miles a day on it, and have not yet had to change the oil.

I asked the question that must be on the tip of everybody's tongue the first time they talk to Bork and Steinhauer: why do they call their van the Food Shark? The name causes a certain amount of confusion with non-English speaking visitors to Marfa, who occasionally step up to the window and want to know what kind of shark is being served. Bork says that the name just popped into his head. "It might have something to do with the way the truck looks," he says. I'm not sure what this says about someone who occasionally calls himself Earth Pig, but wherever it came from, Food Shark has become synonymous with good food in Marfa.

August 23, 2007

WINDMILLS

IF YOU LOOK on your left as you drive north out of Marfa on State Highway 17 you will see one of the most evocative symbols of the Western cattle ranching industry. It is a windmill on the Dixon Water Foundation's Mimms Ranch, and at sunset the tower, wheel, and metal tank are silhouetted against the evening sky, a perfect photo opportunity and one that is frequently taken advantage of by visitors, judging from the number of times I see a car parked on the shoulder there. I doubt if many of those photographers realize the significance of windmills for West Texas and indeed for the entire West. The windmill is a machine that has made life possible on arid land.

Cattle and humans need water, and before windmills came to West Texas the only way a rancher could provide it was to secure title to land with a creek or spring on it. Creeks and springs are few and far between in the Big Bend and across the rest of West Texas, so a lot of good grassland went unused because it was impossible to get water to it. The windmill-powered water pump changed all of this.

Sail-powered windmills, of course, have been around for centuries—we all remember that Don Quixote jousted with one in
Spain—but they were used primarily for grinding grain, which is
why they were called windMILLS, and they had to be manually
set in order for their sails to catch the wind. The self-governing, water-pumping windmill is an American invention. The first
ones were manufactured in the 1850s by the Halliday Wind Mill
Company of South Coventry, Connecticut. They were powered by
a wheel with wooden blades that automatically feathered themselves as wind velocity increased and they had a wooden vane or fin
mounted at right angles to the wheel that kept it pointed into the
wind. The Halliday self-governing system was improved on in the
late 1860s by the Eclipse Wind Mill Company of Beloit, Wisconsin,
and Eclipse windmills, some of them with wooden wheels as large
as 30 feet in diameter, became the most popular windmills on the
Western plains in the 1880s and 90s. The railroads erected them
every 30 miles or so along their tracks to provide water for steam
locomotives, and ranchers used them to pump water from wells
into tanks in otherwise waterless pastures. They are mostly gone
now; you occasionally see their huge wooden wheels in museums
or Western themed restaurants, but a 22 ½ foot example has been
pumping at the Cannon Ranch west of Sheffield, Texas since 1898.
It is now on the National Register of Historic Places.

Metal bladed wheels began to replace wooden wheels in the
1880s, although at least one wooden wheeled windmill was still
being manufactured in the United States in 1940. Metal bladed
windmills were popularized by the Aermotor Company, founded
in Chicago in 1888 and still making windmills today at its factory
in San Angelo, Texas. The iconic windmill on the Mimms ranch

is an Aermotor. There have been many other windmill manufacturers over the years. T. Lindsay Baker's classic *Field Guide to American Windmills* (University of Oklahoma Press, 1985) lists over a thousand brands, ranging from Abbot to Zephyr.

Ranchers welcomed the water pumped by windmills but the windmills themselves were a constant irritant. Their delicate machinery required continual tinkering, and the tinkering had to be done while clinging to a rickety wooden or steel tower, a tower that in the wintertime was likely to be coated with ice. On the earliest windmills the most onerous task was oiling the bearings, which meant climbing the tower at least once a week to fill the grease cup above them. Eventually manufacturers added a closed oil reservoir that could be activated by pulling a wire that ran down the tower to the ground, and that reduced the number of climbing trips, but the reservoir itself still had to be refilled occasionally. Finally, in 1912, the Elgin Wind Power Company, which produced a windmill called the Terrible Swede, introduced its Wonder Windmill, whose working parts were completely enclosed in a recycling oil bath, much like an automobile crankcase. The Wonder gave rise to a number of knock-offs with names like the Demptser Annu-Oiled, the Butler Oilomatic, and the Axtell Ever-Oiled. Lindsay Baker calls the Wonder Windmill the most important single innovation in windmill design in the 20ᵀᴴ century.

Even with the lubricating problem solved, sucker rods came loose, leathers wore out, and a thousand other problems required climbing the tower. Cowboys hated working on windmills, and those who were good enough to get away with it would specify when applying for jobs that they would do anything on a ranch as long as they could do it horseback (which also excluded digging postholes). A new Western occupation, that of windmiller, grew up to fill in the gap. Windmillers understood machinery and were not acrophobic, but there was not always one around when you needed him, and so cowboys continued to climb windmills with wrenches in one hand.

One of the best examples of cowboy humor that I know of involves windmill repair. Paul Patterson of Crane liked to tell about two cowboys who were working on a windmill. The one on the tower dropped his wrench, and just as it glanced off the head of the one on the ground the man on the tower hollered, "Look out!" The man on the ground looked up and said, "What are you gonna do? Throw another one?"

I spent most of one summer living in a log cabin in the mountains above Las Vegas, New Mexico, finishing a book. The cabin had no electricity and no running water, but it had a windmill fifty feet from the front door with a water tap and an outdoor shower. The clank of that windmill at night was sweet and restful. When my wife, Dedie, and I built our house in Fort Davis I thought about drilling a well and putting in a windmill just to hear that clank, but then I thought about the trips up that tower on cold January mornings when the water wasn't running and decided city water was just fine.

August 13, 2015

THE WORLD'S MOST EXPENSIVE DRIVE-IN

THE PIONEER MARFA rancher Luke Brite was a devout member of a Protestant religious denomination called the Disciples of Christ. He and his wife, Eddie, joined the Disciples at a camp meeting held in 1911 by Addison Clark, one of the founders of Texas Christian University. The Brites endowed the Brite College of the Bible, now Brite Divinity School, at T.C.U. They also hired a Phoenix, Arizona architect, Leighton Green Knipe, to design the First Christian Church in Marfa. Knipe gave them a magnificent building whose sanctuary will seat five hundred people. The Brites clearly operated on the If You Build It They Will Come theory.

The only problem was that they didn't come. The Disciples are a small denomination, and even during World War II, when Marfa's population was swollen by two military installations, there were never more than two hundred people in church there, and that was on Christmas and Easter. The congregation eventually dwindled to six, and the church was closed several years ago.

On the other hand, the If You Build It They Will Come theory has worked for other institutions in Marfa. Who would have thought, when Donald Judd arrived here in 1972, that his work would turn Marfa into an international art center where you can hear half a dozen languages spoken on Highland Avenue any Saturday of the year? Who would have thought that you could find three Michelin-quality restaurants and a superb bookstore in a West Texas town of 2200 people? Who would have dreamed that the most remote and thinly populated region of Texas could support an active public radio station? Miracles will happen.

Now a project is underway that will test the If You Build It They Will Come theory to the utmost. Marfa is about to become the site of the world's most expensive drive-in movie theater. The theater will be built by Ballroom Marfa on 8.35 acres of land in Vizcaino Park which has been leased by the Ballroom from Presidio County. According to Melissa McDonnell, the Ballroom's project manager for the theater, the total cost of the project will be $4,500,000.

Drive-in theaters were a common feature of the American landscape in the 1950s and 60s. The first one was built in Camden, New Jersey in 1933 by chemical manufacturer Richard M. Hollingshead, who nailed sheets to trees in his backyard and balanced a projector on the hood of his car in order to determine the proper angles and throw distances. He advertised his theater with the slogan "The Whole Family is Welcome, Regardless of How Noisy the Children Are."

The popularity of drive-ins was a function of the baby boom that followed World War II, when many young families had noisy children. There were just over a hundred drive-ins in the United States in 1946. By 1948 there were 820, and by 1958 there were 5,000. Most of them accommodated 400 or 500 cars, but the Panther Drive-In in Lufkin, Texas, one of the largest in the country, had spaces for 3,000 automobiles. Drive-in owners added playgrounds for the children and concession stands, some of them serving full meals, for adults. Even Marfa, with a population of 3,600, had a drive-in, which opened in 1953 just west of the cemetery and closed six years later.

Drive-ins proved to be a short-lived cultural phenomenon. The development of color television and rental videos combined with rising urban real estate values made them unprofitable, and most of them closed in the 1970s and 80s. In 1960 twenty-five percent of all American movie theatres were drive-ins; today the figure is one and a half percent.

The Ballroom's drive-in is not going to be built on the 1950s model. It will be a twenty-first century drive in. It will only accommodate 90 cars, but it will have amphitheater seating for 1,200 people between the cars and the screen. Melissa McDonnell describes it as "a pedestrian drive-in." It is really an outdoor events space where concerts and performances incorporating film can take place. According to McDonnell, it was inspired by the Red Rocks Amphitheater, a natural amphitheater near Denver that seats 9,450 people and is a popular concert venue. Architect Michael Meredith of MOS, the New York firm that is designing the space, told me that the 40-foot wide, 52- foot high screen will resemble an acoustically coffered bandshell, and the cars will be parked on a series of mounds that will place their occupants at a 90-degree angle to the screen. In designing the structure, Meredith has made use of engineering manuals from the 1950s that contain specifications for drive-in theaters, but he has also consulted with contemporary film curators and projectionists from the Museum of Modern Art and the Museum of Fine Arts, Houston. Meredith knows the peculiarities of the territory here because he was a Chinati fellow in Marfa in 2000. In his formal statement about the project he says, "We hadn't experienced weather as an object until we lived in Marfa, Texas." He is undaunted by the challenge of designing a facility for which there is no precedent in such a remote location; he told me that all of his firm's current projects are in remote locations. When I asked him for examples he said, "We're building an orphanage in Katmandu, a folk school in a village in Jutland, and a house on Georgian Bay in Canada." Meredith clearly understands remoteness and plans to produce a state-of-the-art structure.

Four and a half million dollars is a lot of money to gamble on the If You Build It They Will Come theory. McDonnell says that construction is expected to start next year and the theater is to be completed in the summer of 2015. Whether They Will Come or not remains to be seen. If they do, it will be a great thing for Marfa. If they don't, it will be one of the biggest white elephants in Texas.

February 28, 2013

Editor's Note: The Marfa Ballroom's drive-in theater project was dropped in 2014 due to projected cost overruns.

THE WORLD'S LEAST EXPENSIVE DRIVE-IN

DAVID BEEBE IS an enterprising young man who has anticipated Ballroom Marfa's drive-in theater project by creating his own drive-in movie theater, which he estimates cost $2,500 to build and which is already operating on the lot Beebe leases behind Padre's in Marfa. He calls the lot Airstreamland because it has five Airstream trailers parked on it in addition to a taco stand, a recycling center, and a 1967 Chevrolet Suburban that once belonged to the University of Texas Department of Zoology, where it was known as Murgatroyd.

The Ballroom's drive-in will have a screen that measures 40 by 52 feet. Airstreamland's screen measures 6 ¾ by 12 feet and is constructed from three sawed-off telephone poles, some 2 x 6 planks, and a piece of plywood. Beebe has given it three coats of industrial oil-based paint and plans to add a coat of gray movie screen paint containing glass beads, which costs $300 a can. His projection booth is a metal table with "Cerveza Superior" stamped in each of the four corners, the type of table you used to find in Juarez *cantinas*. His projector is a $400 Viewsonic digital projector, and the sound system is a loudspeaker and a one-half watt transmitter, which does not require a license but which can be picked up on a car radio at FM 90.1 within a two-block radius of Airstreamland. Beebe says he doesn't know how many cars the theatre will accommodate because 80 per cent of his audience arrives on foot and sits on folding chairs to watch the films. In addition to his taco trailer, which is currently only open for lunch, Beebe plans to open another trailer called the Rib Krib, where he and Delfin Lopez will make barbecue for moviegoers.

Beebe describes the drive-in as "a grass-roots, bare bones, guerilla-style project." The idea started, he told me, last fall when Emily Bovino, a Fieldwork Marfa scholar, wanted to project a film on the side of his taco stand, and it just grew. "It's a typical Marfa project," he said. "It wouldn't work if everyone wasn't on the same page."

Beebe says that Airstreamland will be the center of a new Marfa entertainment district. "You can watch a movie for a while, eat some barbecue, and then drive to Padre's, Grilled Cheese, or Planet Marfa and still pick up the sound. It's not even in the center of town, it's in the suburbs." He says that he may ask the city to put up signs that say "Historic Railroad Cultural District" in the neighborhood.

Beebe's conversational style is richly-textured, rapid-fire, and circuitous, and it is sometimes hard to tell when he is joking. He probably could get the city to put up historic district signs, because he has been a respected member of the Marfa city council since 2008. Here is an example of his style. When I asked him how he decided to run for city council, he immediately said, "You can't fight city hall." Then he paused for a few seconds, obviously organizing his thoughts, and started telling me what a hard time he had finding a place to live when he first moved to Marfa from Houston in 2006 as a co-owner of Padre's. He could not find a house or apartment to rent that he could afford, he said, so he planned to live in the building that was to become Padre's while it was being remodeled. The contractor told him that would be impossible because there was no electricity or running water. Beebe described to me in some detail the condition of the building and the impossibility of living there.

Then the scene of the narrative shifted to Houston and the Continental Club, which Beebe managed before coming to Marfa. A customer had left an old Airstream trailer in the club's parking lot, a trailer that was in terrible condition because it had been in the Florida Everglades for many years. Beebe vividly described the mold and rot in the trailer and told me how a Houston gang had tagged it with their graffiti; how the owner of the Continental Club had told the owner of the Airstream to get it out of the parking lot, offering to store it in the yard behind the club for $500 a month; and how he had eventually persuaded the owner to sell it to Beebe.

Beebe than described how he had gone to the Marfa city hall to make sure that it would be legal for him to live in a trailer parked on the street and how, after a month of repeated inquiries, had been told by the then city administrator that it would be fine. He told me how much time and money he had spent fixing up the derelict Everglades Airstream and towing it to Marfa and how, after he had been living in it here for a month, he was summoned to Mayor Dan Dunlap's office, where he was politely told that the former city administrator had been wrong and that he was violating a city ordinance by living in his trailer. "The mayor was very apologetic," Beebe said, "but he showed me the ordinance and there it was;

there was no doubt about it. He gave me two weeks to find another place to live."

At that point, Beebe said, "I thought, this town is crazy and I'm planning to open a club here? I decided I would go to every city council meeting from then on and learn how this place works." He did, and when the 2008 election rolled around Mayor Dunlap asked him to run for city council, saying that he obviously had an interest in city government. Beebe did and won a seat, and has been a committed and productive member of the city council ever since.

My conclusion from listening to Beebe is that he has not only superb narrative skills but considerable political skills, and that when he decides to do something it will be done thoroughly and well. I don't think Marfa will have to wait for the Ballroom's project to be finished to have a first-class drive-in theatre, and I think Marfa will hear a lot more from David Beebe.

April 4, 2013

THE PLAYBOY MARFA CAPER

EVERYONE IS BEING so negative about the 40-foot high neon bunny on a stick that is Playboy Enterprises' contribution to the outdoor sculpture garden that is growing up along U.S. 90 west of Marfa that I decided that I had better drive out and have a look at it myself. I was out of town when it suddenly appeared, and all I knew about it until last night was what Beto Halpern wrote about it in Thursday's paper and what Lauren Klotzman had to say about it in the on-line art blog *Hyperallergic*. Now I've seen it. I hate to pass an aesthetic judgment on it. After all, I'm a historian, not an art critic. I'll just say that I agree with my friend Anthony DeSimone, who is quoted in *Hyperallergic* as saying, "Worst thing ever to happen here. End of story." As everyone knows, Anthony has impeccable taste. You only have to look at his socks to realize that. I will add that it is the ugliest and most offensive structure that I have seen in a long time.

But I am an optimist. I like to look at the bright side of things, to make lemonade out of lemons. I also have a deep respect for the English language and for calling things by their right names. I may be the last person in America who calls challenges problems. So I think the first step in making lemonade out of the neon Playboy bunny is to call it advertising instead of art. It prominently displays Playboy's corporate logo, it was paid for by Playboy Enterprises, and it was designed and erected by an employee of that company. Ergo, it is advertising.

Once that is clear to everyone, we can proceed with the lemonade. Why not create the world's first outdoor museum of corporate advertising along U.S. 90 between Marfa and Valentine? The Prada installation west of Valentine could serve as one bookend (and please don't try to tell me that is not advertising; it is just not as heavy-handed as Playboy's contribution) and the Playboy bunny could be the other. In between, artists could be commissioned to produce sculpture based on famous corporate logos.

The most prominent spot, perhaps halfway between Prada and Playboy, should go to Texas's most famous corporate logo, the red Pegasus that graces the top of the Magnolia Hotel in Dallas. When the 29-story skyscraper was completed in 1922 the architect, Sir Alfred Bossom, declared it the "tallest building between Mexico City and the North Pole," but in 1934 the Magnolia Oil Company, which then owned the building, decided to extend its height by adding an oil derrick supporting two 30 by 45 foot steel and porcelain flying red horses, its corporate logo, to the roof. The horses, one on each side of the derrick, were outlined in red neon and revolved. They deteriorated over the years and in 1999 they were replaced with exact reproductions made by the Dallas firm of Casteel and Associates. I'll bet Casteel and Associates would be happy to accept a commission to install another set of reproductions in the new Marfa Garden of Advertising.

One of America's most famous corporate logos is the V-8

symbol developed by the Ford Motor Company, an elegant in-
terlocked letter V and numeral 8. It referred to the v-shaped,
8-cylinder engines used in Fords between 1932 and 1953 and it
appeared on the radiator badge and hubcaps of the Fords of my
childhood. Those cars were simply referred to as "V-8s," and the
symbol embodied power and speed. It was a 1934 Ford V-8 that
inspired Clyde Barrow to write a letter to Henry Ford telling him
what a fine getaway car he built. I can see a 100-foot high V-8
symbol towering above a 1934 Ford on a concrete platform. I
would suggest that the window and windshield glass be removed
from the Ford before it is placed on the platform to discourage
drive-by pistol plinkers. Not that anyone from the Big Bend would
ever do that that, but visitors from big cities are notoriously free
with firearms when they get into the countryside.

Another classic corporate logo is the Lucky Strike cigarette
package, a red circle on a white background with the words "Lucky
Strike" in the circle, designed by Raymond Loewy in 1942 to replace the old dark green packages. The change was heralded by a
series of ads proclaiming "Lucky Strike Green Has Gone To War"
and explaining that the copper used to manufacture the green ink
was needed for the war effort. A giant slab-like white Lucky Strike
package, rising out of the prairie near the gate to the Ryan Ranch,
would be a nifty addition to our outdoor museum. Special light-
ing effects could be employed to change the color of the package
from white to pre-war green and back every five minutes. Viewers
parked on the highway shoulder waiting for the change could be
entertained by loudspeakers playing the Lucky Strike commercials
from the Jack Benny radio show, an auctioneer chanting bids for a
bale of tobacco and ending, "Sold, American!"

Having introduced special effects, I'll bet some Marfa film guru could come up with a projection system that could project the famous MGM lion logo roaring on a 100-foot high screen of smoke ejected into a pasture alongside U.S. 90. The MGM motto that appears on a ribbon around the lion's head, *Ars Gratia Artis*—Art for the Sake of Art—would be particularly ironic in this context.

There are many other candidates for inclusion in our new museum: McDonald's Golden Arches, Taco Bell's mission bell, KFC's chicken bucket. The possibilities are limited only by curatorial imagination. Of course, the installations, as in all museums, should have labels, and the labels should include an explanation of the origin of the logos. The label on the Playboy bunny should include a quote from an interview Hugh Hefner gave to Oriana Fallaci for *Look* magazine in 1968. In explaining the bunny logo, Hefner said, "I chose it because it's a fresh animal, shy, vivacious, jumping, sexy. First it smells you, then it escapes, then it comes back, and you feel like caressing it, playing with it. A girl resembles a bunny."

June 20, 2013

THE VIN FIZ FLYER COMES TO MARFA

 I HAD MY first encounter with the Vin Fiz Flyer when I was six years old. We were living in Washington, D.C., and I was spending a Saturday at the Smithsonian Institution with my father. This was before the National Air and Space Museum was built, and several historic airplanes, including the first one built by the Wright brothers, were suspended from the ceiling of the Arts and Industries Building. We had just finished examining the Wright brothers' plane when my father spotted the Vin Fiz Flyer hanging nearby. It looked like a big box kite with wings, made out of polished wood struts and covered with fabric. The words "Vin Fiz" and a bunch of grapes were painted on the bottom of the lower wing. There were two wooden propellers behind the wings, connected to the engine by what looked like bicycle chains.

My father explained that the airplane had been used by Cal Rodgers to make the first transcontinental airplane flight in 1911. "I saw it when he landed in Fort Worth," my father said. "I rode my bicycle out to Ryan's Pasture to see it. It was the first airplane I ever saw. It sounded like a motorcycle up in the sky."

Calbraith Perry Rodgers (he was named after his great-grandfather Matthew Calbraith Perry, the U.S. naval officer who opened Japan to foreign trade in 1853), was what in his day was called a sportsman. He lived in rooms above the New York Yacht club and raced yachts and motorcycles, and in 1911 he decided to learn to fly. He went to Dayton, Ohio and paid the Wright Brothers $850 for flying lessons and then he bought an airplane from them. His pilot's license, issued on August 9, 1911, was number 49.

The first thing Rodgers did after getting his flying license was to enter the Chicago International Aviation Meet, at which two dozen European and American aviators competed for prizes. Rodgers walked away with $11,285 in prize money. He was a daredevil and would try anything.

Emboldened by his success in Chicago, he then entered the William Randolph Hearst transcontinental flight competition, which offered a $50,000 prize to the first aviator to fly across the United States in 30 days. Rodgers bought a second airplane, an EK Flyer, from the Wright brothers, and found a sponsor, the Armour food company, which was introducing a new grape-flavored soft drink called Vin Fiz. The Armour Company agreed to provide a special train consisting of a Pullman buffet car, a day coach, and a "hangar car" housing a completely-equipped workshop and spare parts that would follow Rodgers's plane, and to pay Rodgers $5.00 for every mile he flew east of the Mississippi and $4.00 for every mile west of the river. When Rodgers balked at the reduced rate for the less populous western miles, the company's publicity agent told him, "Even three-foot high jackrabbits don't buy Vin Fiz."

Rodgers left Sheepshead Bay, New York, on September 17, 1911, and arrived in Pasadena, California 49 days later on November 5, forfeiting the Hearst prize but becoming the first aviator to cross the United States in an airplane and a national hero. He flew in hops of 50 to 200 miles at about 60 miles an hour, landing in fields and pastures to refuel from the train that followed him and eating and sleeping on the train. He spent as many days on the ground as he did in the air, as he wrecked the plane 16 times on take-offs and landings and it had to be repaired each time by the mechanics on the train. By the time he got to Pasadena he had used up six wings, eight propellers, four propeller chains, two engines, two radiators, two tails, four fins, and one elevating plane. One of the mechanics said that the only original parts of the plane left were the vertical rudder and a drip pan.

Rodgers, who stood six feet four, flew crouched on a corduroy saddle on the plane's lower wing, with his feet resting on a bar below the wing. The four-cylinder engine pounded away beside him. His back was against the gasoline tank and a second gasoline tank was suspended over his head. He usually flew at between 2,000 and 4,000 feet and had absolutely no protection from the wind and rain. His flying attire was a business suit, over which he wore leather leggings and a leather motorcyclist's vest. On particularly cold days he stuffed newspapers under the vest.

He navigated by following the railroad tracks, flying along the Erie from New York to Chicago, the M.K.T. from Chicago to San Antonio, and the Southern Pacific from San Antonio to Los Angeles. He told reporters that the roughest part of the trip was the flight over West Texas between Del Rio and El Paso, as the country was broken up by canyons and mountains that generated strange air currents and provided few landing places.

Rodgers left Del Rio on October 26, 1911, and flew along the Rio Grande to Sanderson, where he spent the night aboard his train. High winds kept him on the ground in Sanderson all of the next day, and on the 28TH he hit a fence taking off, which meant that a wing had to be repaired. He finally got into the air about noon that day and flew to Alpine, where he landed for half an hour to refuel, and then to Marfa, where he landed in a field just south of the railroad tracks. He was on the ground in Marfa for about an hour before flying on to Sierra Blanca. His plane was surrounded by crowds at every landing spot.

Rodgers did not live to enjoy his fame. He spent the winter of 1911–1912 in California and was killed on April 3, 1912, when his plane suddenly plummeted into the ocean while he was giving an exhibition flight at Long Beach. His tombstone in Pittsburgh, Pennsylvania is topped by a bronze model of the Vin Fiz Flyer and bears the words, "I endure, I conquer."

January 27, 2011

THE MARFA ARMY AIR FIELD

I WAS AMUSED to pick up the *Big Bend Sentinel* a couple of weeks ago and see a story on the front page about someone who wants to build a motor raceway on the site of the old Marfa Army Air Field and then turn to page 10 and see a public notice saying that the Corps of Engineers was seeking information to determine if there were any unexploded munitions at that site. Let's hope they get the munitions cleaned up before the Porsches and Corvettes start racing.

The Marfa Army Air Field, established by the War Department in February 1942 as an advanced pilot training base, was the biggest thing that ever happened in Marfa, bigger even than the filming of *Giant*. The airfield, which was east of town on the south side of the road to Alpine, covered 2,750 acres and had six asphalt runways and 250 buildings. At its peak in April 1944 it had a total complement of 575 officers and 2,144 enlisted men and it employed 604 civilians. In addition, there were 1,009 student pilots training at the base, using 500 airplanes. The base post office employed five civilians and 25 military mail clerks. There is no reliable estimate of how many local girls married men stationed at the base.

One of those girls was Georgia Lee Jones, who married Lieutenant Chauncey M. (Fritz) Kahl, a pilot instructor, in May 1944. Their first home was an apartment in a house on Highland Avenue, just north of the courthouse. "The base created a housing shortage in Marfa," Georgia Lee told me. "People rented extra bedrooms out, and turned garages into apartments." The housing crisis spread beyond Marfa; Indian Lodge in Davis Mountains State Park was used to accommodate cadets' wives, and military families occupied the married students' housing on the Sul Ross campus. Eventually a 172-unit housing area for married civilian employees, called Marpine, was built on the base.

Fritz Kahl and his fellow pilot-instructors trained Army Air Corpsmen to fly twin-engine planes, graduating one class a month from February 1943 to May 1945. All in all, nearly 8,000 men went through the Marfa Advanced Flying School. The graduation ceremonies were monthly public events, with a parade, a military band, tours of the base, aerial demonstrations, and an evening dance. The basic training plane was the Cessna AT-17B, nicknamed the Bobcat but sometimes called the Bamboo Bomber because of its wood and fabric wing construction. Toward the end of the war, Beech AT-11s and North American B-25s were added to the flight line. The B-25 was not a trainer but a light bomber, the same plane that Colonel James Doolittle's squadron used to bomb Tokyo in April 1942.

With almost 300 new pilots in the air each month there were bound to be accidents. Several instructors and pilots were killed when their planes crashed or, on one occasion, collided in midair. One AT-17B simply disappeared; its wreckage was found two weeks later on the Juan Prieto ranch near Ruidoso, along with the

102

bodies of the instructor and pilot. In one bizarre incident, an instructor and his student strayed from the practice area and ran out of gas; they crash-landed on a sandbar on the Mexican side of the Rio Grande south of Castolon. Both pilot and student survived, but the Mexican government demanded that the disabled plane be moved out of Mexican territory. While arrangements were being made to winch the wreckage across the river, armed guards from the Marfa base were placed at the crash site, and the store at Castolon, where there was a primitive landing strip, became the supply base for the winching operation. Fritz Kahl was placed in charge of flying the supplies and guards to Castolon, and in a memoir he described that landing strip as "up-hill and down-hill with a dog leg about two-thirds of the way from the down-hill end." Every flight in and out of Castolon involved a white-knuckle take-off and landing, and the flights went on for several days.

In addition to danger, or perhaps because of it, the base generated frenzied wartime gaiety. There were some pretty hot bars in Marfa, including a place called The Little Red Bar that Georgia Lee Kahl said "ladies did not go into," and a dance hall called the Marfa Joy. The focal points for more sedate entertainment were the officers' club and the U.S.O. building in town, where dances attended by local families as well as base personnel were held nearly every weekend and where Mario Lanza, who was stationed on the base as a non-commissioned officer, sometimes sang (a separate U.S.O. was maintained for black soldiers). There was also a post theatre which opened in December 1942 with a variety show that featured ventriloquist Edgar Bergen with his two dummies, Charlie McCarthy and Mortimer Snerd, and cowgirl singer Dale Evans; several months later a review called "WACz A Poppin'" (after the title of a Broadway show called "Hellz A Poppin'") was playing there.

In September 1944 the first contingent of Chinese Air Force cadets arrived to be trained to fly B-25 bombers, three hundred of which were supplied by the United States to the Chinese government through the Lend-Lease Act. Georgia Lee Kahl remembered her husband's saying that the traditional army instructional methods had to be modified for the Chinese cadets because of their sensitivity to losing face by being criticized in front of their fellow-pilots. Eight groups of Chinese pilots were trained at the Marfa base before the war ended.

In May 1945, shortly before the war in Europe ended, the army announced that the pilot training program in Marfa would be terminated, and the Marfa Army Air Field became a redeployment center for the Troop Carrier Command, where pilots were brought for reassignment or discharge. The base was permanently closed in December 1945.

There seems to be no record of how many of the young men who trained at Marfa Army Air Base survived the war, but if the general survival rate for bomber pilots applied to them, only half of them lived long enough to come home with memories of Marfa.

March 17, 2011

THE U.S. CAVALRY IN MARFA

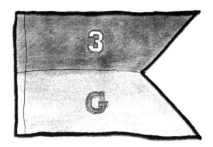

A FEW MILES south of Washington, D.C., on the Maryland side of the Potomac River, is an imposing stone fortress called Fort Washington. It was built in 1824 so that the British fleet could never again sail up the Potomac River and menace the national capital, as they had in 1814, when the British burned the city. Its construction was a classic case of locking the stable after the horse is gone.

The same thing could be said of Fort D.A. Russell at Marfa, now the home of the Chinati Foundation. Fort D.A. Russell started out in 1911 as Camp Marfa, a scattering of tents in a pasture south of the railroad tracks in Marfa, the temporary base of two troops (about 100 men) of the Third U.S. Cavalry. The cavalrymen were sent to the Big Bend from Fort Sam Houston in San Antonio to try to control the arms smuggling into Mexico that had reached epidemic proportions with the outbreak of the Madero revolution against the government of Porfirio Diaz the year before. The arms smuggling was a violation of federal law, and, as the Border Patrol had not yet been established, the army was the only enforcement agent the government had.

The cavalry spent five futile years in the Big Bend, trying to intercept smugglers with about as much success as the Border Patrol now has in turning back illegal immigrants. Then, in 1916 the army's mission changed dramatically. On May 5 of that year, 60 armed men crossed the Rio Grande from Mexico and attacked the little communities of Glenn Springs and Boquillas, Texas, both now in Big Bend National Park. They looted the stores at both places and killed three U.S. army soldiers and a seven-year old boy at Glenn Springs. At Boquillas they kidnapped the storekeeper and his assistant and took them into Mexico with them.

In response to the raid, President Wilson ordered the National Guard of four states to the Big Bend, and Camp Marfa suddenly became the headquarters for a major military operation. A dozen army subposts were established along the Rio Grande, all of which were supplied by wagon train and pack mules from Camp Marfa. The Sixth United States Cavalry established its regimental headquarters there. The soldiers and their horses remained under tents, but the tents covered a lot of ground. The raids continued through 1917 and 1918, and several punitive cavalry expeditions into Mexico were launched from Camp Marfa.

In November 1918 World War I ended. The army had a huge appropriation for fiscal year 1918–1919, and another for 1919–1920. It seemed sensible to use some of it to improve the army facilities along the Mexican border. Between 1919 and 1921 184 permanent structures went up at Camp Marfa—barracks, officers' quarters, stables, blacksmith and machine shops, a theatre, an officers' club, a gymnasium. Buildings also replaced tents at the subposts along the river, and a stone fort was erected in Vieja Pass. The army was now ready for any raiders who dared to cross the Rio Grande.

But 1920 was also the year that Mexico achieved some degree of political stability under President Alvaro Obregon, the one-armed general who overthrew Venustiano Carranza in 1919. The raids stopped and never resumed. The cavalry settled into a somnolent and pleasant existence at Camp Marfa, pumping about half a million dollars a year into the local economy and providing a stream of bachelor officers to serve as escorts and, in some cases, husbands for ranchers' daughters. Marfa became an army town. The cavalry officers, many of whom had served in the Philippines, Cuba, and Europe, elevated the tone of local society. There were dances at the officers' club and the Paisano Hotel, and polo matches on Wednesday and Sunday afternoons, followed by polo teas at the officers' club. In 1930, the year that Camp Marfa was promoted to a fort and re-named Fort D.A. Russell, a First Cavalry polo team went to Mexico City on a special train to play a series of matches against a Mexican army team, taking a group of prominent Marfans and their wives with them. The Mexican team played return matches in Marfa, bringing along a 60-piece brass band which played for a series of dances at the Paisano Hotel in the evenings.

Fort D.A. Russell kept Marfa afloat during the first years of the Depression, but early in 1932 the axe fell. The Hoover administration announced that as an economy measure the army would close 53 military posts and Marfa's fort was on that list. Texas's congressional delegation swung into action to save it, but to no avail. As a last ditch effort, Marfa rancher Luke Brite, whose ranch had been raided in 1917, went to Washington to plead with his fellow-rancher, Vice-President-elect John Nance Garner of Uvalde. Garner listened sympathetically and sent Brite to see General

Douglas MacArthur, the army chief of staff. MacArthur told Brite that not only was Fort D.A. Russell redundant, the cavalry itself was redundant. The days of border raids were over, MacArthur said, and if they ever resumed airplanes from Fort Sam Houston in San Antonio could reach the Big Bend in three hours. He told Brite that the fort would close on January 1, 1933 and the First Cavalry would be shipped off to Fort Knox, Kentucky, where they would learn to drive tanks. That was exactly what happened. The First Cavalry held a final mounted review on December 14. One horse, Louie, too old at 31 to be of further use to the army, was draped in black, shot, and buried on the grounds, a symbol of the regiment's demise as a mounted unit. The regiment's other horses were sent to other cavalry regiments in Texas. The men of the First Cavalry left Marfa in a convoy of 84 trucks on January 2, 1933 and the gates of Fort D.A. Russell were locked behind them.

As things turned out, the growing threat of war in Europe brought about the reopening of the fort in July 1935, but it was re-opened as a mechanized field artillery training base, and the clop of horses' hooves were never again heard on its parade ground.

May 5, 2011

THE HIGHLAND HEREFORD ROUGH RIDERS

EVERY AMERICAN HAS heard of Teddy Roosevelt's Rough Riders, the volunteer cavalry unit that Roosevelt and Colonel Leonard Wood took to Cuba in the Spanish-American War, but how many people have heard of the Highland Hereford Rough Riders? I certainly had not, until I started reading old issues of the *Big Bend Sentinel* in the Marfa Public Library in connection with some other research that I was doing.

The Highland Hereford Rough Riders grew out of the days of panic, confusion, and anger that followed the Japanese attack on Pearl Harbor on December 7, 1941. Oddly enough, the *Big Bend Sentinel* of December 12, 1941 (the paper came out on Fridays then) does not even mention the attack or the war; the big story on the front page is about an upcoming Rotary Club meeting.

I suppose by then everyone knew what had happened, and there was enough local news to fill up the paper. However, the next issue, December 19, is full of stories about emergency preparations at Fort D.A. Russell, a planned blackout practice, sales of Defense Bonds, ladies flocking to join the Presidio County Red Cross, and a report on a Marfa man who sustained injuries when the Japanese bombed Clark Field in the Philippines. Buried on page four is a story about the Rotary Club meeting mentioned in the previous week's paper. It seems that at the meeting, which took place on December 16, rancher George Jones proposed the organization of a home defense unit composed of "men who ride horses and shoot rifles."

The unit, Jones explained, should include at least 100 horsemen and a back-up force of pickup truck drivers who would trailer the horses to points where they would be needed. Another member, W.B. DeVolin, was quoted as saying, "this is a cavalry country, not one for infantry." The club president, Albert Logan, chimed in that "a man on a horse was of much more value in this country." Jones threw in an added advantage: if the unit were organized quickly, he said, it could participate in the Sun Carnival parade in El Paso. After this discussion, the members patiently listened to a book review of Dorothy Thomson's *Political Guide*, but it is clear that they left the meeting ready to join the cavalry.

The Friday evening after the Rotary Club meeting, December 19, there was a mass meeting at the Marfa City Hall to discuss defense measures. Most of the talk amounted to instructions from Lieutenant Colonel Bertram Frankenberger, the commander of Fort D.A. Russell, about how to organize blackouts if Japanese planes should appear over Marfa, but R.I. Bledsoe also announced that a home defense cavalry unit was being formed to counter the threat of Axis saboteurs slipping across the border. Of course, this was less than 25 years after the border raids during the Mexican Revolution, and the vulnerability of the border was on everyone's mind.

The next Friday afternoon, December 26, 74 ranchers gathered in Marfa. George Jones opened the meeting with a speech saying that the unit was being organized "not just for getting publicity" but for serious business, and if people joined they had better be ready to saddle up and head out at any time. Everyone present was asked to step forward and sign a register listing the equipment they could contribute to the unit—horses, saddles, guns, pickup trucks, and trailers. The *Big Bend Sentinel* listed the names of those who registered. They included every prominent cattleman in Presidio, Brewster, and Jeff Davis Counties.

Shortly afterward the annual meeting of the Highland Hereford Breeders Association, a group formed in 1918 to market Hereford cattle raised in the Big Bend, was held in Marfa. Virtually all of the men who had signed up for the cavalry unit were members of the Association, and at the Association meeting George Jones announced that the new unit would be called the Highland Hereford Rough Riders. He also announced that Governor Coke Stevenson and Brigadier General J. Watt Page, the adjutant general of Texas, had approved the unit and that it would have the legal status of a county home guard unit, subject to the orders of the sheriffs of the three counties it would serve. Most of the members were well above draft age.

The apogee of the Highland Hereford Rough Riders came on Saturday, January 24, when the members assembled at the Bloys Camp Meeting Grounds for a formal swearing in and review. General Page was there with his staff, and so was the Mexican general in command of the Juarez garrison and his staff. In spite of George Jones's insistence that publicity was not the organization's goal, cameraman Jimmy Lederer of Universal Newsreels turned up to film the proceedings so the rest of America in their local movie theatres could view the ranchmen's regiment assembling. John Stroud, an entertainer and banquet speaker from Amarillo who impersonated the rustic character "Old Whiz," supposed foreman of the Frying Pan Ranch, was on hand. The Highland Hereford volunteers galloped past Lederer's camera in a column of fours and flourished their rifles, then dismounted and stepped smartly up to a table to sign the regimental roll. There were speeches and everyone sat down to a barbecue dinner prepared by Hayes Mitchell, Frank Jones, and B.H. Davis from donated beef.

Ted Harper, who at 94 may be the only surviving member of the Highland Hereford Rough Riders, was there that day. He remembers it vividly, and told me, "We had our horses and our guns and we were ready if they needed us. The country was pretty wide awake—we didn't know what to expect."

By February 1942, it became evident that the first stages of the war were going to be fought in the Pacific and not in the Big Bend. As a consequence, the Rough Riders seem to have faded away; at least, there is no more mention of it in the newspaper. A Texas Home Defense Company was organized in Marfa in March, but they were infantry. The Highland Hereford Breeders Association is still around, of course. There are a lot of cattlemen's associations in the Southwest, but I'll bet it is the only one that ever had its own cavalry unit.

September 22, 2010

BLACKWELL SCHOOL'S LOST HISTORY

A FEW SATURDAYS ago I attended the Blackwell School Alliance's Spring Open House and had a chance to say goodbye to Joe Cabezuela, one of the Alliance's founders and its president for the past nine years. Cabezuela, who graduated from Blackwell in 1960, five years before the school closed, has been the main man behind the preservation of the old school building, overseeing its acquisition from the Marfa Independent School District after it was abandoned, securing its designation as a Texas Historic Landmark, and obtaining funds and donations that have resulted in many improvements to the aging adobe building. Cabezuela is moving to El Paso, but he will continue to serve on the Alliance board.

Blackwell served as the elementary school for the Hispanic population of Marfa from 1908 until 1965. While Texas law did not require the segregation of Mexican-American school children in the way that it did African-American children, most Texas school districts established separate elementary schools for Mexican-Americans, reflecting the prejudices of the last century. In Marfa, where in 1920 74% of the population was Hispanic, that school was Blackwell. There was no separate Hispanic high school because it was assumed that no Mexican-American children would continue to high school, even though a young man named Juan de la Cruz Machuca became the first Hispanic to graduate from Marfa High School in 1911, and by the 1960s nearly all Blackwell students went on to Marfa High. Blackwell was closed in January 1965 when a new elementary school was opened and Marfa's schools were finally integrated.

The building that the Alliance has preserved was apparently built in 1908. Before that date a one-room adobe building on Galveston Street served as the Mexican school, and one teacher taught all of the grades together. In 1908 there were two teachers and about 100 students. The new building had a Romanesque doorway and a bell tower and the teachers called it "the cathedral." By 1947 the campus had grown to include four buildings and 17 classrooms, with 16 teachers and 600 students. Blackwell School was a significant Marfa institution.

In spite of its importance to the community, researching the history of Blackwell School is a Herculean task and a historian's nightmare. The early records of the Marfa Independent School District have been destroyed or lost, and there is no entry at all for Blackwell School in the index of Cecilia Thompson's two-volume *History of Marfa and Presidio County*, published in 1985 and considered to be the bible of Presidio County history. Joe Cabezuela and Richard Williams of the Marfa and Presidio County Museum have done a heroic job of assembling newspaper clippings about the school, and those and the memories of students and teachers are about all anyone has to go on at present.

Some of the most valuable newspaper clippings are a series of articles that ran in the *Big Bend Sentinel* in the late 1980s under the heading "Blackwell School Memoirs," evidently the outgrowth of the reunions organized by the Blackwell Ex-Students Association. The memoirs were contributed by both former students and former teachers, and they have absolute gems of information scattered through them. John Fortner described the school building as he first saw it in 1914, a three-room adobe house with a belfry, a coal house, and two outside toilets. The main building was divided into one long room in front and two smaller classrooms in back, each with its own outside entrance. This is the earliest description of the building that I have been able to find. Myrtle Barnett Shepard recalled teaching at Blackwell from 1919 to 1921, when she and the principal shared responsibility for 100 students, some of whom were older than she was. She was paid $60.00 a month. Quintin Williams mentioned a principal in the late 1940s who was known to the students as *Cara de Tecolote*, Owl Face. Betty Newsome, who taught at Blackwell in the late 1950s, remembered that her girl students played jacks at recess and taught her games called Tortilla and Tarantula, while she taught them Around the World and Sky Rocket. Many memoir writers recalled that corporal punishment for infringement of school rules was applied from the fourth grade on, the instrument being a paddle that was called "the board of education," a common term in schools all over the country when corporal punishment was the norm.

In the absence of documents, the Blackwell School Association has launched a unique oral history project to try to capture memories of the school and incorporate them into a public presentation. Lisa Bateman, a New York artist and a faculty member at Pratt Institute, has made four trips to Marfa and conducted 35 interviews with former students. Her goal is to incorporate the words of the interviews into what she describes as "a site-specific audio art installation" that will be installed in the school building. She has successfully completed a similar project at a former African-American school-house in North Carolina. While Bateman realizes that oral history is as much about memory as it is about history —she told me that she has recorded so many versions of one incident that she thinks it may have happened several times—her interviews will provide invaluable clues to historians who may be trying to piece the history of Blackwell and Marfa's Hispanic community together.

Joe Cabezuela's successor as president of the Blackwell School Alliance is Gretel Enck, an energetic woman who moved to Marfa last year from Colorado and is employed by the National Park Service at Fort Davis National Historic Site. Enck brings to her new position many years of experience with the Park Service, including five years at Manzanar National Historic Site in California, where Japanese-Americans were interned during World War II. Those years, she says, were her inspiration for wanting to be involved with issues of civil rights and social justice, issues that are relevant to Blackwell's segregated past.

Thousands of tourists come to Marfa every year, drawn by the town's reputation as an artistic mecca. They stay a few days, sample the restaurants, the galleries, and the Chinati Foundation, and leave without any sense that Marfa has a thriving Hispanic community that has been part of the town since the 1880s and has a story of its own to tell. With Enck's guidance, and the help of all of the people who have dedicated their time and talent to maintaining Blackwell over the years, Blackwell School could become the place to tell that story. It is definitely worth telling, and it is a story our visitors need to hear.

June 2, 2016

MARFA PEOPLE

WEIRD MARFA AND CAMP BOSWORTH

 MY WIFE, DEDIE, and I were enjoying a drink in the White Buffalo Bar at the Gage Hotel in Marathon after the Museum of the Big Bend's Heritage Dinner there several weeks ago when we overheard a young fellow at the next table telling the two people that were with him about his recent visit to Marfa. It seemed that the only descriptive adjective he could muster was "weird." "It was weird, man," he said. "I went to Marfa to see all the weird artists there and I got into this weird place that was like a church and there was this weird dude there who had this huge wooden pistol that opened up like some kind of weird bar. It was really weird." I knew right away that he had stumbled into the gallery that my cousin Camp Bosworth and his wife, Buck Johnston, have in the old Mexican Methodist Church on West Dallas Street. But he was in error about one thing. It was not weird, it was Wrong, which is the name Buck and Camp chose for their studio when they decided to open it to the public several years ago.

Buck and Camp were among the first people that Dedie and

I met when we moved to the Big Bend 13 years ago. We had a common friend in Dallas who told us to look them up and we quickly discovered that, although they had only been in Marfa for a year, everyone in town knew who they were. They were famous for two things. One was the glass block wall on one side of their West Dallas Street property. The glass blocks are irregularly shaped globs of waste from a glass factory that Buck and Camp had encountered on their travels; they arranged to buy a load and incorporated them into a rock wall they were building along the east side of their residential lot. In the mornings the rising sun shines through the glass blocks, creating a wonderful luminosity in their breakfast room next to the wall. The other thing was a film they made called "Marfa Dogs." As Camp explained it, there was a free ranging dog, part Chihuahua and part cow dog, that was a rover in Marfa. No one seemed to know who he belonged to or where he lived, but he was all over town. Buck and Camp followed the dog for several days in their car, shooting film of its wanderings, and turned it into a five-minute movie, with music by Ray Freese. It is hilarious.

We met and became fast friends. I discovered that Buck grew up in Oklahoma and knew how to noodle catfish, that is, catch them with her bare hands, a talent that I have always admired, and that Camp was an artist who loves stories and has a keen sense of the absurd.

Camp (which is short for Campbell) is a Southerner and says that his art is rooted in his Southernness. "It's the Southern way to want to tell a story," he says. "I try to create a specific place where my stories exist." His big painted wood collage, done in 1998, that hangs in the Alpine coffee shop Plaine is a good example. It is called "A Truckload of Art" and it depicts an overturned and burning semi with paintings scattered on the pavement beside it. It is based on a satirical song by Lubbock singer-songwriter Terry Allen about a truckload of art sent to the West by New York artists to enlighten the yokels that met with disaster. It is a tall tale in painted wood.

After moving from Dallas to Marfa, Camp got fascinated by the border way of telling stories, through the songs known as *corridos*, ballads about outlaws, killings, and tragic love affairs, and especially by *narcocorridos,* songs about the exploits of *narcotraficantes*, dope smugglers. His art came off the wall and became groupings of carved and painted three dimensional objects. In 2010 he created a show at The Marfa Book Company called "The Ballad of Chalino Sanchez" (Sanchez was a singer of *narcocorridos* who was murdered in Mexico in 1992). The work in it included a 3 ½ -foot high wooden .45 automatic pistol that opened up to reveal a bar, a huge carved and painted dollar sign, a gigantic wooden spur, bundles of wooden currency and a carved portrait of Chalino brandishing his trademark .45. Since then Camp has created other groupings of carved and painted objects referring to border culture, most recently a show at the Old Jail Museum in Albany, Texas called *"Al Otro Lado"* (On the Other Side).

I asked Camp if any drug lords had bought his work and he said no, but at the Houston opening of his Chalino Sanchez show a very engaging Mexican gentleman wearing an expensive silk suit, an open shirt, and a large medallion on a gold chain around his neck had asked him all sorts of questions about his work. "We became such good friends in such a short time," Camp said, "that I asked him if he was a *narcotraficante*. He said no, but his brother was."

I stopped in Camp's studio the other day to see what he was working on now and found him just completing a nine-foot wide, seven-foot high belt buckle that was commissioned by the San Antonio Spurs. The buckle is adorned with a symmetrical composition of Texas symbols: the façade of the Alamo cradled in a horseshoe is surrounded by armadillos, rattlesnakes, buzzards, six-shooters, blossoming prickly pear, hummingbirds ("I just like them," Camp told me) and, yes, basketballs. It is an imposing piece of work that will be suspended from the ceiling of the Spurs' A.T.&T. Center stadium in San Antonio. The buckle is not wood but is carved out of high-density urethane, a material that is easy to carve but is much lighter than wood. "The buckle only weighs 600 pounds," Camp said. "If it were wood it would weigh twice that."

I had known Camp for several years before I learned that we were cousins. His parents came to Marfa to visit and Harry Hudson organized a dinner party for them. In an attempt to show them that their son had respectable friends in spite of his being an artist, Harry invited Dedie and me and Cecilia Thompson to the party. In the course of the evening Camp's mother mentioned that her grandfather was Robert E. Lee Dick of Galveston, whose mother happened to be my great-grandmother's half sister. Robert E. Lee Dick's brothers were named Stonewall Jackson Dick, Jefferson Davis Dick, Francis Marion Dick, and Raphael Semmes Dick. You can't get more Southern than that.

October 15, 2015

DESTINATION WEDDINGS ARE the thing. Prospective brides and grooms, best men and maids of honor, bridesmaids and grooms-men, parents and guests, sometimes hundreds of guests, now fly to Caribbean islands or Hawaiian beaches or the south of France to do what they used to do in the little church around the corner or the little brown church in the vale. The wedding guest no longer beats his breast because he hears the loud bassoon; he beats it because he has shelled out thousands of dollars to go to someone else's wedding at a Jamaican resort.

When I was growing up in Fort Worth in the 1950s Turner Falls, Oklahoma, was a popular destination for young people who wanted to, or had to, get married. That was because Turner Falls was only 60 miles north of the Texas state line and in Texas a young woman could not get married without her parents' consent until she was 18 and there was a mandatory three-day waiting period between getting the license and tying the knot, but in Oklahoma the minimum age for a female was 14 and there was no waiting period. As soon as you crossed the Red River heading north you began to see billboards that said "Marriage Information Five Miles," and some justices of the peace advertised that they were available 24 hours a day. Turner Falls featured a 24-hour J.P. in the nearby town of Davis, several motels with honeymoon suites, and a 77-foot waterfall ("the Niagara of the Arbuckle Mountains') that was lit up at night with colored lights and could be turned on and off on demand like a backyard water spigot. All you needed to have a destination wedding at Turner Falls was a car and gas money to get you there and an extra 10 bucks, five for the license and five for the J.P.

The fact that Marfa has become a wedding destination that is somewhat less expensive than Versailles and considerably more elegant than Turner Falls is partially due to the allure of the scenery but largely due to the efforts of Lizzy Wetzel, with whom I spent a delightful afternoon a couple of weeks ago. She told me that she was working as the events manager at El Cosmico two and a half years ago when she and the El Cosmico manager, Sarah Cork (now Sarah Bolen), noticed that couples who wanted to get married at El Cosmico needed a lot of help. "They didn't know where to get a cake or where to hire a band," Wetzel said, "so Sarah and I set up a business to help them. Sarah was the business wizard and I was the creative side. We called it Magic Hour Marfa and thought we might get three weddings a year." Cork left the partnership to move to Austin, and Wetzel is now running Magic Hour by herself. She told me that she has coordinated 13 weddings and other events since January. including the big Valentine's day party in Valentine, which she produced for the Big Bend Brewery in collaboration with Nicki Ittner.

She hastened to add that while she is managing the business by herself, she is not producing weddings by herself. "My last wedding involved 250 guests from New York," she said, "and 65 people in Marfa helped me with it." She started to enumerate them. "Allison Scott baked 250 individual dessert pies for the rehearsal dinner at the Sproul Ranch. Andy Peters arranged for me to rent Marfa school buses to get the guests out there. Krista and Brandon catered that dinner and a lunch at the Chinati arena, which Kelly Sudderth helped to arrange. Shawn Adams smoked meat for one of the meals. Katie Rose baked two amazing wedding cakes. The Hotel St. George catered a reception. Ashley North Compton and Nicki Ittner helped manage the staffing. Gory Smelley ran the sound." She tapered off. "It takes a village...," she concluded.

Wetzel is a practicing artist who says she no longer has time for her own work. She grew up in Austin, majored in art at the University of North Texas, and worked as an art teacher in Dallas before moving to Marfa in 2013. She regards a wedding as an artistic creation, and enjoys designing the accessories—table runners, vases, place mats—and turning them over to friends who are craftspeople to produce. "It's better to make things than to buy a bunch of garbage," she said. "There's too much trash that happens at weddings and I'd like to avoid that as much as possible." The economic impact of Wetzel's weddings on Marfa must be considerable, but she says that she has never taken the time to calculate exactly what the figure is.

I asked her why people wanted to get married in Marfa, thinking that the reason must have something to do with the buzz in the national press about the town, but she said that most of her weddings involved at least one person with a personal tie to Marfa or at least to West Texas. Sometimes, she added, a couple will have family members on both the east and west coasts, and rather than have one group fly all the way across the country they will decide to bring both groups together "in the middle of nowhere."

Wetzel says that, for a Marfa wedding to go smoothly, it is essential for couples to understand how far they will be from a big city and what the town's limitations are. "I try to tell them clearly and honestly from the start what to expect. If they haven't been here before that's a big red flag. I tell them they may be disappointed unless they check it out first." Since a Wetzel-organized Marfa wedding is not cheap, she is anxious to avoid disappointment. So far, she has had no disappointed couples, and I doubt if she will. She has 15 weddings booked between now and the summer of 2017. Since she is so clearly a perfectionist, you can be certain that whatever is put into her hands will come out all right.

At the close of our interview I asked Wetzel if she had any local competition and she said, "Who else would want to do this? I'm not even sure why I do it." I think that she just likes to make people happy.

June 16, 2016

TIGIE LANCASTER AND MULES

LAST YEAR AT the St. Paul's Episcopal Church ice-cream social in Marfa a woman with a ruddy complexion, short gray hair, and very blue eyes drove up to the church in a rubber-tired buckboard pulled by a mule. She asked a small boy standing at the curb to go in and get her a dish of ice cream, and then sat in the buckboard and ate it. Her name is Tigie Lancaster, and she has lived in Marfa since 1998. The mule's name was Hollywood Doc. Well, actually, it was just Doc, but Lancaster says that he had been in so many movies that she called him Hollywood Doc. Doc, who died last spring, was a big mule, 16 and a half hands high. His mother was a Kentucky thoroughbred mare and his father was a Mammoth jack. "He was the mule of my dreams," Lancaster told me the other day. "He was everything you would want in a mule." When I asked her exactly what she meant by that, she said, "Not many mules would let you put a tutu on them." Then I remembered that Doc was the mule that Lancaster entered in the Beautiful Mule contest in Fort Davis last year. He not only wore a tutu but had simulated ballet slippers on his hooves. Doc had other good qualities, too, according to Lancaster: "He had a superior attitude around horses—you could see that he didn't approve of their kicking and running around. He was real smooth—he didn't have any rough, bouncy qualities. He was unflappable. He was a special mule."

Although Lancaster is basically a horse person, she has had a lot of experience with mules. When she was a child in Dallas, she was fascinated by the mules that pulled the garbage wagon through her neighborhood, and she persuaded the garbage man to let her climb up beside him when he came by and ride to the end of the block. Her grandmother was horrified, but her mother said, "There's no point in telling her not to do it. She'll just do it anyway," which seems to have been a pattern in Lancaster's life. A few years later, when she was at a girls' boarding school in Colorado Springs, she was introduced to an army mule named Hambone who could jump with thoroughbreds. She sometimes went fox-hunting with the El Paso County Hounds, and one of the army officers at Camp Carson used to bring Hambone along on fox hunts. He could sail over fences with the best of them. Lancaster got to ride Hambone once, and she told me that it was like riding in a Rolls-Royce. Hambone became her standard of "a real doing mule."

Lancaster's first mule, however, was not up to Hambone's standards. "He was a Shetland mule, a handsome strawberry roan with white stockings," she said, "but he had a cheating heart and was not generous. He had been trained to pull but you had to re-train him every day, and if he got a chance to let you have it, he would. He was the opposite of Doc in every way." Most mules, Lancaster was quick to add, are not like that, although they are independent-minded. "Mules are smarter than horses," she said. "Horses aren't Einsteins and they can be bullied into doing things they shouldn't do, but mules don't like bullies and they won't go anywhere that isn't safe."

Mules get their good qualities from donkeys, Lancaster told me, and she is also fond of donkeys—in fact, she has four of them in her pasture right now, named Black Jack, Apple Jack, Bottom, and Pearl Lite. "The only animal I ever rustled was a donkey," she told me. This was in the late 1950s, she explained, and she had come out to the Big Bend for a short vacation. She drove her pickup to the store at Lajitas and asked the man there if she could drive on down to the river, and he told her that she had better leave her truck at the store and walk to the river, as someone might steal her hubcaps if she parked it on the river bank. She took his advice and walked through the brush to the river, where she found a donkey tethered to a tree. The donkey was saddled and bridled, and there were two big gunny sacks on the ground beside his feet. She looked in the gunny sacks and discovered they were full of hubcaps. Impulsively, she untied the donkey, got on him, and rode him along the river for a while. When she finally got back to her truck, she said, "I hated to part with him. I reasoned that anyone who was stealing hubcaps wouldn't prosecute me for stealing a donkey, so I put the tailgate down and he jumped right into my truck. I stopped in Fort Stockton and bought some stake sides and drove back to Dallas with him. I never felt guilty about taking that burro. There were plenty of them around and the guy who owned it probably would have taken my hubcaps."

Mules and donkeys are really a sideline to Lancaster, who has spent most of her life training horses and teaching riding. I asked her how she got into the horse business, and she told me that during her sophomore year at Bennington College she got interested in the writings of Eugene V. Debs, five-time Socialist candidate for president and founder of the first railroad workers' union. "I came home that summer and started telling my grandfather about my admiration for Eugene V. Debs," she said. "Well, my grandfather was president of the Texas and Pacific Railroad, and he said that if that was what I was learning at Bennington he was going to take me out of there, and I could either go to Sweet Briar or the University of Texas. I said I wasn't going to either one. I had a friend in Dallas who had polo horses, so I leased a stable from him and started boarding polo ponies and training jumpers, and I've been doing that ever since." And she's been speaking her mind ever since, too.

November 12, 2006

TONY CANO AND THE CHINGLERS

TONY CANO GREW up poor and on the wrong side of the tracks in Marfa. He recently wrote a book about his youth, which he published through his Reata Press in Canutillo, Texas. It is called *The Other Side of the Tracks* and it will tell you what it was like to be Mexican in Marfa 50 years ago.

Cano grew up in the 1950s. His father was a fine cowboy and was a ranch manager on Wayne Cartledge's 9K Ranch on the Texas-New Mexico line, but he was a heavy drinker. Cano's mother left him when Cano was in the first grade, moving to Marfa with her three children and taking a job as a waitress. She had a difficult time making ends meet. In a recent phone interview, Cano told me that sometimes he and his brother would come home from school for lunch and there would be nothing in the house to eat but cornflakes.

Marfa's elementary schools were segregated in the 1950s, and, like all Mexican-American children, Cano went to Blackwell School. But when he reached the seventh grade he enrolled in Marfa Elementary, the Anglo-American school whose graduates went on to Marfa High School. *The Other Side of the Tracks* grew out of the prejudice that Cano experienced there and at Marfa High, and out of the ways that he and a small group of friends devised to fight it. The novel is about the adventures of a group of Mexican-American teen-agers who called themselves the Chinglers, a word derived from a Spanish verb that cannot be translated in a family newspaper. The book is a frank and unflinching picture of what it was like to be poor and Mexican-American in Marfa in the 1950s. It should be required reading for every newcomer to Marfa because it explains some of the tensions that still underlie the idyllic images of Marfa and its arts community that have recently appeared in national publications.

The Chinglers broke a taboo by secretly dating Anglo-American girls. Fifty years later, Cano still remembers the sting of that particular prejudice. "You couldn't date Anglo girls," he told me. "You couldn't even talk to them in the hallway. We did it because they told us we couldn't." He told me about one Anglo boy who was in love with a Mexican-American girl. He and a Mexican-American friend had an arrangement by which they would pick up each other's dates; then meet and exchange girls for the evening, meeting again before taking their respective non-dates home. Another unspoken rule was maintaining a racial balance on high school athletic teams; in the novel a coach is fired for playing an all-Mexican-American basketball team, even though it is a spectacularly winning team. Cano puts his finger on the far-reaching ramifications of high school athletics in a small Texas town; something else that some newcomers to Marfa may have a hard time understanding.

The book is more memoir than novel. The ending is somewhat clumsy, and Cano told me that was the only part that did not really happen; all of the other incidents are factual. He said that he cast it as a novel "for legal reasons." When word got out in Marfa that he was writing a book several people threatened to sue him if he used their names in it, and that put him on guard.

Cano told me that he wrote the novel "as therapy." Even as an adult, he said, he had a lot of anger about the way Mexican-Americans were treated in Texas. "Writing the book took a monkey off my back. I learned to put the past behind me," he said. *The Other Side of the Tracks* is not Cano's only book. He and his wife, poet Ann Sochat, have published a Dutch oven cookbook and a book of poems and ranch reminiscences, *Echoes in the Wind.* Their most recent collaboration was *Bandido,* a biography of Cano's great-grandfather, the revolutionist and bandit Chico Cano. *The Other Side of the Tracks*, however, was a solo effort on Cano's part. He told me that he credits his self-confidence as a writer to two of his Marfa English teachers who saw him as more than a Mexican-American troublemaker. "Mrs. Emma Lou Howard taught me how to stand up and talk to a group, and Ms. Mary Lou Kelley made me sit on the front row my senior year and motivated me to do well. If it were not for Ms. Kelley I would not have graduated from high school."

Tony Cano went on from Marfa High to have a career worthy of another book. When he graduated from high school, he told me, his mother gave him $68 and said, "You're a man." He ended up in El Paso, where he got a job working in a Mr. Quick hamburger stand. "When I was twenty-one," he told me, "I said, 'Tony, is this it? Is this what you are going to do the rest of your life?'" He enrolled in Texas Western College, now The University of Texas at El Paso, went on to complete a B.A. at the University of Missouri, and did graduate work as a teaching assistant at the University of Hawaii.

Cano eventually got into the garment manufacturing business in El Paso and ended up the owner of his own company, Tony Cano Sportswear. Cano's factory became a leading producer of sports jackets for auto racing teams, a narrow but profitable niche. Cano told me that came about because in 1981 he went to Phoenix to see his first auto race. He was impressed by the skill of the drivers, and after the race he went down to congratulate the winner, Bobby Unser. One thing led to another, and he became a regular weekend volunteer on Unser's pit team, eventually being assigned to holding the pit board, the blackboard that tells the driver how many laps he has to go. He designed a set of jackets for the Unser team, and so many other drivers admired them that the next year eight of the 33 teams at the Indianapolis 500 were wearing Tony Cano jackets.

Cano is now retired and travels all over the world with his wife. He says that someday he will write a sequel to *The Other Side of the Tracks*, and it will have a happy ending.

December 1, 2011

LEE BENNETT & THE SECRET HISTORY OF MARFA

 MARFA HAS A secret history, the history of its Spanish-speaking families, whose stories have not yet been told in print. Some of those families were settled along the Rio Grande and were ranching along Alamito Creek long before Marfa came into existence. Some came from Mexico in the 1880s and 90s to work at the military post at Fort Davis, or in the mines at Shafter and Terlingua, and were drawn to Marfa by the opportunities for more regular employment, higher wages, and a better education for their children. The majority came in the years between 1910 and 1920 as refugees from the violence that accompanied the Mexican Revolution. In 1910 30% of Marfa's population was born in Mexico; by 1920 the figure had jumped to 74%. Spanish-speaking families have always been an integral part of Marfa's history, but very little has ever been published about them.

The stories of these Spanish-speaking Marfa households would be completely lost to historians if it were not for the efforts of one remarkable woman and her students. Lee Bennett came to Marfa with her parents in 1925, when she was four years old. She grew up here, finished high school here, and married her high school sweetheart, Bob Evans, whom she met at Bloys Camp Meeting when they were both 12, shortly after she graduated from Baylor in 1942. They were married at the post chapel at Fort Riley, Kansas because Evans was in the Army. He was killed in the Normandy landings, and his young widow started teaching school. In 1948 she married a rancher named Murphy Bennett, but she continued to teach intermittently. I first met her in 1969, when I was working for the Texas State Historical Association in Austin, because the Association oversaw the Texas Junior Historians and Bennett sponsored a prize-winning Junior Historians club at Marfa High School.

One of her teaching techniques was to ask her American history students to write papers about their own family's history. She showed them how to interview their parents and grandparents, how to look for documents like naturalization papers and marriage certificates, how to interpret family photographs. In short, she taught them the rudiments of the historian's investigative skills. Not only that, she placed their finished papers, and the photographs they collected, in the Marfa Public Library, where they reside as the Junior Historian Files. Those files contain the histories of at least seventy of Marfa's Hispanic families, many of whom were refugees from the revolution. They include astonishing stories of courage and endurance.

Some of the histories take on a mythic quality. Arthur Fuentes wrote about his great-great-great uncle, Francisco Fuentes, who died in Marfa at the age of 105 in 1944. Uncle Chico, as he was known in the family, was born in the mountains of Mexico in 1839 and as a young man had fought the French and served in the army that brought Porfirio Diaz to power. He became an outlaw, crossed the Rio Grande, worked for a while in Fort Davis, settled down and raised a family in Ruidoso, and ended up in Marfa, where he owned several rent houses. Relying on his father's memory, Fuentes wrote, "He never did like to sleep in a bed and he never did like to eat in a house. He used to take his food outside to eat."

Some of the stories preserve minute details. Bentura Contreras hauled freight from Marfa to Shafter, Presidio, and Ruidoso in the 1890s and early 1900s. Seventy years later his 90-year old widow told their great-grandson about his freight business. He had two wagons, each pulled by a team of seven mules. She remembered the names of the mules: La Zorerra, La Naranja, La Maja, La Sota, La Nica, La Pola, La Nene, La Tane, El Zarco, La Concha, El Tórtolo, El Venado, and El Negro. The fourteenth draft animal was a mare named La Palomina, whose bell kept the mules close to her.

Jesus Cabazuela's life, as recounted by his granddaughter Nora Cabazuela, was fairly typical of the men whose families made up Marfa's Spanish-speaking middle-class in the 1920s and 30s. It also demonstrates the permeability of the border in the early 20TH century. He was born in San Lucas, Chihuahua in 1879 but shortly after his birth his family moved to Fort Davis and then to Shafter, where his father and two older brothers worked in the silver mine. He started school in Shafter, but after he finished the second grade his family moved to San Antonio del Bravo, Chihuahua, and he did not return to Texas until he was in his 20s, when he crossed the Rio Grande and went to work as a cowboy on the Brite Ranch outside of Marfa. After several years of cowboying he moved to Candelaria, Texas, directly across the Rio Grande from San Antonio del Bravo, married a local girl and opened a barber shop, and, during the Border Troubles in 1917 and 1918, worked as a scout at the cavalry outpost there, becoming a U.S. citizen in 1917. In 1920 he and his wife moved back to Marfa, where he used his savings to buy a gas station and a small tourist camp. He later added a grocery store to his holdings. He retired in 1948, prosperous enough to maintain a winter home in Mesa, Arizona.

Max Cortez's life, chronicled by his great-granddaughter Martha Cortez, had a somewhat similar trajectory. Cortez was born in Aldama, Chihuahua, in 1867, the son of a tailor. In 1877 his family moved to Ojinaga, and at the age of 13 he was hired by a Fort Davis rancher, George Perrin, and moved to Fort Davis to live on the Perrin ranch. As a young man he worked in a saloon in Fort Davis, serving drinks to soldiers from the Fort and earning extra money by taking photographs of them, as Lucillia Perrin had taught him the rudiments of photography. He married a Fort Davis girl, Francisca Lujan, and in 1900 they moved to Marfa, where they opened a small grocery store in their adobe house on Alamito Creek. That house was destroyed in a flood in 1904 which swept away everything the Cortez family had. They made a fresh start in a new house on Dallas Street, and the grocery store they opened there grew into one of Marfa's major mercantile stores, selling not only groceries but clothing, china, medicine, coal, and petroleum. Max Cortez believed in progress and was a major investor in both the Marfa Power Company and the Marfa Telephone Company, which were organized in 1908 to bring electricity and telephones to Marfa. He died in 1944, but when his great-granddaughter wrote about him in 1965 he was still remembered for the sacks of candy, nuts, and fruit that he distributed to the children of Marfa from his store every Christmas morning.

Unlike Cabazuela and Cortez, Seferino Ramon was one of the refugees from the revolution. He was a stone mason who lived in a three-room house in a village near Ojinaga with his wife and thirteen children when the revolution came. He and his family fled across the river to Presidio, where they lived in grass hut for a while. Berta Melva Mendias, who wrote the history of Seferino's family for Bennett's class, tells how Seferino died after being in Texas just a year, and how his youngest son, Jose, set out with two of his brothers to find work in Shafter, then a mining boom town. They were hired to work on the Catholic church, and then built several houses in Shafter before Jose set out on his own for Marfa.

In Marfa, Jose found that Fort D.A. Russell was expanding and was advertising for adobe makers. He had never made adobes, but he told the hiring officer that he knew how and quickly picked up the knack on the job. He stayed on in Marfa, married, had five children, and became a prominent building contractor. His name is pressed into the concrete of some of Marfa's older sidewalks. One of his sons, Jose, became a doctor; another, Raymundo, was a teacher.

Not all of the papers are about Hispanic families. Some students wrote about their Anglo ancestors, and some wrote about local businesses. All of Lee Bennett's students made an invaluable contribution to Marfa's history. If you know one of them, go shake their hand. If you are one of them, you have done something to be proud of the rest of your life.

April 6, 2017

HARPER B. LEE, MARFA MATADOR

BACK IN THE 1990s, when I was still a historian at the Smithsonian Institution, I did a good deal of research on the Star-Spangled Banner, the flag that flew over Fort McHenry in Baltimore during the British bombardment of 1814. The flag was preserved in the family of the fort's commander, Lieutenant Colonel George Armistead, and was donated to the Smithsonian by his grandson in 1911. It happens that there is a Marfa connection to the story. It leapt at me out of a stack of old papers in a Baltimore law office, and I'd like to pass it on.

Lieutenant Colonel Armistead was a Virginian. He was born on his mother's family's plantation, New Market, in Caroline County in 1780, while his father was serving as an aide-de-camp to George Washington. His mother was Lucinda Baylor. Lucinda Baylor had a brother named Walker Baylor, and Walker Baylor's children and grandchildren wandered west, first to Kentucky and then to Texas. Baylor University is named after one of those grandchildren, Robert Emmett Bledsoe Baylor. Another grandson, George Wythe Baylor, served as a colonel in a Texas cavalry regiment during the Civil War and after the war became the captain of a Texas Ranger company stationed at Ysleta, near El Paso. That is where our story begins.

One of the rangers in Baylor's company was a young man named James B. Gillett. In later life Gillett became a prominent Big Bend rancher, a director of the Marfa National Bank, a long-time president of Bloys Camp Meeting, and the author, in 1921, of an often-re-printed book, *Six Years With the Texas Rangers*. But in 1881 he fell in love with his ranger captain's daughter, Helen, and married her. She was not quite 16; Gillett was 25. They had two children, both boys, named Harper and Baylor. The marriage was not a success and they were divorced in 1889. Gillett remarried and had another family. In his book, which his second wife helped to edit, he makes no mention of his first wife or of their children.

One of those children, Harper, had a career that was every bit as remarkable as his father's. Under the name Harper Baylor Lee, he became the first *norteamericano* bullfighter. His mother married Samuel Lee, a railroad construction superintendent who took her and her sons to live in Mexico, and Harper grew up in Guadalajara. In high school there he and his friends participated in amateur bullfights in the same way, he later said, that a group of boys in the United States would have played sandlot baseball. After graduation he went to work for his stepfather's construction company but he was still drawn to the bullring and, with the encouragement of a retired matador called El Chiclanero, he eventually decided to become a professional bull-fighter. He made his first appearance as an apprentice in the ring at Guadalajara in July 1908, just two months short of his 24ᵀᴴ birthday. Over the next three years he participated in 52 corridas and killed 100 bulls. He retired in October 1911 after a near-fatal goring in Saltillo.

After his retirement he married a girl from Texas, Roxa Dunbar, whom he had met in Mexico. The wedding was in San Antonio in 1915 and the two old Texas Rangers, Colonel Baylor and Captain

Gillett, Harper's grandfather and father, both attended. Except for a brief meeting the year before, Captain Gillett and his son had not seen each other for 25 years. To mark the occasion, Harper announced that henceforth he would be known as Harper B. Gillett. He and Roxa moved to Marfa and for a few years in the 1920s Harper managed his father's Barrel Springs Ranch. Pansy Espy, Captain Gillett's granddaughter, remembers Harper as the kindest, gentlest person she ever knew. "I don't see how he could have ever been a bullfighter," she said when I asked her about him the other day.

The reconciliation did not last, and Harper and Roxa moved back to San Antonio, where Harper died from cancer in 1941. Roxa Robison of Crows Nest is named for Roxa Gillett, and her brother Harper was named for the bullfighter.

There are a lot of Armistead descendants in Baltimore. While I was researching the Star-Spangled Banner one of them, a prominent lawyer, invited me to his office to look at a file of family papers. The file included letters from George Washington to Lieutenant Colonel Armistead's father and letters from Lieutenant Colonel Armistead's nephew, the Confederate general Lewis Addison Armistead, as well as a dozen other prominent Virginians. But the document that excited me most was a letter written in 1909 from Guadalajara, Mexico, on letterhead stationery that said "Harper B. Lee, Matador de Toros." It was addressed to one of the Baltimore Armisteads and it said that the writer's grandfather Baylor had told him when he was a boy of his connection to the Armisteads and the Star-Spangled Banner and asking for more information. It must have surprised the daylights out of the Armisteads when it arrived.

August 12, 2004

CECILIA THOMPSON, MARFA'S DRAMA QUEEN

THE FIRST TIME that Cecilia Thompson directed *The Glass Menagerie* John Tower played the role of Tom Wingfield. That was in Wichita Falls in 1960, where Tower, who served as a United States Senator from Texas from 1961 until 1985, was a professor of government at Midwestern University.

Thompson says that Tower had a good sense of drama and made an excellent Tom Wingfield. Thompson must have made an impression on Tower, too. Several years later she received a postcard wishing her well, mailed from the U.S. Senate post office and signed "Tom Wingfield."

Thompson has another reason to remember that particular production. The afternoon before the final performance the leading lady asked if she could spend that night at Thompson's house. Thompson thought the request odd, as the woman lived in Wichita Falls, but being a generous and hospitable soul she agreed. The next morning she discovered that the lady had packed her car the night before and at sunrise had driven away from Thompson's house to a new relationship in Dallas, leaving her husband and children behind in Wichita Falls.

Nothing quite so dramatic happened after the final performance of *The Glass Menagerie* that Thompson directed at the Crowley Theater here in Marfa earlier this month, nor is it likely that any of this production's cast will be taking a Senate seat soon, although they all have the poise and stage presence to get themselves elected to one.

But this production has been memorable for Thompson in another way. It is the first time she has had a chance to bring Tennessee Williams's characters to life on a stage in front of people she grew up with.

Thompson's grandfather S.A. Thompson was a pioneer settler of the Big Bend, a rancher, surveyor, and business partner of Alfred Gage, founder of the Gage Ranch. Thompson grew up on her father's ranch between Marfa and Fort Davis, a place later known as the Poor Farm. She bridles a bit at that name, which she says was given to the place by the man who bought it from her father because he claimed he could not make a living from it. "It was 1930," she says, "the depths of the Depression. You could have said the same thing about any ranch in the area. No one was making a living."

Thompson's career took her a long way from home. As a student at Sul Ross in the late 1930s, she fell under the spell of drama teacher Annie Kate Ferguson, who, she says, "infected a lot of us with the madness." From Sul Ross she went to the University of Iowa, then a center for innovative theater (Tennessee Williams was a student there), where she got her master's and doctor's degrees, and then on to a career as a professor of theater at several universities.

She worked with some of the great directors and playwrights

of the 20ᵀᴴ-century American theater, including B. Iden Payne, Lynn Riggs, and Paul Baker, and she also put in a few years in commercial theater, which she says was much more challenging than teaching. For a while, she lived in New York and wrote soap operas to support herself between engagements.

But eventually Thompson came home to the Big Bend to help care for her aging parents, and when she got here she started a second career as a historian, writing a two-volume history of Marfa and Presidio County that was published by Nortex Press in 1985. Her stage became the past, and her actors the people she encountered going through courthouse records and newspaper files.

But forty years in theater is a hard habit to break, and three years ago Thompson returned to the stage in Marfa by directing a production of Thornton Wilder's *Our Town,* followed this month by *The Glass Menagerie.* This might not seem so remarkable except that Thompson will be 85 in April. When I asked her if this would be her swan song, she just smiled and reminded me that one of her mentors, B. Iden Payne, ran the theater department at the University of Texas until he was 94.

February 10, 2005

BANJO BILLY FAIER

A COUPLE OF weeks ago my wife, Dedie, and I spent a memorable Saturday afternoon on the patio of the Famous Burro in Marathon listening to a group of local musicians who had gathered to honor the memory of Billy Faier. Faier, who died on January 29 at the age of 85, was a world-class banjo player who gave informal concerts at Marfa Farmstand, the Plaine coffee shop in Alpine, and other venues in the area. Most of the people in his audiences, who loved his music and called him "Banjo Billy," probably did not know that Faier had been a seminal figure in the folksong revival movement of the 1950s in New York, where he played with the likes of Pete Seeger, Rambling Jack Elliot, Erik Darling, Barbara Dane, Ed McCurdy, Dave von Ronk, and the Reverend Gary Davis.

Billy Faier started playing the banjo long before most of the musicians who gathered at the Famous Burro to honor him were born. He took the instrument up in 1947, and Riverside Records issued his first recording, *The Art of the Five String Banjo,* with jacket notes by Pete Seeger, in 1957, followed the next year by a second record, *Billy Faier: Travelin' Man.* But Faier never got bit by the publicity bug, and while his friends formed groups and gave concerts and became famous, he devoted himself to experimenting with the banjo and seeing what it would do. He would not accept the fact that the instrument had limitations. He once spent a year transposing a fiddle tune called "The Last of Callahan" for the banjo. He arranged South American ballads and Elizabethan love songs for the banjo. He could play Bach on the banjo.

Faier grew up in Brooklyn and as an adult lived in New Orleans; in San Francisco; in Mendocino, California; in Woodstock, New York. He played the banjo and supported himself with odd jobs, working as a San Francisco cable car conductor and as a juggler in a traveling carnival. In Woodstock he ran an art gallery called The Light Box and made picture frames. He put out a record about once every 10 years, and they were treasured by banjo aficionados. He was fond of saying that his records brought him more friends than money and that was probably a better deal anyway. For a while in the late 1950s he published a folk music magazine called *Caravan,* and he had a radio show on a New York FM station called "The Midnight Special," which came on from midnight to 2:00 AM on Saturday nights.

Faier moved to Terlingua in 2001, and I heard him play at the Marfa Pachanga in 2003. He did a gospel song called "The Great Assembly" which sounded strangely familiar to me, reminding me of my days as a graduate student in New York forty years earlier. I went up to him at intermission and asked him if I had not heard him sing "The Great Assembly" at a folksong club called Gerde's

Folk City in New York in the fall of 1961. He said, "You probably did. I sang there every Wednesday night for a couple of years." Several weeks later I drove down to Terlingua to interview him for a "Rambling Boy" column, and we became friends.

Faier could be a difficult friend. He had strong opinions about how nearly everything should be done and was not shy about voicing them. Shortly after we met he was playing at a jam session organized by Wendy Wright every Friday evening at the Paisano Hotel, and he complained to me about the difficulty of driving back to Terlingua after those sessions, as he did not see well at night. I told him that he was welcome to use our guest room in Fort Davis any time he wished, and he said, "How about next Friday?" He showed up that night with a dog, which he had not mentioned, and the next morning he came into the kitchen in his bathrobe and stood by Dedie at the stove while he instructed her *exactly* how to cook his bacon, which Dedie did not take kindly to. However, I got the impression that he had a good deal of experience with friends' perturbed wives. He did not stay with us again, but our friendship continued unabated.

Saturday's gathering was organized by Wendy Wright, who first met Faier in 2001 when he and some friends played a gig at Ben's Lounge at Ruidosa. Wright was just learning to play the guitar, and Faier became her mentor, pushing her to play pieces she did not think she was ready for and teaching her to perform them flawlessly. Faier's last public performance was with Wright at Joe's Café in St. Louis, Missouri in June of last year. You can view it on You-Tube.

On Saturday afternoon Wright was at the Famous Burro early, setting up an elaborate buffet of snacks, arranging for free beer and wine to be served to the guests, and setting up chairs for the musicians on the patio. By 4:00 PM about 50 friends of Faier's had gathered. J.P. Schwartz and Charles Maxwell were there with their guitars; Paul Graybeal with his mandolin, and Gary Oliver with his accordion. A slide guitar player named Charlie had come all the way from England for the event. Michael Combs from Terlingua was there, wearing a battered Stetson patched with black electrician's tape, playing the harmonica and keeping time by tapping a punched-out tambourine with his feet. Other men and women I did not know joined the group with their instruments as the sun got lower.

The star of the afternoon was Faier's grandson Christopher Wand, who had come from California with his father, Nico Wand. Christopher is a handsome blond young man. He is 19, a recent graduate of Novato High School in Marin County and a dynamite banjo player. He was playing his grandfather's banjo, with "Billy Faier" spelled out in embossed letters on the leather strap across his back, and as we left for a dinner date in Marfa he was leading 14 musicians in a spirited rendition of Faier's trademark song, "The Great Assembly." It was like having Billy back for an afternoon.

March 10, 2016

WE ALL KNOW that Marfa is a center for the visual arts and that people come from all over the world to see the minimalist installations at the Chinati Foundation. Most of us know that several important films have been shot in Marfa, starting with *Giant* in 1954. Many people are aware that Marfa is a gliding and sailplane mecca, and that international sailplane competitions have been held here. Some folks even remember that in the 1920s Marfa was known all over the West as the source of pure-bred Highland Hereford cattle. But as far as I can tell not more than a dozen people know that fifty years ago Marfa was famous in the aviation world for the hand-made airplane propellers built here by Ray Hegy.

Ray Hegy was a genius, a daredevil, and a fine craftsman, and there is no published biography of him. I have had to piece his story together from scattered newspaper clippings and the memories of the few people left in Marfa who knew him. There were never very many of those, because he was a very private man. I am indebted to Dr. Tom DeKunder of Schertz, Texas for most of my information about his early life. DeKunder befriended Hegy shortly before his death in 2000 and sent me a collection of clippings about his career before he moved to Marfa in the late 1940s.

Hegy was born in Wisconsin in 1904, the year after the Wright Brothers made their first flight, and he started out in life as a cabinetmaker. But he got into aviation at the age of 21 when he answered an ad for expert cabinetmakers to build wooden airplane propellers at the Hamilton Aero Manufacturing Company in Milwaukee. He made laminated wooden props from birch and white pine for both commercial and military aircraft, as well as mahogany props for navy dirigibles. Years later he remembered that the dirigible props had to be hollowed out by hand to reduce their weight, and were then covered with fabric and painted navy gray.

Hegy got the flying bug himself in 1928 and quit the propeller factory to become a barnstormer, doing stunt flying at carnivals and circuses all across the country. A clipping from a 1930 Hartford, Wisconsin newspaper includes a photograph of Hegy and his friend Norman Zunker standing in front of a single-engine monoplane that they have just built; a later clipping describes Hegy parachuting from the wingtip of a plane piloted by his brother "before the gaze of thousands" at a Fourth of July celebration. A third clipping, dated March 3, 1939, identifies Hegy as the pilot of a plane from which "the veteran Negro parachute jumper, Suicide Willie Jones" jumped over Chicago's Dixie Airport. Jones's gimmick was that he jumped out of the plane at an altitude of 31,000 feet but did not open his parachute until he had fallen nearly six miles and was 1,000 feet above the ground.

The next clipping in DeKunder's file is dated 1944. It shows Hegy in an Army Air Force captain's uniform while he was making aerial photographs of the Amazon River in Brazil from a Grumman Goose, a twin-engine amphibian. After the war he went to work for a San Antonio aerial mapping service, and that was what brought him to Marfa. "I was here on a mapping job," he told an interviewer in 1969, "I liked the people, loved the climate, and after comparing it with winters in Wisconsin I decided to live in Texas."

Hegy married a Marfa schoolteacher and they bought a house on Texas Street. He built the airplane that made him famous, a tiny red biplane that he called the Chuparosa, the hummingbird, in a two-room shop behind that house. Hegy drew the plans for the plane in chalk on the wall of his shop in 1950; the plane was not finished until 1959. It was made largely from parts from other planes and was powered by a 65-horsepower Continental engine, with a propeller built by Hegy. The Chuparosa was often described as the world's smallest airplane. It was just the right size for Hegy, who stood about 5'4" and weighed 120 pounds at the most. Hegy flew the Chuparosa to the Experimental Aircraft Association's annual show in Rockford, Illinois, all through the 1960s. Its propeller was so widely admired that Hegy began to get requests from all over the country for custom-built propellers, and he started making them in his Marfa shop.

Fritz Kahl, whose typewriten memoirs his widow, Georgia Lee, graciously let me examine, estimated that Hegy made 4,000 propellers in his shop before his death. He made them from laminated wood, and it took him 10 to 12 days to build one, but he always worked on several at a time. He shipped them all over the United States. Kahl painted a vivid picture of Hegy walking down the street to the Marfa bus station with a boxed single-blade propeller as long as he was tall over each shoulder.

Kahl knew Hegy pretty well because in the summer of 1961 they were partners in something called Humpback Airlines, which used two Cessna 182s to fly Empire Oil Company seismograph crews from Marfa over the Sierra Vieja to the Rio Grande. Kahl recalled that it was tricky flying because they had to take off from the Marfa Airport at 4,800 feet, climb immediately to 7,000 feet to get over the mountains, and then drop to 3,400 feet to land on a strip that was only 1,600 feet long. The strip occupied most of the top of a mesa and was known to the pilots, Hegy and Russ White, as "the carrier." Humpback made six flights a day, three in the morning and three in the evening. The morning flights were beautiful, Kahl remembered, but the evening flights were heartstopping, as the temperatures were over 100 and there were always crosswinds and unpredictable turbulence over the Sierra Vieja. The turbulence, Kahl said, sounded like a rushing waterfall from within the plane cabins. Kahl described Hegy as "a pilot with 10,000 flying hours, an expert at low speeds, short landings, and flying in turbulence." At that time Hegy was nearly sixty years old.

Hegy's shop is still standing behind his house on Texas Street. Documenting and preserving it would be a worthy project for the Marfa and Presidio County Museum.

June 11, 2009

NINA KATCHADOURIAN, JINGLE ARTIST

RADIO JINGLES, KNOWN to my generation as "singing commercials," stick in your mind. That is why they are such successful selling gimmicks. Sometimes they stick in your mind long after the demise of the product. I occasionally hear a voice in my head singing, "Dream girls, dream girls, beautiful Lustre Creme girls / You owe your crowning glory to / A Lustre Creme shampoo." Lustre Creme has not been manufactured since about 1970, but that jingle, sung to the tune of Victor Herbert's "Toyland," still resonates. It is inextricably associated in my mind with a radio program called "Our Miss Brooks," sponsored by Lustre Creme, which I listened to avidly once a week in 1950. I was sure that Miss Brooks, a high school English teacher who spent a good deal of time thwarting the schemes of a blustering and authoritarian principal called Osgood Conklin, had shining golden hair, the result of many applications of Lustre Creme.

I had thought that radio jingles went out with five-cent soft drinks, so imagine my surprise when I started hearing them a couple of weeks ago on KRTS, Marfa's public radio station. The KRTS jingles, however, were not advertising nationally-marketed products. They were extolling local businesses and organizations. " The Times, the Wall Street Journal / The Tribune and the Post / They always miss the kind of news that Marfa needs the most / But the Big Bend Sentinel is on the lookout for the leads / We write the kind of story every Marfan wants to read," a voice sings about the Big Bend Sentinel. "The powerless, the poor, the sick / We lend a hand to all / And just this year a scholarship/ Brought a Swedish student here for fall" is about the Marfa Rotary Club. "When you're feeling troubled / When your world is full of gloom / There's no better antidote / Than picking up a broom" urges folks to visit Ron Cox's broom shop in Fort Davis.

Artistically, these jingles are several cuts above the one about Lustre Creme. In fact, some of them sound like a cross between a Schubert lieder and a Baptist hymn, with a little touch of Louis Moreau Gottschalk thrown in. When I asked around I learned that they were written by a Brooklyn artist, Nina Katchadourian, as part of a show she is participating in at The Ballroom this month. Katchadourian somewhat shyly admits that they aren't pure jingles, but are, she says, "in a gray zone between jingles, songs, and public service announcements—they impart information." There are ten of them, she explained when I talked with her last week, and she hopes that taken together they will form a musical portrait of Marfa.

Katchadourian, who is a fine-boned woman with sparkling brown eyes and animated features, is a well-known visual artist, but she told me that she came to music before art, taking piano as a child and singing with school choral groups. She now plays guitar, accordion, and recorder with a Brooklyn-based band called the Wingdale Community Singers, a group that she says is heavily influenced by the Carter Family and the sacred harp tradition. She is a self-described "faculty brat"—her father, Herant Katchadourian, teaches at Stanford University and she grew up on a block with three Nobel Prize winners. While she is basically a big-city girl, she had some small-town experience before coming to Marfa because she has spent her summers since childhood on the Finnish island of Porto, which has a summer population of about 700 (her mother is Finnish and has written a novel, *The Lapp King's Daughter,* about her childhood in Finland during World War II) .

Writing the jingles was a community-based activity. Katchadourian sent a questionnaire headed "Hello, Stranger, Would You Like a Jingle?" which included questions like, "Describe your typical customer," and "If you were to make up a slogan, what would it be?" to a number of local businesses and organizations. She came to Marfa earlier this summer and met with the folks who indicated that they would like jingles, asking them, among other things, if there was a particular musical style that they would prefer for their jingle. She got busy composing, and then came back and recorded her work at the Marfa Recording Company, with accompaniment by Adam Bork and David Beebe and the help of several other Marfans, including Boyd Elder, whose unmistakable voice intones, "The Marfa Lights—have a little faith" at the end of the Marfa Lights jingle, which essentially says that the Lights believe in you even if you don't believe in them.

Katchadourian has done an admirable job of matching the music to the subject matter. The Marfa Lights tune is plaintive and dreamy, the Get Go jingle has a peppy drum rhythm, the Big Bend Sentinel gets a bullring *pasodoble* introduced by trumpet flourishes, and the Ballroom is sung to a lilting waltz. My favorite is the Rotary Club, which is set to a stately anthem played on the piano. Katchadourian told me that this tune was inspired by all of the national anthems she heard as she watched the Olympics. It fits the international nature and the humanitarian mission of the Rotary perfectly.

Some of Katchadourian's visual art has aural elements. Several years ago she created an installation called "Natural Car Alarms," which had its origin in a hike she once took in a rain forest on the island of Trinidad. High on a mountain peak, surrounded by un-familiar plants, birds, and sounds, she suddenly heard a sound any New Yorker could recognize—a six-tone car alarm. Her guide ex-plained that it was actually a bird. When she got back home she created an installation that consisted of three automobiles whose alarm systems each consisted of six very loud bird calls, recorded by the Macaulay Library of Natural Sounds at Cornell University. The alarms were timed to go off at random, so at some times the cars seemed to be answering each others' calls and at other times they were all screaming at once. "Misunderstandings are a won-derful starting point for art," Katchadourian says.

The Marfa Jingles will receive their premier public perfor-mance tomorrow night at 10:00 PM in the patio of the Thunderbird Hotel. You can buy a CD of them, with a handsome cover designed by Katchadourian, at the Marfa Book Company, and I urge you to do that. It is not every town that gets its own song cycle.

September 25, 2008

157

BILLY D. PEISER, EL INDIO

BILLY D. PEISER of Marfa is the master of a profession that most people think disappeared with Daniel Boone. He is a tracker, and during his 25 years with the Border Patrol here he was so good that he was known all over northern Mexico as "El Indio," the Indian. When the Border Patrol caught up with a party of illegal immigrants out in the brush, one of the immigrants would always ask, "Is El Indio with you?"

Peiser has been retired for 19 years now, but his eyes still light up when he talks about the days he spent on foot, following trails no one else could see across the ranches of the Big Bend. "It was fun," he told me. "I loved the challenge and I liked working outdoors. I wanted to be the best and I was, in this part of the world, anyway." Peiser was known in the Border Patrol not only for his ability but for his stamina and his tenacity. When his granddaughter, Tess Seipp, was in the 5TH grade she wrote a biography of Peiser for a class project. One of Peiser's colleagues sent her a letter about Peiser's pursuit of a man who had broken into a ranch house near Casa Piedra, stolen a gun and some jewelry, and headed for Mexico. Peiser and his partner picked up the thief's trail the next morning and pursued him on foot all day, covering 20 miles of some of the roughest country in the Big Bend, before finally running him to earth about a half mile this side of the Rio Grande. Peiser's colleague wrote, "An officer of less stamina, confidence, and abilities would have given up long ago, but not Billy D. Onward he went with his usual perseverance."

Peiser told me that he had no experience as a tracker before he joined the Border Patrol in 1961, but he had always loved being outdoors. He was born in 1934 and grew up on a cotton farm on the Concho River, near the town of Veribest. He graduated from San Angelo College in the middle of the drought of the 1950s. "We had 200 acres and we made three bales of cotton that year," he told me. "I decided that wasn't for me so I went to work on a gravity crew." He worked on oil exploration survey parties all over the Southwest for a few years and then joined the Border Patrol in Yuma, Arizona. "The soil around Yuma was real powdery," he said, "and it was easy to see footprints." He soon discovered that he had a talent for seeing things other people could not see. "I could see footprints in a drag from a car going 50 miles an hour," he said. A drag, he explained, is the plowed strip that the Border Patrol maintains along the right-of-way of east-west roads near the border, which patrol agents examine daily, looking for indications that someone had crossed it on foot—cutting for sign, Peiser called it.

Once Peiser had spotted the sign, it was his job to follow whoever had made it and, if they turned out to be illegal immigrants, to apprehend them. A large part of his success came from knowing the country. He was transferred to Marfa in 1964, and within a few years, he said, "I knew every road, every windmill, every fence line, every gate. If you didn't know that you could waste a lot of time." Speed was important, he pointed out, "because whoever you're tracking is ahead of you and they are moving, too. You've got to move faster if you are going to catch them." He tried to explain to me how to tell how old footprints were. "If they've got bird tracks or bug tracks in them they've been there a while," he said. Then he added, "Early in the morning new tracks have a different color. They're shinier." When I pressed him for a more precise definition he just said, "They're shinier, that's all. I can't explain it." I suspect he was talking about sheer instinct.

Tracking is more difficult in rocky country, Peiser said. "You keep your eyes on the ground and look for kicked rocks, broken sticks, and crushed grass. It's harder. And then when they get on the railroad tracks and step on the ties it's real hard." Peiser expresses admiration for the evasion skills of some of the men he has trailed. Once he and some other agents were following a trail made by a group that had come up over the Candelaria rim and were headed toward US 90 near Valentine. The agents lost the trail in the grassy flats near the highway, an area of tall grass and shallow gullies. They were sure the group had not crossed the highway, but night fell before they could locate them. The next morning Peiser picked up the trail on the other side of the highway and soon had the immigrants in custody. He asked them if they had seen any Border Patrolmen on the flat the night before, and one of the men turned around and showed Peiser a tobacco stain on the back of his shirt. He had been lying in a gully covered with grass when Peiser had spit out a wad of his chewing tobacco.

Peiser has helped to track lost hikers in the Big Bend National Park, but 99% of his work was tracking illegal immigrants. He says it is a lot easier to track people who know where they are going. "People who have a destination tend to move in a straight line toward some landmark, like Mount Livermore or Needle Peak, and they stop at windmills or tanks for water and leave sign. People who are lost wander around every which way."

Bill Peiser loves being alone in the wide open spaces of the Big Bend. Shortly after I met him five years ago I heard him say something that I think is a key to his character. My wife and I had just moved here from Washington, D.C. and we were still adjusting to the sparse population of Far West Texas. We had spent a Saturday in Midland and were astonished that on the way home we did not pass more than a dozen cars in the 70 miles between Pecos and Fort Davis. The next day, during the coffee hour after church, I overheard Peiser telling someone that he had made the same drive at the same time that we had. "And do you know," he said, "that after we got off the Interstate it was wall-to-wall traffic all the way from Pecos to Fort Davis?"

February 21, 2008

MARY BONKEMEYER AND THE GRITS TREES

 NOT LONG AGO at a party in Marfa I over-heard a woman behind me say, "When I was in college in North Carolina there were some very gullible Northern girls there who wanted to know about the South. So I told them that I had grown up on my father's grits plantation, and that every morning my job was to take my bed sheets and spread them under the grits trees and then shake the trees so that we could have fresh grits for breakfast." I turned around to see that the speaker was Mary Bonkemeyer, the mother of Marfa architect Kristin Bonkemeyer, and that she had an impish grin on her face.

A few days later I sat down with Mary Bonkemeyer at her daughter's and son-in-law Doug Humble's house, where she has been visiting from Santa Fe, New Mexico while a show of her paintings has been up at the Marfa Book Store. Bonkemeyer, who is 87, has been painting for 70 years and her work is as fresh and exciting as it must have been in the 1930s. She is pretty fresh, too. "The most wonderful thing you can have as you grow older," she told me, "is curiosity. I keep asking questions and trying to frame questions and work at them while I'm painting. Right now I like to dream about the Golden Ratio."

Bonkemeyer has always seen things differently from other people. Her father was a Methodist minister in rural North Carolina, and her earliest memory is of disappearing from the parsonage one afternoon to go sit on the eggs in the hen house. "It's my first memory of creating a stir," she said. "When my parents finally found me there was a discussion as to whether or not to punish me. I thought I was doing the right thing." In high school she was kicked out of her home economics class for using a rolling pin backwards. "Everything else I did in high school was backwards, too," she told me. "I was always being sent out of class to go do something else while the class was at work. My report cards always said, 'Mary Alice does not follow instructions'—I hated absolutes."

The one thing that she could do was art. "That grabbed my interest," she said. "In the first grade I loved shaping letters. I could get attention from my penmanship." The public schools she attended in North Carolina did not offer art classes—"That would have been considered frivolous"—but when she went to Greensboro College (where she impersonated a grits planter's daughter), she had an art teacher who encouraged her and persuaded her to transfer to the University of North Carolina, which, she said, "had a serious art program, but not too serious." From there she went on to graduate school at the University of Iowa, where the painters idolized by the faculty were realists like Grant Wood. "But I thought his work was too journalistic," she told me. "I wanted to be a little more Frenchy. I liked Matisse and Picasso, and Jackson Pollock. I would unroll a length of newspaper down the hall of my dorm and splash paint on it. I was interested in the accidental and in chaos and how to make sense out of chaos. I was ahead of my time, but somehow my teachers didn't appreciate it."

One teacher who did appreciate her work was the pioneer Abstract Expressionist Philip Guston, who, she said, "taught me how to look at something and transpose the literal into an altered state. I learned that the literal is not necessarily reality. I learned to take something to the very edge—it's like looking over the edge and saying, 'oooh!' It takes your breath away. An abstraction may be closer to the truth."

In 1940 Bonkemeyer married her college boyfriend, an engineer who was a captain in the Army Ordnance Corps and was stationed in Washington, D.C. They lived in Washington for the next 39 years, while her husband developed weapons for the army. "During the Vietnam war I told my friends he was a ski instructor," she said. In Washington Bonkemeyer's career as an artist flourished. She met Duncan Phillips, a wealthy collector of 20TH-century art who had established a gallery in his mansion near Dupont Circle, now the Phillips Collection. Phillips bought one of her paintings, and then invited her to join a group of artists who met to paint in a studio on the top floor of the mansion. "It was heaven," she said. "Climbing the stairs to the studio I walked past paintings by George Braque and Paul Klee and Picasso." The studio could have been an entrée to Washington social circles; Phillips's wife, Marjorie, painted there, and so did Alice Stanley Acheson, the wife of Secretary of State Dean Acheson. But Bonkemeyer says, "I was the only one who was willing to take chances. The others were just trying to impress whoever was there."

In 1979 Bonkemeyer's husband retired from the Defense Department and the couple moved to San Miguel Allende. "My goal was to find a climate where you could live without air conditioning," Bonkemeyer told me, "and that led us to Mexico." They lived there for ten years. Bonkemeyer was a faculty member at the Escuela de Bellas Artes, where she taught "a lot of young Texans," she says. After her husband's death she moved to Santa Fe, New Mexico, where she now maintains a studio.

I asked Bonkemeyer if her style had changed over the seventy years that she has been painting, and she said, "No, it has just deepened. I feel that I have finally understood how to create light in a painting and how to work with form in a more controlled way, but a painter has to realize that too much control can ruin the creative process. You have to be able to accept the gift of accidents." Then that grin I had seen at the party appeared and she said, "In the beginning I didn't like the literal and I still don't." At 87, Mary Bonkemeyer is still shaking the grits tree.

April 10, 2008

GEORGE JONES DIED more than 30 years ago, but people around Fort Davis and Marfa still talk about him as the consummate cattleman. His son-in-law Rube Evans told me, "He was a good cowboy and a good cowman. They're not the same thing, but George Jones was both. He knew cows and he knew how to make money from them." His niece Georgia Lee Kahl simply said, "He was a great cattleman." He stayed in the business more than 50 years, long enough to know the vicissitudes of the cattle market. He understood the peculiar ranching environment of the Davis Mountains and knew how to exploit it profitably, and although he tried raising cattle in other places he was always most successful on his home ground. He once told his friend Mike O'Connor, "I've driven away from Marfa in a Cadillac three times and I've walked back home three times."

Jones, who was born in Marfa in 1897, was part of the first generation of ranchmen to be born in the Big Bend. His father, W.T.

Jones, came here in 1885 from Coleman, Texas in charge of a herd of cattle. He had a dollar and a half in his pocket when he arrived, but he went to work as a cowboy, saved his money, and started buying cattle. By the time George Jones was 18 his father was one of the largest landowners in West Texas. In this area he had the Crows Nest ranch, the Point of Rocks ranch, and the Kelly ranch, all along what is now the southern leg of the Scenic Loop. He was one of the first Big Bend ranchers to build earth tanks, and one of the first to pipe water from springs to tanks. There is an old story that when George and his brother Frank got their first look at the Pacific Ocean on a trip to San Francisco, Frank turned to George and said, "I hope Papa doesn't ever see this. He'd want to pipe it to the Kelly Ranch."

George Jones's father put him in charge of the 40,000-acre Kelly ranch when he was 18. According to Jones's niece Georgia Lee Kahl, W.T. Jones had sent George off to Hardin-Simmons College in Abilene, but after one semester decided his son was spending too much money and told him, "I'm going to bring you home and show you where this money is coming from." George had started a small money-lending business at school, taking neckties as security, and he told his father he would have to have a tie auction to recoup some of his losses before he came home. He had a reputation in the family for aggressive go-aheadness. As a boy he shared a room with his brother Frank. Every night George, who his son-in-law described as "not the epitome of neatness," would shuck off his dirty clothes on the floor and climb into bed, while Frank would carefully fold his somewhat cleaner ones on a chair. Every morning George would put on Frank's clean clothes and leave Frank his dirty ones.

Jones started raising Herefords on the Kelly ranch during World War I, when cattle prices were at an all-time high. He was extremely successful and remained so through the 1920s, which was a period of relative prosperity in the Big Bend. But in the 1930s the Great Depression and a drought hit West Texas at the same time, cattle prices fell to rock bottom, and Jones moved to Mexico. He bought 3 ranches in Chihuahua and lived with his family in the Victoria Hotel in Chihuahua City. He told his friends that he was disgusted with Franklin Roosevelt and the New Deal and that he was not coming home until Roosevelt was dead, and he did not. After World War II he bought a ranch in Montana, but he always said that he never did as well anywhere as when he ranched in the Davis Mountains.

Jones was an individualist and was the kind of person that a whole cycle of stories developed around. As Mike O'Connor told me, "If you told stories about him today and didn't mention his name everyone would know who you were talking about." One familiar tale has to do with the breakup of the Double Circle ranch in the Chiricahua Mountains of Arizona. W.T. Jones and Joe Espy had leased this ranch in the 1920s, and when the lease expired George Jones and a representative of the Espys were charged with dividing a large herd of cattle evenly between the two owners. The men agreed that they would take turns cutting cows out of the herd, and that at each cut each man would take one good cow and two bad ones. About halfway through the procedure Jones became aware that his counterpart had reversed the agreement and was taking two good cows for each bad one. When they were finished, Jones rode over to him and said, "Well, are you satisfied with your cut?" "Oh, yes," the man said, "I think it's fair." "Fine," Jones told him. "I'll take your half and you take mine." And that's the way it was.

One thing that made Jones so memorable was his facility with words. As O'Connor said, "He was not a talker but he had an inimitable way of rearranging words." Rube Evans told me that once Jones was returning from a cattle-buying trip in Mexico and found the Rio Grande in flood at Ojinaga, with the bridge under water. He tried to cross the river in a small boat, which overturned, nearly drowning him. When he finally got back to Marfa and told his family what had happened his daughter asked him if he had been scared. "Well, I'll tell you," he replied, "it sure does make you love your Jesus." Evans also told me that when he proposed to Jones's daughter Sargie she was visiting his family's ranch in New Mexico. She called her father in Marfa to tell him that she had accepted Evans's proposal, and asked him not to tell anyone until she got home. When she got back to Marfa, she said to Jones, "Papa, did you tell anybody?" "No," Jones replied, "I'm just as ashamed of it as you are."

Jones died in 1977, just a few days short of his 80TH birthday. When I asked Rube Evans how to sum up his character, Evans said, "The one thing that I want to impress on you is that George Jones was one hell of a man." He must have been.

May 1, 2008

VILIS INDE, LATVIAN PATRIOT

ON A RECENT Friday night I found myself wearing a nightshirt over my street clothes and playing the part of a dying father in a reading of the Latvian national epic play "The Golden Horse" at the Marfa Book Company. The reading was in honor of the 150ᵀᴴ anniversary of the birth of the play's author, Janis Rainis. It was being held in Marfa because Vilis Inde, the co-owner of Marfa's inde/jacobs gallery, has translated Rainis's play into English and published it with an introduction explaining the play's significance as a plea for Latvian independence (Rainis wrote it in 1909, when Latvia was still part of the Russian Empire, and cast it as a children's fairy tale in order to get it past the Czar's censors). The standing-room-only audience included seventeen Latvians from all over the United States and Canada—one came from St. John's, Newfoundland—who gathered in Marfa to listen to scenes from Inde's translation, surely the largest gathering of Latvians ever seen in the Big Bend. The publication, the performance, and the presence of so many Latvians confirmed my belief that Marfa is the most cosmopolitan small town in Texas, if not in the entire United States.

Inde, whose parents immigrated from Latvia in the late 1940s, grew up in the Latvian community of Minneapolis, Minnesota. He told me that he first encountered Rainis's play at the age of 11 when the Latvian Lutheran Sunday school he attended produced it in the original Latvian. He was in the production, but he says he can't remember what part he played, although he is sure he was not the star. Inde's family spoke Latvian at home and when he was in high school he spent part of his senior year as an exchange student at the Lettische Gymnasium, a Latvian-language high school in Muenster, Germany. He went on to St. Olaf College in Northfield, Minnesota, where he graduated with a double major in art history and psychology in 1981, and then went to law school at the University of Minnesota. He practiced law in Minneapolis and New York for 12 years but then, he told me, "I decided that I didn't want to work 80 hours a week for the rest of my life," and he left his law firm. "I didn't know how I'd be able to live," he said, "but I've always been able to take steps toward what would satisfy me."

Inde went back to Minneapolis and wrote his first book, *Art in the Courtroom* (Praeger, 1998), a book he says is found "only in law libraries and museum libraries," dealing with legal cases involving art that arose from the culture wars of the 1980s. Shortly after that he began to think about translating Rainis's play, but he didn't actually get down to work on it until he and his partner, Tom Jacobs, moved to Marfa in 2005 to open an art gallery.

Inde spoke about the Latvian diaspora, the tens of thousands of Latvians who, like his parents, fled Latvia after World War II to avoid Soviet domination and ended up in the United States, Canada, and Australia. He wanted to do something that would keep Latvian culture alive among the younger generation of this diaspora, and he hit on the idea of translating Rainis's play into colloquial English. "I wanted to write something that children could read and talk to their Latvian grandmothers about, something that would tie the generations together. Rainis's play, with its powerful Latvian folk symbols, was the perfect vehicle." As he worked on the translation, he realized that he was doing it specifically for his nephew, the son of his brother who had married an American and did not speak Latvian with his family.

The translation was published in 2012 with the help of the Cultural Foundation of the American Latvian Association. It immediately became controversial. Sarma Liepinš, the past president of the American Latvian Association, who came to Marfa from Boxford, Massachusetts for the reading, explained why: "The play was originally written in a rhythm and with a rhyme scheme that reflected the rhythm and rhymes of traditional Latvian folk songs. Vilis's translation abandoned that rhythm and those rhymes to make the text more accessible in English, and this offended some academics and traditionalists." Inde says he committed another sin by using contemporary English. "For example," he explained, "there was an earlier translation in the 1970s that translated the title as 'The Golden Steed.' I called it 'The Golden Horse.' No kid today knows what a steed is. I wanted people to read my translation and pass it on."

The wounds seem to be healing, however. Inde is working with the National Library of Latvia in Riga to bring out a new edition with an additional chapter that will explain the links between the symbols in the play and the architecture of the new library. The play is about the quest of a young man who rides a golden horse up the Glass Mountain to the Castle of Light to awaken a sleeping princess; the Glass Mountain and the Castle of Light, both elements of ancient Latvian folklore, are incorporated into the design of the library's new building, which was completed last fall. Inde's book will serve as a guidebook to the library as well as an explanation of Latvia's history and Rainis's part in it.

The Marfa reading was a smashing success. We did three scenes: the one in which I die, admonishing my sons (Brandon Nagle, Michael Camacho, and Robert Aragon) to remain unified; one in which my youngest son (Michael Camacho) tells an old man (Harry Hudson) about his passion for the sleeping princess, and one in which the seven ravens guarding the princess discuss their vigil, croaking all the way (Francis Keck Benton, age 9, and Nalu Gruschkis, age 12, were the youngest ravens). Inde told me that the best part of the evening for him was hearing the words that he had written read by so many people. "When I heard the reading I thought, oh my God, this is alive!" he said. He added that one of the Latvians had told him that it was fantastic to hear the words of their national poet read with a Texas drawl. That's Marfa.

April 9, 2015

WILBORN ELLIOTT THE BEE MAN

HAMILTON FISH AND Sandra Harper came from New York to be there. Presidio County Attorney John Fowlkes and his wife Lauren were there. Marfa mayor Dan Dunlap and his wife Anne were there. New York filmmaker Lacy Dorn was there. All of the beauty and chivalry of Marfa, as the old newspapers used to say, gathered in Buck Johnston's and Camp Bosworth's back yard last Friday night to help Wilborn Elliott celebrate his 90TH birthday with a pot luck supper and a horseshoe shaped honey cake aglow with 90 candles.

Elliott, with his ready smile and trademark suspenders, has been a familiar figure in Marfa ever since he moved into town from Casa Piedra 20 years ago. He is known as the Bee Man, and until a couple of years ago his honey was a regular item at the Marfa Farmstand. He also raises chickens and functions as the town's one-man welcoming committee, and at Friday night's party he hobnobbed with the scores of young people among Marfa's art community that he has befriended.

I had a long talk with Elliott the next day at the Farmstand.

When I asked him why he started keeping bees he said, "to keep from starving." He explained that his father died when he was two years old, and his mother decided to take her children and move from Fort Stockton, Texas, where Elliott was born, back to her parents' farm in western Kansas. Her father was a beekeeper, and so young Wilborn grew up among bee hives. In 1933 hard times and an extraordinarily cold winter made Elliott's grandfather decide to sell out and move his family to Texas. Elliott said his mother did not want to live in a town, "where her children would roam the streets," so they moved to the Big Bend and settled down at Johnson's Ranch on the Rio Grande, 130 miles south of Alpine and one of the most isolated places in Texas. "Times were very hard in Texas in 1933," Elliott told me, "and my grandfather said to my mother, 'let's go into the bee business.' My mother said she didn't want anything to do with bees because she didn't want to get stung, and my grandfather said she was going to get stung no matter what business she went into so it might as well be by bees." Elliott attended the one-room San Vicente school and helped with the hives after school.

When he finished the seventh grade, his mother sent him to Española, New Mexico, to live with his paternal grandparents and attend McCurdy Mission School there. He was 14 and he hitchhiked all the way from the Johnson Ranch to Española. He was drafted into the Navy in 1943, a month after he graduated from McCurdy, and spent the war at Pearl Harbor, where he was trained as a torpedo mechanic. When he came home he found that his mother had purchased a small farm at Casa Piedra. "She remembered World War I, and how when the war was over the veterans walked the streets looking for work, and she wanted my brother and me to have something to do, so she gave us this farm," Elliott said. That was when Elliott started in the honey business in earnest.

"I brought 10 hives of bees from Johnson's Ranch to Casa Piedra," he told me, "and a few years later I had 80 hives." Each hive, he explained, contains about 30,000 bees. In some good years, years with lots of rain, he was able to gather 20,000 pounds of honey, but it was usually less than that. He sold the honey to grocery stores and filling stations in Alpine, Marfa, Fort Davis, and Fort Stockton, and sometimes shipped special orders to customers in the East and even in Europe.

It takes about a year for a hive of bees to produce enough honey to store a usable surplus, Elliott said. He explained that some beekeepers wait until fall to harvest the honey, "like farmers with their crops," but he liked to get it while it was fresh, in May. "That's when the mesquite and catclaw blossom, and that honey is good, clear and white. The best honey is from the whitebrush, that blossoms for only ten days or so in May (he was talking about the plant known to botanists as Privet Lippia). After that it's all weed honey, which is red. It's baker's honey." Elliott would actually harvest two crops of honey, white honey in May and red baker's honey in the fall.

I asked him about starting new hives and he explained that bees swarm in the spring, and all that you have to do is to find a swarm on a tree limb and coax them into a box with a screen wire lid and move them to their new hive. "If you get the queen in your box the other bees will follow their mama right in," he said. Elliott did not like to work bees wearing a net on his hat; he couldn't see what he was doing, and he didn't like to wear gloves, either. A Marfa lady once saw him moving a swarm without any protective equipment and told everyone in town that he was immune to bee stings. "It wasn't that at all," he said. "Bees are smarter than people think. When they swarm they're looking for a new home, and when you move them they know you are helping them find one so they won't sting you."

"I sure miss my bees. I've been around them for 75 years," Elliott told me. He stopped keeping bees two years ago because he could no longer stay on his feet long enough to tend the hives. Several years back a young bull knocked him down and smashed his left leg below the knee; at the time he told his friends, "that bull just wanted to play with me." However, he still has chickens and sells their eggs at Marfa Farmstand every Saturday. He told me that he keeps chickens "just to have something to do. I'd go crazier than I am now if I just sat around the house and thought about the old times," he said. Judging from the number of people who came up to visit Elliot while we were talking, I don't think he will be at home alone with his thoughts very often.

April 23, 2015

ROBERT GUNGOR AND THIRD WAVE COFFEE

BACK IN THE Dark Ages of the late 1950s I was the part owner of one of the hippest coffee houses in Fort Worth, a place called the Coffin on Park Hill Drive near T.C.U. It was a dean of students' nightmare. We stayed open until 2:00 AM. We had a resident beatnik who wore a monk's robe and recited his own poetry while thumping a pair of bongo drums. We had a folksinger, a young woman who wore a black leotard and sat on a stool strumming a guitar and occasionally breaking into "I Gave My Love a Cherry" or "The House of The Rising Sun." We had dim lights and tables with candles in wax-covered Chianti bottles on them. We had a second-hand espresso machine that broke down regularly. We had everything we needed to run a Greenwich Village coffee house except an accountant who could tell us how much it cost to keep the place open, and so we went broke after six months. But I thought from that experience that I knew something about coffee houses.

Until I met Robert Gungor.

Robert Gungor is the presiding genius behind Marfa's newest

coffee house, Do Your Thing, located in the old lumberyard across the street from the Get Go. Gungor, a rotund man in his early 30s with a neatly-trimmed beard and an evangelical manner (his father was a non-denominational preacher in Tulsa, Oklahoma and Gungor is a graduate of Oral Roberts University there), sat with me in Do Your Thing one cold morning a couple of weeks ago and filled me in on developments in the coffee-house business since I left it.

I was part of the First Wave, he told me. The First Wave was composed of coffee houses, mostly in Greenwich Village and in San Francisco's North Beach, that were inspired by the indigenous Italian espresso parlors in those neighborhoods. Their owners simply added performers to the traditional mix of tile floors and marble-top tables and attracted young hipsters instead of elderly Italian gentlemen. The Second Wave, Gungor explained, came along in the 1980s with the expansion of Starbuck's into a national chain, followed by Starbuck's imitators. Gungor himself is the Third Wave.

Gungor has been a coffee-house aficionado since the age of 15, he told me. That was when he started working for a Second Wave coffee house in his native Tulsa called Nordaggio's, owned by a man from Seattle. "I was his most loyal and excited apprentice," Gungor told me. Gungor worked for Nordaggio's for seven years, while at the same time he played piano and keyboard in a series of Christian bands. On a band tour to Seattle he met David Schomer, the guru of Third Wave coffee shops.

Schomer, Gungor explained, is a Seattle native who as an engineer spent years calibrating measuring devices for Boeing. As part of a mid-life crisis he opened a mobile coffee cart on Seattle's Capitol Hill, and he quickly discovered that no one had ever applied scientific techniques to the brewing of espresso. His coffee cart turned into a permanent coffee shop, Vivace, and Vivace became a laboratory for the development of the perfect cup of espresso.

Schomer broke the process of brewing coffee down into a number of separate steps, from buying the beans to pouring the steamed milk into the coffee once the coffee is in the cup. He experimented with each step, attempting to find the method that would achieve the best-tasting cup of coffee. For example, he determined that the flavor of the beans is best when they are ground in a burr grinder at less than 900 revolutions per minute; that the hot water that is infused into the ground beans must be exactly 203.5 degrees Fahrenheit, and that the infusion must take place over exactly 25 seconds.

Schomer disseminated his discoveries through a book, *Espresso Coffee: Professional Techniques*, published in 1994, and through DVD's and hands-on classes that he teaches at Vivace. Over the next twenty years Schomer's gospel spread slowly across the country, resulting in Third Wave coffee shops in San Francisco, New York, Boston, Austin, Boulder, and, of course, Seattle.

Gungor, who had left the coffee house world for a career in music (he is a composer who works under the name Wilderman), didn't come to Marfa to open a coffee house. He and his girl friend, Simone Rubi (also a musician), came here from California in December 2013 to make a record at Gory Smelley's studio. They planned to stay three months. Back in San Francisco, they had patronized a Third Wave coffee shop called the Blue Bottle. They missed their Blue Bottle coffee, but they fell in love with Marfa and decided to extend their stay for a year. "Then," Gungor said, "We decided to open a Blue Bottle pop up."

The old lumber yard seems to be the perfect place in spite of the fact that customers have to push a heavy sliding metal door open to get inside on cold days. Gungor and Rubi buy their roasted espresso beans from Blue Bottle, and Gungor explained that they only use them from 4 to 10 days after they have been roasted, when their flavor is at its peak. They set up the shop with all of the equipment needed to achieve Third Wave perfection but it is a little short on furniture and other amenities: customers can sit at one big table or one small table or in two low-slung chairs, and heat is provided by a gas brazier filled with rocks in the center of the room. The walls are raw plywood hung with coffee sacks. However, the coffee is delicious, very possibly the best cup of coffee you ever tasted.

And definitely the most decorative. The day that I sat down to talk with Gungor, he made me a cup of cappuccino. After he had filled the cup, he picked up a pitcher of steamed milk and manipulating the cup with one hand and the pitcher with the other, drew a little palm leaf on the surface of the coffee. That, he explained, was latte art, the signature of a Third Wave coffee shop. It didn't alter the taste of the coffee, but it made the interior of Do Your Thing seem almost elegant.

January 29, 2015

DIRK VAUGHAN, REFORMED COP

 PEOPLE MOVE TO Marfa from all over, and come from all kinds of backgrounds, some of them surprising. Dirk Vaughan is a case in point. Most folks know Vaughan as the smiling, friendly fellow who waits on them behind the counter at the Get Go, or who used to be a waiter at the Blue Javelina, or was behind the desk at the Paisano for a while, or drove them to Midland in the Marfa Flyer, or delivered stacks of the *Big Bend Sentinel* to local businesses early on Thursday mornings. Vaughan has done all of those things since he and his companion Elizabeth Redding moved to Marfa in 2006. Who would have guessed that in an earlier life Vaughan was a Denver cop, and a very good one?

Vaughan told me about his law enforcement career over coffee one morning at Squeeze Marfa. He even brought along what he calls his Pig File to verify what he was telling me, pulling out a certificate saying that he had graduated from the Denver Police Academy on January 27, 1978 and other documents certifying to further training and employment in both Denver and Aurora, a Denver suburb. The certificates added up to 13 years of police work.

I asked Vaughan how he had decided to become a cop and he gave me a straight answer. "It was all because of a blonde-headed girl with a fantastic figure," he said. "I was a senior in high school, and her father was a Denver cop. He kept urging me to apply for the Denver police training program, and I figured that if I did, I'd have a better chance with the girl. It didn't quite work out that way, but when I looked into it I discovered that it was like being handed a college education and a career on a silver platter. It was a really good deal." The training program, Vaughan explained, paid for college courses at Denver Community College and offered the enrollee part-time civilian employment at the Denver Police Department while he was taking them, plus a guarantee of an eventual job as a Denver police officer. The only problem, Vaughan said, was that there were 10 slots in the program and 800 applicants for them. Vaughan applied and, after going through a series of written, oral, and physical exams designed to weed out unsuitable applicants, got one of the slots. Eighteen months later he had a badge, a gun, and a beat.

When I asked Vaughan what he liked best about being a policeman, he had to think a minute. "I was always a good athlete in high school. I played soccer and I was a cross-country runner, and I always liked mental challenges, too. When I became a cop I realized that police procedures—the rules of search and seizure and the pyramid of escalating force, what you do in response to what the person you are trying to arrest does, were a game with complicated rules that challenged me and a physicality that appealed to me. I should add," he went on, "that I grew up in a white-bread, middle-class family in Arlington, Texas, where policemen and firemen were positive role models. They stood for fair play, honesty, and justice. I wanted to be one." After another pause he said, "I was the cop you wanted to meet. I was out to resolve any situation in a way that was beneficial to everyone."

Did his idealism survive working the streets as a cop? "Nope," he said. "It fell away like feathers from a dead bird. I stopped being a good cop." I asked him to explain, and he said, "In order to be a good cop, you have to have compassion and discretion; you have to engage in every interaction as a humane person, and that is costly. A robotic cop, the kind who just goes by the book, is a tired cop. He's dealt with too many savage and irrational situations. I got tired and I realized I was becoming a savage."

Vaughan gave me an example of what he meant. He and two other officers went to a trailer court to arrest a 17-year old girl who had stabbed her boyfriend, although not fatally. The girl admitted the attack but said it was in self defense. Vaughan explained that they would have to take her to jail and book her, that she would be charged with assault with a deadly weapon, and that her parents could follow them and make bail for her and bring her back home. The girl got hysterical and started screaming that she was not going to jail, locking her hands under the seat of a chair she was sitting in. Her father, a huge man, "nothing but muscles and hostility," as Vaughan put it, started advancing towards Vaughan, with his wife pulling on his shirt, trying to hold him back. The other two officers had their hands full trying to get the girl out of the chair, out of the trailer, and into the police car. They finally dragged the chair, with the girl still gripping it and screaming, out the door of the trailer and down the sidewalk to the car, while Vaughan kept backing away from the enraged father. Finally, when Vaughan was at the bottom of the trailer's steps and the father was looming above him at the top, Vaughan drew his nightstick and, breaking away from approved police procedure, said, "M_____r, if you take one more step I'll break your head open like a melon."

"I didn't intend to hit him in the head," Vaughan told me. "I was going to try to break his kneecap. But I knew that if this was going to work I had not only to make him think I was going to kill him, but that I would enjoy doing it." Vaughan's bluff worked, but he knew from that moment that his days as a policeman were drawing to an end. "You build a persona of blue suit invulnerability," he said, "but you are stained by it."

It took Vaughan several more years, plus the fatal shooting of a uniformed colleague and good friend by an armed robber and a high-speed chase in which Vaughan killed a drunk driver who made a left turn in front of his police car, to resign from the force, but, looking back, he says he made the decision that night on the steps of an enraged man's house trailer.

Visiting with the affable Vaughan over the counter of the Get Go, who would know?

September 5, 2013

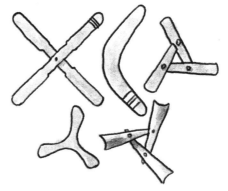

THE SHETLAND ISLANDS are north of Scotland in the North Sea, due west of Bergen, Norway. In the wintertime they are among the least hospitable inhabited places in the world. Scott Hawkins of Marfa used to travel there in the winter with a circus, the Clown Jewels, which also made winter tours of the Orkney Islands, south of the Shetlands, and of northern Scotland. The circus was a New Age animal-free circus, with a core group of professional performers who produced a play interspersed with jugglers, acrobats, and giant inflatable puppets. Hawkins built and manipulated the puppets. "For instance," he explained when I talked with him in Fort Davis last week, "there was a point in one of the plays where an actor would say, 'Give us a hand,' and a giant hand would appear behind him. That was my contribution."
"It was a life-changing experience for me," Hawkins said. "I was twenty-three and had just come back to Britain after two years as a volunteer in rural Nigeria, and the return was a massive culture shock. My values had been changed and I no longer fit Britain. My name is Scott so I went to northern Scotland, Scott-land. I thought there might be something for Scott there, and there absolutely was."

What Hawkins found, he said, was a big house where a group of professional actors lived, surrounded by a forest full of hoboes and nomads, New Age travelers with shamanistic beliefs, something similar to an American hippie commune but with a purpose. "There were people living in teepees, people living in trucks parked in the garden. There was a core group of five skilled professionals, and about twenty others who helped out, and then we had contract performers. In the winter we traveled in a double-decker London Routemaster bus and performed in a tent. In the summer we used three buses that converted into a three-sided stage." The Clown Jewels, Hawkins said, filled a real need in northern Scotland and the islands. "Our shows were sell-outs. We went to isolated places where there was real poverty." The circus received generous grants from national and regional arts councils. "This was in 1988, and we were a total expression of that age, a shamanistic community funded by the government that fulfilled a social need."

Hawkins learned to juggle, walk a slack rope, and ride a unicycle in the Clown Jewels, and then he and a female Clown Jewel formed their own circus and toured Great Britain for the next fifteen years. "It was called Turnaround Arts," he said, "because we believed that people could be empowered by creative group activity. We set out to change the world. We learned that the best we could do was to change people, at least for a moment." Hawkins built a giant inflatable dinosaur and played the role of Professor Crazybones In Search of the Last Living Dinosaur. He wore a pyrotechnic device of his own design on his head that emitted flames when the script called for his brain to overheat. The first time he tried it out, he said, it burned holes in his hair and he had to re-engineer it.

Designing things like pyrotechnic headwear is Hawkins's forte. He is a natural innovator. He grew up in Stevenage, a postwar "new town" north of London. When he left school at sixteen he was apprenticed as an electronics engineer in the town's main industry, British Aerospace, and learned to design and fabricate metal objects. In Nigeria he became an improviser; the school he was teaching in had no typewriters so he made wooden keyboards in order to teach typing. In the Clown Jewels, he said, "I built a dragon that ate little children." It was made out of wind-surfing sail fabric and fiberglass hoops, and had mechanical jaws.

While touring with Turnabout Arts, Hawkins became a part-time student at the University of Sheffield and earned a degree in industrial design. After graduation, he joined the faculty as a lecturer in industrial design and did research on a subject so esoteric that he had to explain it to me several times, finally saying, "Just say that it has to do with the way that sound informs our perception of three-dimensional space." As a result, he built several devices he describes as "para-musical instruments" and holds patents on several products that make use of sound for therapy and relaxation. Far easier for me to grasp is his interest in what he calls "obscure bicycles." He recently built a bicycle from spare parts he found around Marfa. It looks like most bicycles except that the handlebars are behind the seat.

After several years of teaching, Hawkins discovered that his time at the university was being increasingly consumed by administrative tasks, and he decided that it was time to wipe the slate clean and start over again. He and his circus partner had parted, and he subsequently met and married Metta Carlsen, a Danish art conservator. When she was offered a job as the conservator at the Judd Foundation, they moved to America, arriving in Marfa last November. With the exception of a short trip through Arizona and New Mexico following Carlsen's initial job interview, Marfa, Alpine, and Fort Davis make up Hawkins's entire experience of the United States. "In a way," he says, 'the Big Bend is like northern Scotland. The towns are small and isolated, but there is a regional sense of community. Everyone knows each other."

When I asked Hawkins what was ahead for him in Marfa, he pulled a cross-stick boomerang out of a bag he was carrying. "I've bought a sander, a band saw, and a heat gun, and I've opened the Red Frog Boomerang factory under a shelter half in my back yard," he told me. In addition to the cross-stick models, he plans to make boomerangs he has named the Longhorn, the Horseshoe, and the Texas Flying Star.

When Hawkins said he had been in Marfa since November, I asked him if he had bought a pair of cowboy boots yet. "No," he said, "I don't feel I'm quite entitled to wear cowboy boots yet." Then, after a pause, he added, "When I sell my first Longhorn boomerang to a Texan, then I'll buy my cowboy boots."

So if you see a tall fellow with a short ponytail riding a bicycle with the handlebars behind the seat down Highland Avenue, stop him and tell him you want to buy a Longhorn boomerang.

August 2, 2012

JACK AND DOC, THE PANCHO AND LEFTY OF MARFA

I SPENT A Friday morning a couple of weeks doing what I enjoy almost more than anything and don't get to do often enough. I sat at a kitchen table in Marfa with a couple of gentlemen in their eighties drinking coffee and listening to them trade stories. Jack Brunson and Doc Whitman have been friends for more than half a century. They first met in the Border Patrol, which Brunson joined in 1951 and Whitman in 1955. They worked together for nearly twenty-five years, until they both retired on the same day in 1978. They are very different in appearance and manner. Brunson is short and gregarious; Whitman is tall and reserved. Brunson is a seasoned raconteur; Whitman often communicates with a quiet smile. But their common life in the Border Patrol has given them plenty to reminisce about.

When Brunson and Whitman joined the Border Patrol, its agents in the Southwest spent most of their time tracking down aliens who were working here illegally and returning them to Mexico. Agents were not popular with ranchers and others who were dependent on these aliens for cheap labor. Brunson told a story to illustrate the double hazards of his job. He and three other agents had gone to Lajitas to check on some Mexicans who were working in a uranium mining operation there. When they arrived they saw the men at the mouth of a cave in the side of a mountain above the spot where the mine was being blasted out. Brunson and two other men scrambled up the mountain toward the cave while the fourth agent, Buck Newsome, stayed on horseback below. Brunson pulled himself up on a boulder that broke loose and rolled down the mountain, leaving him stranded in a precarious spot. He shouted for help, and Newsom rode up the slope and threw two lariats to the agents above him, who tied them together and pulled Brunson to safety. In the meantime the mine owner appeared in a pickup truck, driving toward Newsome and yelling at him. Just before he reached Newsome there was an explosion that blew the right front wheel off the truck. The mine owner jumped out of the cab and started cussing at Newsome, wanting to know why the agents were shooting at him. Newsome looked down from his horse and said, "They're not shooting at you, you ran over a dynamite cap." The man stopped in mid-sentence, looked at the ground, and said, "I've been telling them boys to be more careful with that dynamite."

One of Brunson and Whitman's former colleagues was Bill Jordan, a six-foot-six Louisianan and former Marine who was famous within the Border Patrol for the speed with which he could draw his pistol. Jordan liked to stand facing another agent with his pistol holstered and ask the agent to clap his hands when he saw Jordan start to move. When the agent brought his palms together Jordan's pistol would be between them. Brunson once asked Jordan, "What good does all that fast-draw practice do you?" Jordan answered, "Well, when I go to check out a bar I know I'm not going to come out a dead man." After Jordan retired from the Border Patrol he became a field representative for the National Rifle Association, giving fast-draw demonstrations on a number of television programs. He invented a special holster that was used by the Border Patrol as long as they carried revolvers.

Brunson and Whitman agreed that in their days the Border Patrol had a higher standard of marksmanship than other law enforcement agencies. "We had to qualify as marksmen with our pistols four times a year," Whitman said. "We carried .38 Specials, most of them Colts." Brunson said he only fired one shot at a person during his career. "And I didn't shoot at him," he emphasized. "I shot near him." Brunson explained that he and his partner had pulled up to a ranch house near Bakersfield and "the bunk house just exploded. My partner took off after a bunch on foot and I was trying to head one off in the car. He jumped into a canyon and ran up the other side, turned around, and gave me an obscene gesture. I had a tremendous sinus headache and I was mad and thought I'd just scare him, so I fired a shot to what I thought was one side of him. The bullet hit the ground right between his feet. He took off running and then he'd stop and vomit and then run some more and stop and vomit again. It cured any desire I ever had to use a pistol. I drew my gun again, but I never fired it."

The men talked about some of the local lawmen they had worked with. Jim Nance, the sheriff in Sanderson, had a high-powered rifle that he was extremely proud of. He liked to demonstrate how it could propel a bullet through a steel rail at close range, until one day the bullet hit the flange of the rail and ricocheted back and winged him. After that he just told people what it could do.

Whitman, who was a master tracker—"I still keep my eye on

the ground when I walk," he said—recalled tracking a man who had stolen a rifle from a ranch near Marathon all the way to Black Gap with Sheriff Jim Skinner of Alpine. "Sheriff Skinner didn't allow hats or caps at his dances," Brunson interjected. "If he had to ask you a second time to take it off it came off with a blackjack." Whitman recalled asking a couple of young men from Alpine if they knew Sheriff Skinner. "We sure do," they said, putting both hands on top of their heads as if to protect then.

While we were talking a man knocked on Brunson's door to deliver three beautifully boxed dolls that Brunson had won at a Border Patrol retirees' raffle. "They've been around the office for a month," the man said. "Nobody knew whose they were." "Jack doesn't look like a man who would play with dolls," I put in. "You haven't known him very long," Doc Whitman said with a slow smile.

September 8, 2011

DOWN ON THE RIVER

THE PEOPLE OF LA JUNTA

 IF YOU TURN off Farm to Market Road 170 on the northeast side of Presidio and drive a few blocks toward the river, you will find a dirt street that ends at a large vacant lot covered with mesquite and chaparral. The lot is fenced, and a faded sign says that it is a Texas State Archaeological Landmark and forbids trespassing. When I was there last month it was 108 degrees. Dogs were lying in whatever shade they could find in the yards of the cinder block and adobe houses that line the street, and a radio somewhere was playing conjunto music. The fenced lot, which is the property of the Texas Historical Commission, is known to archaeologists as the Millington Site. My friend Andy Cloud at Sul Ross State University's Center for Big Bend Studies tells me that people have been living more or less continually on and around it since about 1200, a few years before Marco Polo made his first trip to China. The human skeletons that Cloud and his colleagues excavated there last winter could have been the ancestors of whoever it was that I heard playing the radio down the street.

The Millington site is part of a string of archaeological sites that run along both sides of the Rio Grande between Ruidosa and Redford and along both banks of the Rio Conchos between Ojinaga and Cuchillo Parado. The sites represent a group of settlements at a place that was called La Junta de los Rios by the Spanish, a reference to the confluence of these two rivers. The sites along the north side of the Rio Grande, and one on the south side, were first excavated by Sul Ross archaeologist J. Charles Kelley and his colleague Donald Lehmer in the late 1930s. They tell a story of human endurance and resilience and, like many archaeological sites, they raise questions that only further excavation can answer.

The La Junta sites were the home of a people that the Spanish had several names for. Cabeza de Vaca, who first encountered them in 1535, called them the Cow Nation, "los de las vacas," because they hunted buffalo. Later explorers called them first the Patarabueyes, "ox-kickers," and later, the Jumanos. Archaeologists differ on whether or not the Patarabueyes and the Jumanos were the same people under different names, or whether the Jumanos were later occupants of the Patarabueyes' villages, but everyone agrees that when Cabeza de Vaca and his companions stumbled into their villages someone had been living along the rivers for at least 300 years, growing corn, beans, squash, and gourds in the fertile alluvial soil. In the 1300s and early 1400s the villages consisted of pit houses with walls made of river cane or sotol, thatched roofs, and floors sunk several feet below the ground; some had benches of puddled adobe around the walls. The La Junta villages were part of a trade network that centered on Casas Grandes, in north central Chihuahua, and reached all the way from Yucatan to the Pacific. Kelley's and Lehmer's excavations turned up shards of pottery from Casas Grandes as well as from the El Paso area up the river, and sea shells from the Pacific Ocean that were traded through Casas Grandes, where archaeologists have found rooms stacked to the ceilings with similar shells. The Casas Grandes trade network collapsed about 1450, and the people at La Junta learned to do without the shells and to make their own pottery, simple buff-colored pots, some of which were decorated with incised marks or brownish-red paint. Kelley and Lehmer found pieces of that pottery, too. In the 1680s and again about 1715 Franciscan missionaries came to the La Junta villages and built some thatched chapels and at least one, down the river near Redford, out of adobe. The missionaries gave the villages Spanish names; the Millington site was San Cristobal. Kelley and Lehmer found a Spanish coin dated in the 1750s there, as well as shards of the Mexican majolica pottery that the Franciscans used. Sixty years later, in the site near Redford, Andy Cloud found a tiny metal Cristo, the figure of the crucified Christ that would have been fastened to a crucifix.

These artifacts eloquently tell part of the story of the people of La Junta, but there are two unsolved mysteries about them: where did they come from, and where did they go? Archaeologists have two theories about their origin: they were either indigenous to the region, the descendants of the Paleoindian hunters and gatherers of the Big Bend, who discovered agriculture on their own; or they were a Jornada Mogollon people from southern New Mexico who migrated to La Junta already knowing how to farm. Historians claim that they disappeared sometime before 1720, because Spanish documents no longer refer to Jumanos living at La Junta but instead describe that area as being occupied by Apaches. There is a theory to explain that, too: the Jumanos eventually became assimilated with their traditional enemies, the Apaches, and simply became the Apaches that the Spanish reported living around La Junta. But right now there is not a great deal of tangible evidence to support any of these theories.

The Millington Site came to public attention in the summer of 2003 when a Presidio city maintenance crew digging a trench for a water line along its eastern edge uncovered several human burials. Andy Cloud and a team from the Center for Big Bend Studies went to Presidio to document the disturbance (the burials turned out to be prehistoric), and then returned last winter to reopen the trench and salvage the disturbed burials. Over a 3-week period they found a pit house, 2 unidentified structures, and 5 burials, all part of the village that Kelley and Lehmer had excavated in the 1930s. They also collected a pretty good pile of Mexican majolica pottery shards, which makes Cloud think that they were working near the site of the 17TH and 18TH-century chapels. On top of that, they provided a free lesson in archaeology for the crowds of high school students who gathered all day long to watch them work; a few even volunteered to help out. All of this has whetted Cloud's appetite for more archaeological work at the La Junta sites, which he hopes to get started on this winter. Some of it may tell us with more certainty where the original occupants of La Junta came from and where they went.

July 20, 2006

FORT LEATON

FORT LEATON IS, in my opinion, the one must-see place in the Big Bend. It is located on Farm to Market Road 170—the River Road—just a few miles southeast of Presidio. It is not unique—there are other fortified adobe houses in the Big Bend in various states of preservation, including Milton Faver's elaborately restored ranch house at Cibolo Creek Resort, which looks far better now than it did when Faver lived there—but Fort Leaton is by far the biggest and the most evocative of these houses. It is now run as a museum by the Texas Parks and Wildlife Department and is well worth the $3.00 admission fee. I always take people who come to visit us there, even in the summer, when it can be 106 degrees in the parking lot.

Fort Leaton was a private fort, an Indian trading post, a landmark on the Chihuahua Trail, a place once described by a U.S. Army general as "a den of outlaws," and the residence for more than fifty years of the Burgess family, some of whose descendants still live in the Presidio area (they were not the outlaws the general was referring to). Like all old houses, it contains several layers of history, and that is what fascinates me about it.

The original Fort Leaton, probably a building of five or six rooms, was built by Ben Leaton in 1848 on the ruins of an 18ᵀᴴ-century Spanish structure. Leaton was an enigmatic figure about whom not much is known, and what is known is not much to his credit. He was probably born in Kentucky or Virginia, and he was a mercenary scalp-hunter in northern Mexico in the late 1830s, paid by the Chihuahuan government to kill Apaches and bring their scalps in as evidence of their deaths. He probably conspired with the *alcalde* of Presidio del Norte (now Ojinaga) to swindle the farmers who were living on the site of Fort Leaton out of their land through a series of forged deeds. He undoubtedly traded guns and ammunition to the Apaches for stolen horses and mules, and he incurred the official wrath of the Mexican government for doing so, being described in one document as "committing a thousand abuses." On the plus side, he was lauded by several travelers for his lavish hospitality and "reckless profusion." He had three children with a woman named Juana Pedraza, to whom he may or may not have been married, and he died in 1851. No one knows where his grave is.

After Leaton's death the story of Fort Leaton gets complicated. It involves unpaid debts, foreclosures, and three murders. The short version is that Juana Pedraza married one of Leaton's employees named Hall, who had an even worse reputation than Leaton. He got into debt and borrowed money from Leaton's old business partner, John Burgess, who had become wealthy in the freighting business. Hall put the fort up for security. He failed to repay Burgess and was killed in an argument with one of Burgess's sons who was trying to evict him. Burgess and his family moved into the fort but Burgess was then killed in a Fort Davis saloon by

Hall's step-son Bill Leaton, who himself was killed in a gunfight a few years later by the chief of police in Presidio del Norte.

Burgess's son, Juan Burgess, and his wife Paz Landrum Burgess, continued to live in the fort after the elder Burgess's death. They raised fifteen children there and probably added enough rooms to Leaton's original structure to bring it to its present total of 40. They led quiet, peaceful lives, raising barley and vegetables and selling off bits of land when they needed extra money. The fort lost its identity with Leaton and was called *el fortin de los Burgess*. When Marfa historian Alice Shipman interviewed the Burgesses in 1922 she found that Paz Burgess could speak only a few words of English but that she was immensely proud of their son Ricardo, who had fought in France a few years before. Juan Burgess died in 1927; Paz followed him in 1929. They are both buried in the cemetery at the fort.

The one story that everyone seems to know about Fort Leaton turns out not to be true, or at least not to have happened there but elsewhere. According to the story, Ben Leaton invited all of his Apache friends to a big housewarming feast when he completed the fort. They ate and drank all night, but when Leaton woke up the next morning he found that the Apaches had departed with all of his horses and mules. A few months later he threw another feast and invited the same Apaches back. This time he hid a cannon in a room adjacent to the dining room, and a few hours into the party he excused himself, went into the next room, and fired round after round of canister shot into the feasting Apaches, completely annihilating them.

The story has never made any sense. Why would a man kill all of his trading partners and destroy part of his own house in the process? I recently did a little detective work and discovered that the story was first published in the *El Paso Herald* for November 12, 1922, as part of an interview with Leaton's grandson Victor Ochoa, who was born several years after Leaton's death. Ochoa has been mentioned in this column before. He was probably not the most trustworthy source for information about anything.

A little more detective work revealed that in 1837, long before he built Fort Leaton, Ben Leaton was part of a band of scalp hunters led by James Johnson in southern New Mexico who murdered the Apache chief Juan Jose Compa and a dozen of his band by firing a small cannon hidden under some saddles into them while they were gathered around a sack of parched corn, a gift from Johnson. Undoubtedly Leaton told his children this story, and they told their children, and somewhere in transmission it got garbled and set at Fort Leaton.

For some reason it is the Burgesses that I am attracted to, rather than the flamboyant Ben Leaton, but Leaton gets most of the attention at the fort and in the literature about it. People tend to be more interested in scoundrels and Indian fighters than in peaceful farmers.

August 20, 2010

VICTOR OCHOA, REVOLUTIONIST, inventor, and sage, may be the only native of Presidio County whose papers are in the archives of the Smithsonian Institution. Well, Ochoa was not technically a native of Presidio County, because he was born across the river in Ojinaga, but he had deep roots in Presidio County. He was the grandson of Ben Leaton, the Mexican War veteran and Indian trader who built Fort Leaton on the north bank of the river about 1848. His father was Juan Ochoa, who was running a sawmill in Fort Davis when he married Leaton's daughter Isabella. At the time of Victor's birth in 1860 his father was the U.S. Collector of Customs in Presidio, but he lived on the Mexican side of the river. Victor Ochoa became a naturalized United States citizen in 1889.

Ochoa first came to public attention in 1892 as the editor and publisher of *El Hispano-Americano*, a Spanish-language newspaper in El Paso. That was the year that a faith healer in Sonora, Teresita Urrea, inspired a rebellion against Mexican dictator Porfirio Diaz, and Ochoa's paper supported the rebellion. Diaz banned the paper's circulation in Mexico and threatened to imprison any Juarez merchant who advertised in it. Ochoa responded by raising troops in El Paso to invade Mexico and overthrow Diaz himself, offering $75 a month to anyone who presented himself at the newspaper office with a pistol and 100 cartridges. A photograph of Ochoa from that period shows a dashing figure with a short beard and a flowing moustache, posed in a charro costume with silver horseshoes down his trouser seam, a serape flung over one shoulder and a pistol at his belt, every inch a revolutionary.

Ochoa's little army was disastrously defeated by Mexican federal soldiers at Namiquipa, Chihuahua, in January 1894. Ochoa escaped by disguising himself in a federal uniform and made his way back to Texas, but his troubles had only started. The Mexican government put a price on his head, and the United States government charged him with violating the Neutrality Act. He went into hiding, but in October 1894 he was arrested in Fort Stockton and held in the county jail there.

At Fort Stockton Ochoa revealed his true genius. He befriended Sheriff Royer, who was up for re-election, and the sheriff invited him to address a public meeting of the Mexican population in Spanish on his behalf. Ochoa readily agreed and made a long speech in Spanish, most of which was an appeal for support of his revolutionary movement. The audience applauded and cheered, the sheriff waved and smiled, and Ochoa was returned to jail. A few nights later an armed group of Mexicans showed up at the jail, demanded the keys, and freed Ochoa. The Texas Rangers caught up with him in a billiard parlor in Pecos, where he willingly surrendered. One of the Rangers called him "the boldest and most daring off-hand man I have met." On the train to El Paso he was treated as a hero, with people coming on board at every stop to shake his hand. In spite of a spirited defense by future New Mexico governor Octaviano Larrazolo, a federal judge in El Paso found Ochoa guilty on the Neutrality Act charge and sentenced him to two and a half years in the Kings County Federal Prison in Brooklyn, New York.

But it wasn't Ochoa's revolutionary activities that got his papers into the Smithsonian. It was his career as an inventor. When Ochoa got out of the federal pen, he decided not to return to El Paso, perhaps thinking of the $15,000 bounty that the Diaz government was offering for him, dead or alive. In fact, he planted an article in an El Paso paper saying that he had died, and settled down in Paterson, New Jersey, where he remained for the next 15 years. During those years, Ochoa patented and sold a fountain pen holder, a magnetic streetcar brake, an electricity-generating windmill, and a pair of adjustable pliers. His greatest efforts, however, were devoted to flying machines. He established the International Airship Company and built several prototype airplanes he called ornithopters, all of which featured wings that oscillated like those of a bee and were powered by a combination of light gasoline engines and magnets. The ornithopter never got off the ground, nor did another Ochoa aerial invention, a combination automobile-airplane with folding wings called the Ochoaplane. But the prescient Ochoa was quoted in the Paterson newspaper in 1909 predicting that someday airplanes would fly around the world at an altitude so high that local weather conditions would not affect their passage.

The years in Paterson may have been Ochoa's best years, and they were certainly the years that won him a place in the Smithsonian Institution. But the overthrow of Porfirio Diaz in

1911 and the ensuing civil war in Mexico drew him back to the border. He could not stay away from the smell of gunpowder. This time, instead of raising his own army, he put his inventive powers to work developing waterproof containers that could be used to smuggle ammunition across the Rio Grande to the revolutionists, while counterfeiting Villista currency on the side and working as a secret agent for both the Orozquistas and the Carrancistas. He was back in his element. Unfortunately, in 1915 he was caught in El Paso with a boxcar full of ammunition destined for Mexico and was sentenced to two years at Leavenworth Penitentiary, which he served from 1917 to 1919. By the time he got out the revolution in Mexico was in its waning days, and Ochoa faded into obscurity.

He surfaces once more in the historical record. In 1933, at the age of 73, he was selling shares in something called the Caballos Mining and Development Company, which he established to develop a lost Spanish gold mine in New Mexico that he claimed to have a map to. He spent his last years in Mexico, where he died in 1945. A great-granddaughter, Elizabeth V. Ochoa, donated his papers to the Smithsonian in 1997.

David Romo, who wrote about Ochoa in his book, *Ringside Seat at a Revolution* (Cinco Puntos Press, 2005), described Ochoa's airplanes as "examples of turn-of-the-century *rasquachismo* at its best—brash, shoddy, makeshift, ambitious, even a bit comical, but with definite flashes of brilliance." Those words might describe Victor Ochoa's whole life. It is the flashes of brilliance that make him interesting.

May 22, 2010

HORSE AND WAGON DAYS IN PINTO CANYON

LAST WEEK I drove 200 miles to Midland in order to spend half an hour having the computer on my car adjusted by the Honda dealer there and then drove 200 miles back home. This little jaunt caused me to reflect once again on how mobile the automobile has made my generation, as compared to my grandparents', and on the extent to which it changed ordinary lives in the last century. Of course this is not a new idea; it is a commonplace of history textbooks. But sometimes you can be aware of an idea without really understanding its implications until some experience brings them home to you. In my case I never completely appreciated the impact that the automobile had on our culture until I had the opportunity 30 years ago to ride about five miles down a paved highway in a mule-drawn wagon . The trip took nearly two hours. It was a very hot summer day, and as automobiles whizzed by us I suddenly understood with razor-sharp clarity what a powerful urge the desire to own an automobile must have been to farmers in the 1920s. Without automobiles, people on farms and ranches led painfully circumscribed lives, going into town once a month at most, sometimes only twice a year.

Not long ago Jeff Fort, owner of the Pinto Canyon Ranch south of Marfa, gave me a document that dramatically illustrated the difference between life in the Big Bend in the pre-automobile age and life here today. The document was a typed, single-spaced memoir written by Dora Amelia Wilson Dowe (known as Millie to her family), whose parents settled in Pinto Canyon in 1907. The Wilson family, which consisted of Millie, her parents, and Millie's two younger sisters, lived in Alpine and ran cattle in the Glass Mountains. Millie was 10 years old when they decided to move to Pinto Canyon.

Millie's father, J.E. Wilson, had filed on eight sections of public land in Pinto Canyon, and state law required that in order to obtain full title he had to live on it and make $300 worth of improvements within three years. In January 1907 the family gathered their cattle, packed their worldly goods into a two-horse wagon, and started for their new home. A neighbor, Hart Greenwood, and his father went along to help Millie's father with the cattle, and Millie's mother drove the wagon.

When they got to the head of Pinto Canyon they discovered that the road stopped there, and only a trail led down into the canyon. In order to get the wagon down the trail they passed a pole through the spokes of the rear wheels, set the brakes, and tied a rope to the rear axle. Hart Greenwood tied the other end of the rope to his saddle horn, and Millie's mother inched the team and wagon down the trail. It got dark before they reached the bottom, and they had to stop at a level place and make camp for the night. The next day they got all the way into the canyon and moved into a one-room rock house with a dirt floor that had been built as a goat camp. That was their home for the next three years. Millie tells in her narrative how her father was kicked by a horse the second day they were there and ended up with a broken leg. It took the doctor from Marfa two days to reach them on horseback. That would be about a 45-minute drive today.

While Millie's father was laid up, a neighbor named Jose Prieto looked after the cattle and did their grocery shopping for them. The nearest store was at Ruidosa, 16 miles from their homestead. Millie says that Prieto would ride to the store horseback, leading a packhorse to bring the groceries back on. He could make the trip there and back in one long day. If he had gone in a wagon, she says, it would have taken a week.

When her father recovered from his broken leg, the first thing the family did was to build a kitchen onto the rock house, so that they could set up the stove they had brought in the wagon from Alpine and her mother would no longer have to cook meals over a campfire. In order to move the rocks for the addition they cut down a forked walnut tree and wired poles across the fork. They tied a singletree to the trunk and harnessed a gentle mare to the singletree, and they had a sled they could use to haul rocks on. Eventually, they built a three-room adobe house with wooden floors a little way up the canyon.

Other families wanted to move into Pinto Canyon, so Millie's father rode horseback to Marfa and petitioned the county commissioners to build a road into the canyon. The commissioners eventually consented, and once the road was built the Mart Sutherlins, with six sons and five daughters, settled at the head of Horse Creek Canyon, and the George Sutherlins with two more children settled at the point where Horse Creek and Pinto Canyon meet. The Prietos filed on land below the Sutherlins. They also had several children, so there was an obvious need for a school. The county built a one-room school on Horse Creek, and all of the children rode burros to school, about a six-mile round trip for most of them. Millie describes how they staked the burros in the school yard so that they could graze, and how she and her classmates watered them at lunch time.

The first teacher at the school was a Miss Sue Woodward. Millie's father took his wagon to Marfa, a distance of 35 miles, to pick the teacher up and bring her to her new school. The trip took all day each way. Millie went along for the ride. She says in her narrative that it was her first trip out of Pinto Canyon in three years.

If I can drive to Midland and back in half a day, we must have made progress since Millie was a little girl. On the other hand, a recent article in the *New York Times* says that automobiles traversing midtown Manhattan on weekdays average 6.3 miles per hour, not a whole lot faster than my mule-drawn wagon ride. Progress must depend on where you live.

April 8, 2010

THE ONLY ANGLO WHO EVER MADE WAX

THE OTHER DAY I sat at a kitchen table in Alpine and talked with a man not much older than I am who grew up in the nineteenth century. By this I don't mean that he was born before 1900—in fact, he was born in 1936—but that he grew up in the same conditions that prevailed in the Big Bend in the 1880s. His name is William Dodson, and he is the father of Presidio County sheriff Ronny Dodson. Shortly after we started talking he showed me a photograph of his parents' first home below the Chisos Rim, on his grandfather's ranch near Dodson Spring. It consisted of a rock-walled dugout with a sotol roof and a tent pitched beside it. Even though the picture was taken in 1930, the only 20TH-century object in it is a Model-T Ford in the background.

Dodson's father, Dell Dewey Dodson, died when Dodson was two, and his mother, who was 23, married a 16-year old *vaquero* from across the river named Sotero Morin. "He had green eyes," Dodson told me, "a *guero*." The re-marriage so traumatized Dodson that he couldn't talk until he was 10 years old, and he still speaks with a slight lilt. His stepfather had a hard time getting work on ranches during the Depression, and so when Dodson was seven the family started making candelilla wax for a living. Candelilla wax, Dodson explained, is the substance that coats the tube-like leaves of the candelilla plant, and after it is refined it has a number of industrial uses ranging from cosmetics to waterproofing. During World War II, he said, it was used to coat the hulls of ships.

For seven years Dodson and his three siblings lived with their parents in a tent in a series of candelilla camps in southern Brewster County. They had a wagon and 12 burros, and every day they would go out to pull candelilla plants up. They pulled the plants up with both hands, roots and all, all day long. "We worked like dogs," Dodson told me. They tied the plants into bundles with rope and loaded them on the burros, four bundles per burro, and at the end of the day drove the burros back to the camp and stacked the bundles. After two or three weeks of pulling, they would have a stack "as high as a house," as Dodson put it, and he showed me a photograph to prove it. Then they would spend four or five days cooking the wax off the plants.

This was done in a metal vat that was buried in the ground at the camp. The one the Dodsons used was about eight feet long, four feet wide, and four feet deep, and was made in Alpine by a man named King. "It had his name stamped on it," Dodson said. It had a hole scooped out under it for a fire, which was started with wood and then fed with the remnants of the cooked plants. Dodson's mother and sisters hauled buckets of water from a spring to fill the vat, and then the plants were tossed in and stomped down. When the water started to boil a little sulphuric acid was added to the vat, and the wax started to float up to the surface. "It looks just like oatmeal swelling up," Dodson said. It was skimmed off with a per-forated dipper and tossed into a 55-gallon drum, where it hardened into chunks that could be taken to the refinery in gunny sacks. The refinery was in Alpine, at the Casner Motor Company, a sort of sideline to the automobile business.

The Dodsons moved camp seven times while the children were growing up, loading their vat into their wagon, hitching two of the burros to it and driving the rest along behind. The wax busi-ness worked on a sort of sharecropping system, with the ranchers who owned the land the Dodsons were pulling the plants from providing them with the sulphuric acid and a few basic groceries like beans, rice, flour, vermicelli, and canned tomatoes and taking a share of the wax sales. I asked Dodson what they did for meat and he grinned and said, "we had deer meat year round." Once in a while, he added, a rancher would give them a goat. They bought sugar and coffee in Mexico, he said, because it was cheaper. His older sister Mildred did the cooking and washing.

Dodson told me that when he was 12 years old he had been pull-ing up candelilla and making wax for five years and that he could outwork any man on the river. He has taken good care of himself. Today, at 70, he looks like a man of 45. In fact, when I pulled up to his house and saw him standing in the carport I thought I was at the wrong house, expecting to see a much older man. He is tall, lean, and wiry, with a bushy head of black hair tinged with gray, a narrow face, and very blue eyes. He told me that last month he had hiked 12 miles in the Dead Horse Mountains with one of the rang-ers from Big Bend National Park. "I know that park like the back of my hand," he said.

Dodson's family quit making wax when he was 14 and settled

down in a house at Double Mills, and Dodson finally started on his path into the 20ᵀᴴ century. At 16 he started school at Panther Junction and learned to read and write (he had started in the first grade at Marathon when he was seven but the teacher sent him back home because he couldn't talk) and also to have fun. "I never had fun until I went to school," he says. When he was 18 he joined the Air Force, and then went on to a 30-year career with the Texas Highway Department.

Looking back on his life, Dodson says, "There's lots of ranchers that'll tell you that they made wax, but the fact is that it was the Mexicans that did it while they watched. I'm the only Anglo that ever made wax down here, and I'll tell you, I didn't volunteer."

May 25, 2006

 HISTORIANS USE MANY gateways to enter the past. Some study treaties and diplomatic history; some, wars and military history; some, agriculture and trade and the evolution of settlement. Some even study the development of roads and highways. This past month I joined that last group and spent a good deal of time in the Marfa courthouse looking into the history of roads in Presidio County, and it has given me a totally new perspective on the history of the Big Bend.

The mother road of the Big Bend was the Chihuahua Trail, the wagon road from San Antonio to Chihuahua City that wound from water hole to water hole across West Texas until it turned southward at Burgess Water Hole (now Kokernot Park in Alpine) and followed the course of Alamito Creek to Presidio del Norte (now Ojinaga) on the Rio Grande and then on south to Chihuahua City. That road was laid out by American merchants in Chihuahua City in 1839 and the segment of it that ran down the valley of Alamito Creek eventually became the main road from Marfa to Presidio. That segment is now the Casa Piedra Road. Most of the other roads in Presidio County's road network originally branched off from it.

The road that I have been spending most of my time on is one of those branches. When it was built in 1900, it was called the Marfa-Terlingua Freight Road, and it was the longest and most expensive road built to that date in Presidio County. It left the Marfa-Presidio road about halfway to Presidio and wound eastward across the desert past San Jacinto Mountain, then turned south across Bandera Mesa and the western edge of the Solitario and down into and through Fresno Canyon. At the mouth of Fresno Canyon it turned east again and ended at the Marfa and Mariposa Mining Company's mercury mine, about eight miles west of Terlingua. It was 60 miles long and it cost $1877.50 to build. Its only purpose was to serve the mine, which was owned by Presidio County ranchers James Normand, Tom Goldby, and Montroyd Sharp.

The Presidio County Commissioners' Court minutes reveal that when the road was built James Normand was the county commissioner from Precinct 2, and he persuaded the County Commission to appropriate $1557.50 in county funds for its construction. This was supplemented by $820 in private subscription, probably from the mining company. The contract for construction went to Tom Goldby. I am not implying that there was any hanky panky involved; that was just the way things were done in those days. People ran for county commissioner to look out for their own interests.

In 1900, the largest mercantile store in Marfa was Murphy and Walker, which occupied most of the block where Livingston's is now. Murphy and Walker supplied the Marfa and Mariposa mine with groceries, hardware, merchandise for the mine's commissary, mining machinery, and whatever else was needed, and they received the heavy flasks of mercury that were shipped back to be loaded on the railroad. Everything destined for the mine, and the mercury flasks, moved along the Marfa-Terlingua Freight Road in heavy Studebaker wagons designed to carry 8,000 pounds of freight. The wagons were drawn by teams of six or sometimes 12 mules, harnessed two abreast at the wagon tongue and four abreast in front. The driver rode on the mule nearest the left-hand wheel and operated the wagon's brake with a rope, one end of which was tied to the top of the brake handle; the other end was tied around the driver's saddle horn. The brake handle was counterweighted with a heavy piece of iron tied to it. The iron dragged in the road behind the wagon, leaving a trail in the dust. Unkind people said the trail was used by the freighters to find their way back to Marfa from the mine.

The heavily-loaded wagons moved very slowly, usually taking about eight days to make the 100-mile trip from Marfa to the mine, with the drivers camping out overnight along the road. A waybill in the Archives of the Big Bend for a wagonload of goods shipped to the mine from Murphy and Walker bears a sarcastic notation from whoever received the shipment: "Team galloped in at noon dead beat—96 miles in 96 hours." If you have ever been down the road in Fresno Canyon you would be surprised that they made it at all.

There was also a stage connection between the mine and Marfa. The stage was actually a two-seater mule-drawn buggy, called a hack, that carried passengers and mail to the mine and back three times a week, leaving Marfa at 7:00 AM and reaching the mine the evening of the next day. C.A. Hawley, an ex- schoolteacher employed by the mine as an accountant, made his first trip down the Marfa-Terlingua Freight Road in it in 1905. He noticed that both the driver and the other passenger were carrying pistols and rifles, and he asked if they were expecting trouble along the way. "Oh, no," his fellow-passenger replied. "It's just the custom of the country." In his memoir, *Life Along the Border*, Hawley says that the stage stopped for the night at an adobe house a few miles north of the entrance to Fresno Canyon, where the passengers were given dinner, a place to sleep, and breakfast. They did not have an opportunity to bathe, even though they were covered with dust.

A couple of weeks ago I visited that adobe house with B.C. Bennett, who grew up in it. The Marfa-Terlingua Freight Road still leads to Bennett's Bandera Ranch, but it is impassable beyond that point. The Marfa and Mariposa Mine closed down in 1907 and there has been little traffic on the road since then, although the county now maintains it as far as the locked gate at the Big Bend Ranch State Park boundary. Standing in front of that little house, gazing across the desert toward the spire of San Jacinto Mountain a dozen miles away, it was difficult to believe that the Marfa-Terlingua Freight Road was ever a vital link to anywhere, much less to a mine from which thousands of flasks of mercury were once shipped to Marfa.

June 17, 2010

NO PAPER MONEY DURING THE REVOLUTION

EDMUNDO NIETO IS 90 but he still goes to work every morning in the store that his father, Miguel Nieto, founded in 1913. He lets the clerks do most of the work, but he answers the telephone and greets the customers in Spanish as they come in. He has known most of them all of their lives. "We used to get most of our business from Mexico," he told me, "but since NAFTA they can get most of what they want over there, and now our customers are local."

It was 104 degrees on the street the day that I was in Presidio, but it was cool inside the high-ceilinged old store where I was talking with Nieto. He is a small man, perfectly bald. He spoke to me with such old-fashioned formal courtesy that for a moment I thought he was speaking Spanish, but he was actually speaking impeccable English, and he punctuated his words with a beautiful smile. He told me his father built the store building in 1927, and that he had started working there in 1939. Except for the years during the war, when he was in North Africa and Europe with the 933RD Field Artillery, he has been there ever since. He clearly takes his duties seriously. Whenever the telephone rang, he would wave his hand toward it and say, "*Teléfono*," to one of the clerks, and we were interrupted several times by customers who came over to where we were sitting to exchange a few words of greeting with Nieto, always addressing him as "Don Edmundo."

The store has a beautiful pressed-tin ceiling and the walls are lined with the narrow, closely-spaced shelves that you see in country stores, designed to hold canned goods and boxes of soap and baking soda. The counters have deep drawers with big brass pulls. On one wall is a poster advertising Nocona boots, showing a group of men playing poker at a round table, and another advertising Levi jeans. Between them is a black-and-white lithograph of Buffalo Bill Cody, and next to that is a framed photograph of Nieto's father, a serious-looking man wearing a white suit and seated in an overstuffed armchair. Below the image are the words, "God Bless Our Founder." Some things have been there a long time. Nieto pointed to a brass scale on one of the counters, the kind you weigh vegetables in. "You see that scale over there?" he asked. "I was weighed in that scale." Everything in the store is not old. One part of the building is full of gleaming new refrigerators and washing machines, and I noticed a rack of new bridles, surcingles, and roping ropes. "We sell mostly appliances now," Nieto said, "and other things people need."

Nieto told me something about his family's history. "My father was born in Ojinaga," he said, "but when he was just a boy he went to work for Joe Kleinman, who had a store over here. Kleinman was an Austrian Jew, and he brought a cousin over here from Austria to live with his family and teach the servants to cook Austrian food. My father ate his meals with the Kleinmans, and he said that every meal at the Kleinmans was like a banquet. They didn't have beans and tortillas."

"During the Mexican Revolution," Nieto went on, "Kleinman sold ammunition to both sides on credit, to the Federales and the Villistas. My father was the collector. He went into both camps and got the money. Kleinman told him never to take paper money; to always get gold coins. They always paid, because they stole cattle from the big haciendas in Mexico and drove them across the river and sold them to Texas ranchers, so they had plenty of gold."

When his father opened his own business, he and the Kleinmans remained friends, and Nieto went to Austin to go to St. Edward's University because two of the Kleinman boys had gone there. When he came home to Presidio and started working in the store in 1939, the Kleinman store had closed and the other store in town was Spencer's. Nieto's was the larger of the two.

"We got most of our customers from the farmers along the river, on this side and from Mexico," Nieto told me. "Some of them still came into town in wagons. Saturday was our biggest day of the week. The store was always crowded. For a while we opened on Sunday mornings, because people from Mexico liked to come then. We were a general merchandise store. We sold groceries, staples like canned goods and beans, lard in 25 and 50 pound tins, sardines at 10 cents a can. We carried work shirts and denims, a big variety of yard goods, bolts of cloth, shoes, hardware, harness, guns and ammunition, tinware, kerosene lamps and lamp chimneys and kerosene." Most of their goods came from wholesale houses in Saint Louis, Nieto said, and were shipped by train to Presidio.

The majority of their business back then was done on credit. Nieto explained that a customer would come in and make purchases, and the clerk would write the customer's name and the items purchased down on a sales slip, which came in a little book that automatically made carbon copies. The sales slips were filed in a metal rack, where they were held down by spring clips. Every night after the store closed Nieto's father would go through them and post the amounts in a big ledger under the customer's name. Each customer had several pages devoted to their purchases. The cotton crop along the river came in in September, and the ranchers in Mexico sold their livestock in December, so in the fall and winter months the customers would come in and pay their bills, and the process of extending credit would start all over again. "Those people were all honest," Nieto said. "We never had any trouble collecting our bills." The store accepted both United States and Mexican currency, both silver and paper money. "But no Mexican paper money during the Revolution," Nieto added.

"Nowdays we get too much competition from the big chains on most things," Nieto told me, "so we have shifted our stock to appliances and ranch supplies, and we are doing well." When I left, Nieto walked me to the door, shook hands with me, and invited me to come back and bring my family. I suspect that the Miguel Nieto store will be doing well long after the big chains have gone bankrupt.

August 13, 2009

THE WORST THING
THAT EVER HAPPENED ON THE RIVER

THE MOST SHAMEFUL event in the history of the Big Bend occurred at Porvenir, Texas on the night of January 27, 1918. At about midnight that night a group of Texas Rangers belonging to Company B, stationed at Marfa, rode into Porvenir. They were escorted by 12 soldiers from Troop G, 8TH United States Cavalry. They had told the troop's commander, Captain Henry Anderson, that they were looking for evidence that people from Porvenir had been involved in the recent bandit raid on the Brite Ranch.

When they reached the village, some of the soldiers threw a cordon around it to prevent anyone from slipping away, while others roused the sleeping villagers and searched their jacales. It was a freezing night, and the terrified villagers huddled around a bonfire while the soldiers rummaged through their homes. They found an old shotgun with no shells and several knives, nothing else. Captain Anderson reported to the Rangers, who had not taken part in the search, that they had found no evidence of banditry and added that he knew the people of Porvenir and was sure that there were no bandits there. The Rangers replied that they wanted to question the villagers in Spanish and asked the Captain to withdraw his troops. After the soldiers had moved down the road, the Rangers separated 15 male villagers from the women and children, marched them into a dry creek bed just north of town, and executed them with pistol shots.

The Porvenir Massacre, as it came to be called, was part of the violence that plagued the Big Bend between 1911 and 1920, when armed bands associated with the various revolutionary armies in Mexico raided settlements and ranches on the American side of the border, seeking arms, plunder, and revenge for perceived American misdeeds. During those years the people who lived here were caught up in a pattern of escalating fear, suspicion, and killing. United States troops were stationed along the Rio Grande and the raids from Mexico were followed by reprisals from the Texas side of the river. On Christmas Day 1917, raiders from Mexico attacked the isolated Brite Ranch, southwest of Marfa. Three of the people at the ranch were killed, one by being hanged from a rafter in the ranch store with his throat slit. The executions at Porvenir were seen by some as a just reprisal for the murders at the Brite Ranch. No one was ever indicted or convicted for them, although five of the Rangers involved were dismissed from the service.

I visited the site of Porvenir not long ago in the company of Marfa historian Cecilia Thompson and several friends. It is on the Rio Grande in the extreme western corner of Presidio County, 30 miles through starkly beautiful country down a dirt road from U.S. 90. Our guide was Jim Barrow, who grew up on a nearby ranch. We stood on the little flat-topped hill where the village had been and looked down into the dry creek bed where the men had been shot and then across the river at the scattered houses that make up the town of El Porvenir, Chihuahua. There is no trace of the village on the Texas side now, not even foundation stones. Barrow explained that after the murders, the survivors had fled across the river and never returned. The bodies of the murdered men were buried in a mass grave on the Mexican side, and the army had burned the jacales on the Texas side.

"This was the worst thing that ever happened on the river," Barrow said, shaking his head. "These people were in no way responsible for those raids."

One man who agreed with Barrow was Henry Warren, who was the schoolteacher at Porvenir when the shootings took place. His father-in-law, Tiburcio Jaquez, was one of the murdered men. Warren's attempts to bring the incident to public light gained him the enmity of the military authorities and cost him his teaching job at Candelaria the following year.

According to Glenn Justice's fine book about the border troubles, *Revolution on the Rio Grande* (Texas Western Press, 1992), Warren tried until his death in 1932 to bring the matter into the U.S. Court of Claims, but the court never took action. Warren shared the grief and outrage of the people of Porvenir but, unlike them, he was literate and kept records. He filled several pages of an old ledger with an account of the massacre, including the names of the 15 murdered men and the names of the widows and the 42 orphans that they had left behind. That ledger is in the Archives of the Big Bend at Sul Ross State University in Alpine, and right now it is the only memorial to the men and boys who died at Porvenir.

History is a record of what has happened. People do not always act admirably or honorably, and so all history is not uplifting. But it is important to remember that human beings can be stupid and brutal as well as wise and heroic. The Texas Historical Commission has erected 12,000 historic markers at sites across the state. I think one should be erected at Porvenir, telling what happened there. And I think it should include those 15 names.

January 29, 2004

Editor's Note: Shortly after this column appeared in the *Big Bend Sentinel* I received a telephone call from an elderly Hispanic man in Uvalde. He told me that he had been at Porvenir that night. He had been eight years old and had been herded with the women while his father and his older brother had been killed. He concluded the conversation by saying that he understood that I had said that I thought that there should be a marker there with the names of the murdered men and boys on it. I told him that was correct. "Some of us think that there should be a sign there with the names of the murderers on it," he said, and hung up.

THE NEVILL RANCH RAID

NOT LONG AGO I wrote about a trip I had made with Cecilia Thompson to the site of the Porvenir Massacre. Our guide on that trip was Jim Barrow, who is a deputy sheriff in Marfa. Barrow grew up under the Candelaria Rim and knows that lonely and grotesquely beautiful desert country intimately.

He is a child of the border, with family connections on both sides of the river. His father bought the old Nevill Ranch in 1958 and Barrow grew up in the house that was the target of the Nevill Ranch raid in 1918.

Barrow's wife's family is from Coyame, Chihuahua, and through her he is related to people in all of the communities on the Mexican side of the Rio Grande between Ojinaga and Pilares. He told me that his father-in-law's first father-in-law was the bandit Jesus Renteria, called El Gancho because of the iron hook he wore in place of his right hand. El Gancho was the man who held two downed U.S. Army fliers for ransom in Mexico in 1919.

Barrow said his father-in-law remembered El Gancho as "the meanest old man he ever saw." He would sit on his porch with a .45 pistol and a barrel of cartridges, drinking sotol and shooting at anything that moved—"dogs, chickens, children—he just liked to shoot," Barrow said. Barrow added that he had heard stories about Renteria from his father-in-law for years before he realized that he was talking about the same man Barrow had read about in history books.

On our way to Porvenir, we stopped to eat our sandwiches at the old Nevill ranch house, near the bank of the Rio Grande. The Barrows have improved the place by adding a screen porch and several rooms to the old three-room cottonwood log house, but the outlines of the original structure are clearly visable.

We gathered in the kitchen around a big cast iron range, and while Barrow stoked the stove with firewood from the wood box we talked about some of the people who had lived along that part of the river and entered into its folklore, people like Chico Cano and Hawkeye Townsend and Evans Means. And we talked about what happened in that house on the night of March 25, 1918.

Barrow told us that on that night Ed Nevill was at the ranch house with his son, Glenn, and a Mexican couple who worked for them, Adrian and Rosa Castillo. Nevill's other Mexican employees had asked for their pay and left shortly after the killings at Porvenir, two months previously. Mrs. Nevill and her younger children were staying in Van Horn, where the children were in school.

Just about dusk Ed Nevill heard hoof beats and shouts, and looked out the window to see at least 20 armed men riding toward the house from the river, shooting as they came. He grabbed his rifle and ran out of the front door, shouting for Glenn to follow him.

He made it through a hail of bullets to a draw, where he hid in the darkness. Glenn was shot down just a few steps from the door, and lay moaning on the ground for hours with his knee shattered and part of his skull blown away.

Miraculously, Adrian Castillo got out of the house and into a pasture, where he found a horse and rode him bareback to a military post a few miles up the river which had a telephone connection with Van Horn. Rosa Castillo was not so lucky. Her body was found in the house, riddled with bullets.

From his hiding place in the draw, Ed Nevill could hear his son's moans, interspersed with the raiders' voices as they looted the house and rounded up Nevill's horses. Finally they departed. Shortly afterward cavalrymen from Troop G, 8th Cavalry arrived. Nevill emerged from the brush and helped the troopers carry his son into the front bedroom, where he died just before dawn.

Standing around the stove and looking into the room where Glenn Nevill died, we talked about the reverberations down through time of those events. Barrow said that the horror of that night stayed with Ed Nevill the rest of his life, and that Nevill blamed himself for his son's death.

He must have wondered thousands of times what would have happened if Glenn had gone out of that door first. In the Archives of the Big Bend at Sul Ross State University there is a seven-page letter that Glenn Nevill's sister, Lois Kelly, wrote to Sul Ross historian Clifford Casey in 1972, describing how the events of that night changed her family's life.

Her father gave up ranching and opened a café in Marfa, but until his death in 1952 he would wander around the Mexican section of Marfa after the café closed for the night, knocking on doors and asking questions that he hoped would lead him to the men who killed his son. Some people say he carried a loaded pistol with him on those perambulations.

February 5, 2004

CANON MISSIONER TO THE FRONTIER

LAST WEDNESDAY I was in Redford, talking with Father Melvin La Follette, a retired Episcopal priest who once had the imposing title of Canon Missioner to the Frontier. Father Mel, as he is known for a hundred miles up and down the Rio Grande, came to Redford in 1984 with instructions from the Episcopal Bishop of the Rio Grande in Albuquerque to, he says, "go and spread the Gospel and do what needed to be done." Father Mel interpreted these instructions liberally and over the years he has established missions in Mexico, raised goats, and journeyed to Washington, D.C. to speak up for his Redford neighbors.

Father Mel is a small man with a broad face, short gray hair, a gray moustache, gray stubble on his cheeks, and very wide eyes. He looks like a convivial pirate, a look that is enhanced by a gold loop in his left ear, an adornment he acquired the first time he crossed the equator as a civilian teacher on a navy ship. He told me that he estimated that he had logged a million nautical miles on ten different ships while teaching English literature to sailors in a program that Chapman College ran with the U.S. Navy "until Ronald Reagan killed it," he said.

Father Mel told me that he started out in life to be an academic. A native of Indiana, he got a B.A. in English at the University of Washington and an M.A. at the University of Iowa, where he studied with Paul Engle and the poet John Berryman. He was working on a Ph.D. in Renaissance literature at the University of California at Berkeley when he felt the call to the priesthood and moved to divinity school at Yale. His Chapman College gig was just a break in his clerical career; before taking that job he had served Episcopal churches in New York and California.

When he arrived on the Rio Grande in 1984, Father Mel could have made his home anywhere between Candelaria and Study Butte, but he said that he saw the green fields and beautiful flowers in Redford and thought, "that would be a nice place to live," and he has been there ever since. In 1984 there were small Episcopal congregations at Lajitas and Terlingua Ranch Resort, but Father Mel immediately set out to push his mission field across the border into Mexico. "I just went over to those little villages and asked if they would like to have a mass," he told me. "I told them that Episcopalians were just Catholics without the Pope." Father Mel speaks fluent Spanish, and in a short time he had congregations going in Lajitas, Chihuahua; in Boquillas; and in Palomas, across the river from Redford. On Sundays he traveled 200 miles by pickup and rowboat to serve his flock.

The Reverend Judy Burgess, vicar of St. Paul's in Marfa, told me about attending a confirmation that Father Mel organized in the abandoned Catholic church in Boquillas one summer. "I drove down to the National Park with Bishop Kelshaw from Albuquerque and John Haverland, one of the cathedral officials there. It was about 110 degrees, and when we got to the river and opened the

234

car door it was like a furnace. John, who was from California, said, 'I've never been so hot and I've been to Death Valley.' We crossed the river in a rowboat and rode up to the church in a pickup, me and the Bishop in the back. Father Mel had organized everything beautifully, and the Bishop put on his vestments and miter and did what he was supposed to do. When we finally got back to Study Butte the store was just closing, but they opened back up so that John and the Bishop could get cold beers out of the ice tub. I've never seen two men who wanted a cold beer so badly."

The congregations on the other side of the river all dispersed when the informal crossings along the border were closed after 9/11 and Father Mel could no longer reach them. He is sad about this. When I asked him what the greatest change he had seen in his 25 years on the border was, he said, "I've seen it change from a pleasant, open, neighborly place to a police state." I asked him to elaborate and he said, "Just the other day my neighbor was stopped by the Border Patrol on his way to Presidio and made to show his identification. I've been stopped and asked for my identification." When I asked him what he thought the cause of the change was, he said, "Republicans." Then he mellowed a little and said, "Mostly it's ignorance. People in the middle states just don't understand how we live here. But some of it is just plain prejudice."

When Esequiel Hernandez was killed by Marine snipers in Redford in 1997, Father Mel went with other Redford citizens to Washington to protest the presence of troops on the border. He told me that his eyes were opened when the group went to the Pentagon and were directed to the Office of Low Intensity Warfare. "That was when I discovered that we were in a war zone," he told me, "and that we were the enemy." But Father Mel has maintained his sense of humor and his sense of human frailty. He told me that during the group's meeting with officials of the Immigration and Naturalization Service, they were told that there was no need for them to come all the way to Washington, that the INS had notices posted with a telephone number that anyone with a complaint could call. When Father Mel asked where these notices were posted, the official said that they were in every INS detention center. "I asked him why they didn't put them up in post offices and other public places," Father Mel told me, "and you know what he said? He said that if they did that they'd get a lot of complaints. Imagine that."

At 78, Father Mel now spends most of his time with his striped tiger cat, Fox Mulder, his two dogs, and his flock of chickens. He used to have a herd of 100 goats, the remnants of a community cheese-making project that didn't work out, but he got tired of feeding them. He is still politically active, and there is no doubt where his sentiments are. During our conversation he remarked that he had been in divinity school at Yale at the same time that George Bush was an undergraduate there. I asked if he ever encountered Bush on the campus and he said, with a piratical grin, "No, I spent most of my time in the library."

November 16, 2008

RAYMOND SKILES AND THE BEARS

RAYMOND SKILES IS a man who has spent most of his professional life trying to adjust relationships between people and animals, especially bears. Skiles, a tall, quiet, balding man in his early fifties, has been a wildlife manager at Big Bend National Park for the past 22 years. He is currently the Acting Chief of Science Resource Management at the park. He describes his job by saying that he is responsible for creating ways that animals and people can get along in the park on a day-to-day basis, for directing long-range research on animals that will help preserve them and their habitat, and for providing special protection for the four officially-listed protected species that live within the park's boundaries. But in the long run he spends his time tinkering with the intricate web of relationships that tie humans and animals together, and he has thought a great deal about the nature of that web.

Skiles's tinkering takes place on both micro- and macro- levels. "A lot of my work involves just educating people," he told me, "because you can't educate the animals." It's a tough job, he says. "Most of us are so distant from nature in our daily lives that it is difficult to be cognizant of the fact that we have to modify our lifestyle in a place like the park. Our normal relationship with animals is as pets. We like to feed them, and we look at them as cute and cuddly. It's hard for us to realize that sometimes mountain lions look at us as food, and that it's best to show a little dominance and aggression when we see one." Skiles hastens to add that most mountain lions enjoy a steady diet of deer, javelinas, and skunks, but a few young ones, he says, are willing to try anything, "and they might jump a person."

Mountain lions do not really present a major threat to park visitors, Skiles says. There have only been four mountain lion attacks on visitors in the more than 20 years that he has been in the park, and none of them were fatal. "We tell visitors that if they encounter a lion, they should make themselves as threatening as possible—don't run, don't crouch; shout, throw rocks at it, and that usually does the job," he says. Bears, Skiles told me, present a far more challenging problem in human-animal relationships, not because they endanger visitors, but because what visitors leave lying around campsites can harm bears. "Bears regard trash, garbage, toothpaste, and sunscreen as food, and they are smart and quickly learn how to get into things, and they pass that knowledge on to their young." The Park Service tells people to lock their food in their cars, and they provide bear-proof steel storage boxes at campgrounds. "We're still a little smarter and more dexterous than bears," Skiles says, "so we equip those boxes with latches that require opposable thumbs."

Bears, Skiles says, are one of the park's success stories as far as restoring the balance of an environment disrupted by recent human activity goes. "There were no bears in the park for the first 50 years of its existence," he told me. "They were all killed by hunters before the park was created. But in the 1980s bears started migrating from Mexico into the Chisos Mountains. Some of these were fertile females, and by 2000 there were about 30 bears living in the park. The population subsequently decreased because of drought-induced food shortages, but right now we are back up to 20 or so. They are just getting a toehold here."

Skiles says the animals that he enjoys working with the most are those that are having the hardest time surviving the changes that humans have brought about in their environment. "The mussels and the fish that have lived in the Rio Grande for 8,000 years or so are having a terrible time, because the river that they became adapted to no longer exists. Humans have manipulated it with dams and impoundments, first at Elephant Butte in New Mexico and then on the Conchos in Mexico. Seven varieties of fish have disappeared since the 1950s, and two varieties of mussels."

The problem, he says, is that the periodic floods that swept down the river before the dams were built scoured the mud and silt off the river's bottom and kept it healthy for fish and mussels, who need a rocky, sandy bottom to survive. Accumulated mud on the bottom, plus toxic waste poured into the river, has been hard on the animals that live there. "But there is hope," Skiles told me. "In December the Park Service and the Fish and Wildlife Service put 400,000 Rio Grande Silvery Minnows, one of the four officially-listed endangered species in the park, into the river, and we'll add more over the next two years. The river is somewhat less toxic now than it was in the 1950s and 60s, and things may be better now."

Skiles, whose father's family were pioneer ranchers at Langtry and whose parents met while they were students at Sul Ross, had a typical West Texas boyhood, with lots of hunting and fishing.

When he first started college he majored in English and journalism, but he realized that his true interest was in wildlife, and he switched his major to wildlife management. But, he told me, he also had an interest in people and communication, and so helping visitors to National Parks understand wildlife seemed to be a perfect fit for him, and after graduation he kept taking seasonal jobs in national parks until he was hired permanently. His first seasonal job, providentially, was working for the concessionaire in Big Bend National Park, and he subsequently worked in Colorado, California, Virginia, and Washington, D.C. before returning permanently to the Big Bend in 1987.

Musing on the changes he has seen in the park in the time he has been there, Skiles mentioned the things that have recently chiseled away at the integrity of an environment that has evolved over tens of thousands of years—urban development on the edges of the park, light pollution, the introduction of non-native species of animals and grasses. "But the best thing," he said, "is that most of the landscape has not changed, and I'm glad about that."

February 19, 2009

CHILI AT TERLINGUA

THIS YEAR HALLOWEEN was bookended by the 48th annual Terlingua Chili Cook-off, which started on Monday October 27 and wound up the following Saturday. About 5,000 people were there for the final cook-offs. I was not. My idea of hell is being in Terlingua with 5,000 people.

The first Terlingua cook-off was held in 1967. It was the result of a bet between *Dallas Morning News* columnist Frank X. Tolbert and a Dallas advertising man named Tom Tierney. As I heard the story from Tolbert's son, Frank, Jr., both men were part of a group that met for lunch several times a week at the Baker Hotel. One day at lunch Tierney bragged that he was such an accomplished public relations man he could get a hundred people together anywhere in Texas. Tolbert bet him $100 on the spot that he could not get a hundred people to Terlingua, which in those days had a population of nine. Tierney and Tolbert had both visited Terlingua because their buddies auto racer Carroll Shelby and Dallas attorney David Witt had bought a 200,000-acre ranch there with the intention of subdividing it and selling lots. In order to win his bet, Tierney proposed holding a chili-cooking contest in Terlingua to publicize Tolbert's recently-published book about chili, *A Bowl of Red*. The contestants were to be Wick Fowler, a Dallas journalist who prided himself on his chili, and Dave Chasen, a Hollywood restaurateur who was a friend of Tolbert's. Chasen got sick at the last minute, and the organizers invited H. Allen Smith, a best-selling New York humorist who had just published an article in *Holiday* magazine with the provocative title "Nobody Knows More About Chili Than I Do," to take his place.

Tolbert, Tierney, and Fowler were all members of a group of mock-serious chili fanciers who called themselves the Chili Appreciation Society International. The Chili Appreciators had codified a chili recipe that called for meat, masa, chili powder, tomato sauce, and a few spices, but no vegetables and above all no beans and proclaimed it the only true chili. They issued a series of press releases casting the Terlingua contest as a match between righteous Texas traditionalists and an upstart Yankee who put beans and sweet peppers into his chili. Their purpose, according to Gary Cartwright's account of the event in the December 11, 1967 issue of *Sports Illustrated*, was to lure Smith to Texas, humiliate him, and call attention to themselves and Tolbert's book. They were only partially successful.

The contestants and their supporters converged on Terlingua on Friday October 20. The Dallas group landed at the dirt airstrip on the Shelby-Witt ranch in three chartered planes. Shelby and a plane load of Los Angeles friends, which included a man in a monk's robe and sandals who gave his name as Father Duffy and a musician called Ormly Gumfudgin, The World's Only Living Bazooka Player, arrived a few hours later. Father Duffy was accompanied by two women friends. Their presence had repercussions in

242

Dallas because the Dallas group had told their wives it was to be a stag party, and when word of Duffy's girlfriends got back to Dallas some of the Dallas wives hired a small plane which buzzed the contest the next day, showering the spectators with thousands of little yellow cards printed with messages such as, "Congratulations, you get the children" and "We'll arrange the alimony to fit your budget." The cards were signed "Terlingua Women's Auxiliary."

The invited guests had been instructed to bring nothing but a sleeping bag and a toothbrush. School buses supplied by President Brownie McNeil of Sul Ross ferried the visitors from the airstrip to the Chiracahua Ranch, where a planeload of beer flown out earlier and a barbecue dinner prepared by Lyndon Johnson's personal barbecue chef, Walter Jetton, awaited them. After dinner they spread their sleeping bags in the ranch house yard and crawled in. They were awakened before dawn by ranch manager Harold Wynne, shouting, "Get up! Get up! It don't take long to spend the night at the Chiracahua!" while a cowboy named Tooter galloped his cutting horse up and down the narrow spaces between the rows of sleeping bags, waving a bottle of beer.

The cooking was set to start at noon on the porch of the Terlingua store. Smith arrived about 10:00 AM, looking refreshed after a night at the Ponderosa Inn in Alpine. Fowler showed up about 11:30, red-eyed and a little worse for the wear. The two men set up their gas rings and pots on the store porch, and started cooking while a string band from Fort Stockton entertained the crowd of about 500 that had gathered. There were three judges, one chosen by Fowler, one by Smith, and one by the Chili Appreciation Society International, which meant that the odds were stacked against Smith two to one. Fowler's judge was Floyd Schneider, a vice-president of Lone Star Brewery. Smith chose Alpine Justice of the Peace Hallie Stillwell, presumably on the grounds that her oath of office would compel her to render an impartial verdict. The Chili Appreciators designated David Witt.

When the chili was ready the judges were blindfolded and spoons from each pot were guided to their mouths. Stillwell tasted first and voted for Smith's concoction. Schneider was next and made it a tie by voting for Fowler. When the first spoon was guided to Witt's mouth, however, he spit its contents out, fell down, went into convulsions, and croaked, "I can't go on! I need to see a doctor!" He then declared a one-year moratorium on the chili cook-off, ensuring that the whole show would be repeated in 1968 and, apparently, ad infinitum.

In my opinion this was a big mistake. Most jokes are only funny the first time, and 500 people are about as many as Terlingua can accommodate comfortably. I would have enjoyed being at that first cook-off, but not the next 47.

November 14, 2014

EVERETT TOWNSEND, SHERIFF AND HUSBAND

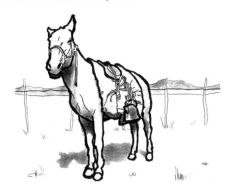

EVERETT E. TOWNSEND, Texas Ranger, deputy U.S. marshal, mounted U.S. customs inspector, three-term sheriff of Brewster County, state legislator, and father of Big Bend National Park, is remembered by Alpine old-timers as a pretty tough customer, a fearless lawman who would not back down from any confrontation. But there is a document buried in a genealogical treatise in the Archives of the Big Bend that reveals a tender side to Townsend.

Townsend, born in 1871, came to the Big Bend in 1894 to take a job as a mounted customs inspector in Presidio, and shortly after that he met and married Alice Jones, who was living on the Circle Dot Ranch near Marathon. After her death in 1940, Townsend wrote a description of their life together which was published in Sharon Anne Moehring's *The Gonzales Connection: The History and Genealogy of the DeWitt and Jones Families,* not a book your average reader would be browsing through. But as a portrait of a marriage Townsend's account is definitely worth reading.

It begins with Townsend's description of his first meeting with Alice. He was returning to Marathon from a horseback scout on a cold February day and about two miles south of town he saw a buggy coming toward him with two ladies in it. The horse was rearing and plunging between the shafts, frightened by the corpses of two burros that were lying beside the road. Townsend spurred forward, took charge of the horse, and escorted the ladies past the dead burros. One of the ladies was "pretty as a peach," and he admired the way she handled the frightened horse. After this first encounter with Alice, he wrote, "I found it convenient to scout pretty regularly around the Circle Dot." One month after their first meeting he proposed to her, and that fall they were married.

They set up housekeeping in Presidio, in two rented rooms with dirt floors. Townsend had a good salary, $3.00 a day plus a per diem for horse feed. "That was all we had except for our love for each other, as I had saved nothing," he wrote. Allie, as he called her, had a gray Spanish pony and loved to ride, and she accompanied her husband on scouts. "We rode many long and weary miles up and down the Rio Grande," he wrote. "Our packhorse carried all the equipment we used, which included bedding, cooking utensils, food, and a little 'war bag' for her. We cooked on open fires, sometimes in the rain." At the end of their first year of marriage, Townsend calculated that they had ridden 1,000 miles together. "Although courageous in every other way, she was never bold enough to wear trousers or ride astride," he wrote. "She used the sidesaddle and was a good rider as well as a graceful one."

At home Allie introduced Townsend to the practice of saying grace before meals. "She insisted and in fact saw that we began every meal right by returning thanks to God for it. When we were alone it was not hard for me to go ahead, but when we had company at meals as we frequently did such as river guards, rangers, cowboys, and sometimes out-treats [outsiders?], I found it pretty hard to respond to her signal and proceed. However, she kept at me until I mastered my embarrassment. During our 45 years of partnership we have rarely missed saying grace even when our tempers were up and I must acknowledge that we both had tempers."

In 1898 Townsend lost his job as a customs inspector due to a change in political administrations, and he and Allie had two tough years, spending one winter with their sick baby in a tented dugout on the Iron Mountain ranch. Townsend eventually got a job managing the 200,000-acre HL Ranch. His work took him away from home for days at a time, and Allie managed the home ranch. "I always left one man or more at home with her," Townsend wrote, "sometimes as many as a dozen. She never pretended to boss them, but she saw that they did their work. They loved and respected her. She could cross her legs, sit on her boots and talk their own language to them." She was a crack rifle shot and could shoot chicken hawks out of the sky with a .30-30. "I would not shoot against her [with a rifle]," Townsend wrote, "for she could always beat me. She did not like to shoot a pistol so I remained the head of the family in that respect."

Once a much younger and bigger man—"a notorious character," Townsend called him—walked into Townsend's office and, without warning, assaulted him. Townsend grabbed a monkey wrench and started hitting him on the head with it. They grappled, knocked over the stove, and were rolling around on the floor when Allie, who had heard the noise from the sidewalk, came running into the office with Townsend's pistol in her hand. When she saw Townsend covered with blood she grabbed the other man by the hair and shoved the cocked pistol in his face. Townsend said she would have killed him had he not wrenched the gun out of her hand. He introduced his account of this incident by saying, "Allie never faltered at any undertaking when my interest or welfare was at stake."

At several points in the narrative Townsend describes tight spots he and Allie were in together, such as sleeping with loaded guns at their sides while guarding the Presidio customs house against a threatened attack by Mexican bandits and being on a ranch in Chihuahua during the Escobar revolt. Shortly after the Mexican incident the Townsends went to visit some friends in Philadelphia, and during a discussion about a proposed trip to New York Allie said that she did not want to spend the night there because she was afraid of what might happen in the big city. Her eastern friends thought this was hilarious, but Townsend wrote, "I couldn't see that she was far wrong and we returned that night to Philadelphia. Both places were appalling to me as well as to her."

In summing up his life with Allie, Townsend wrote, "She was a royal pal and ever strove to do more than her part of the labor. She never sat by to be waited upon." That is the highest compliment a West Texan could pay to anyone.

September 19, 2013

A THREE-ROOM flat-roofed adobe house in the sun-baked ruins of Terlingua Ghost Town is the last place in Texas that I would look for a fine letterpress printer, but that is where Lauren Stedman set up her shop and where it is flourishing today as the Menagerie Press. One room of the building is crammed with wooden type cases, their drawers full of fonts of metal type; one room has three big printing presses in it; and the third room, actually a hallway between the two bigger rooms, has a card table in it that serves as Stedman's office.

Stedman is a slim fair-skinned woman with short red hair, blue eyes, and powerful-looking arms and hands. She came to Terlingua in 2005 from Fort Bragg, on the northern coast of California. "I wanted to get out of the fog, the wet, the cold, the trees," she told me. "For 30 years I woke up every morning and looked out of the window to see if the sun was shining, and 90 percent of the time it wasn't."

Her roots, however, are in the Big Bend. Her grandfather, Fountain Moreau Miller, came to Fort Davis in the early 1900s and grew up on his uncle's apple orchard in Limpia Canyon. Stedman was born in Fort Davis but her father was in the Air Force and she spent part of her childhood in Europe and graduated from high school in the Philippines.

Stedman moved to northern California with her husband and infant son in 1969 "because that's where things were happening," she told me. "Would you have described yourselves as hippies?' I asked her. "Absolutely!" she said. She did not think of herself as an artist then, but she said she had always enjoyed working with her hands and making things. "When I was a child," she told me, "My friends would be saying, 'What shall we do?' and I would say, 'Let's make something,' and they would say, 'Whaaa?'" In the mid-80s, she went to work for her friend Zida Borcich, who was setting up the letterpress studio in Fort Bragg that later became Studio Z. Stedman was her printer's devil, the assistant who mixed the ink and fetched the type. She discovered that she loved setting type. "It's more immediate than typing," she says, "and you have to pay so much attention to detail that it's actually relaxing." She decided then that someday she would have her own letterpress. It took her 15 years to fulfill that dream.

When she arrived in Terlingua she had two big Chandler and Price platen printing presses, one made in 1900 and the other in 1925, and a more modern and compact Vandercook press. After leasing her adobe studio from Bill Ivey, she realized that she had not thought about how to get the presses, each of which weighs nearly a ton, into the building. She persuaded a friend with a bulldozer to blade a road so that she could maneuver the truck that they were loaded on up to the building and then unloaded them with what she described as "an off-road forklift" belonging to another friend. He lowered the presses one at a time onto iron-pipe rollers placed near the building's back door. A third friend who had a pickup with a winch parked his truck at the front door, ran a cable through the building and out the back door, and winched each press up a ramp and into the building, where more friends rolled them into place. Stedman says that she got her business going with "a little help from my friends, as the song says." She showed me a card she had printed up to announce the opening of her business. It had a list six inches long of people who had helped her get started.

Stedman combines old and new technology in her work. She hand-sets type on her printing presses, but she will occasionally lay out a combination of words and illustrations on her computer, send them electronically to a platemaker in Michigan who uses the pdf to produce a magnesium plate which Stedman can then lock into her press and print from. She showed me samples of her work: business cards; wedding announcements and invitations; bookplates; party invitations for the annual Green Scene party, an environmental extravaganza that used to be held annually in Terlingua. She did their invitations for two years running. The first year's was printed on pieces of beer cartons; the second year's on long strips of paper that were wrapped around empty tin cans and mailed. Her samples included the only hand-set political campaign card I have ever seen, a clean design in dark brown type with reddish-brown ornaments on tan stock done for David Fannin when he ran for the Marfa city council, and some very handsome Christmas cards. Stedman told me that several years ago she produced a set of Valentine's Day cards, "but no one in Terlingua sends Valentines," she lamented.

Some of Stedman's work is definitely fine art. She has just

printed a set of broadsides for Marfa artist Nicholas Miller, each one consisting of several lines of type in the International Phonetic alphabet centered on a sheet on creamy white paper. She sometimes makes her own paper, but says that at the moment this is just a hobby. "I'm building a house right now, but when I get through with that I may get serious about papermaking."

Stedman has a wry sense of humor. She showed me a card that she had printed up, a copy of a sample card that she had found in a case of old type that she had bought. It read, "Coupon for one free pair of space pantie's for the girl that think's her ass is out of this world." She had included the two misplaced apostrophes that were in the original. "Some of those old printers had weird senses of humor," she said, "and weird ideas about punctuation."

Stedman says that there has been a renaissance in letterpress printing in the past decade. More universities are offering courses in it; letterpress studios like hers are popping up everywhere; and there is a recognizable small press movement. She compares it to the microbrewery movement. A microbrewery is just opening in Alpine, but Lauren Stedman's Menagerie Press has been in Terlingua for seven years. We always knew Terlingua was ahead of the curve.

July 5, 2012

THE ARABIC TOMBSTONE AT EL INDIO

THERE IS A mysterious tombstone with an Arabic inscription in the El Indio cemetery between Presidio and Ruidosa. The tombstone commemorates two Lebanese peddlers, Ramon Karam and his fourteen-year old son, Salvador, who were murdered by bandits near El Indio in 1918. When I started asking about it I found that no one in Presidio or El Indio knew who placed the tombstone there, or when, and no one knew much about the Karams, either. The matter became a cause celebre in Marfa last December when Field Work Marfa artist-in-residence Emily Bovino produced a performance piece about Ramon Karam at Padre's, and a giant poster depicting the tombstone was created to decorate one of the walls there. I wrote a column about the tombstone and Bovino's performance piece, which had a lot of cockroaches in it.

Shortly afterwards I received an e-mail message from Raymond Karam, a lawyer in San Antonio. Someone had shown my column to him and he wrote, "Lonn, that was my grandfather and his oldest son, Salvador. I have a picture of the whole family taken on that fateful day when the father and the oldest son set out as peddlers." Karam's message went on to give more details about the family and ended by inviting me to call him, which I did the next day.

Raymond Karam is an ebullient-sounding man in his early 50s. He was born in McAllen, Texas, went to college at St. Mary's University in San Antonio, finished law school there, and has practiced law in San Antonio ever since. "The story that you wrote about was central to our family history," he told me. "I've known it all my life." He explained that his father was Elias Karam, Ramon Karam's next-youngest son after the murdered Salvador. "Elias wanted to go with his father and brother that day. He was 12, and he had his gun ready. His mother chased him around the wagon with a belt to make him stay home. After his father was killed, he had to be the man of the family. He looked after his mother and raised his siblings."

Karam explained that his grandfather had emigrated from Barhalioun, Lebanon, to Mexico about 1900, bringing his wife and children over from Lebanon a few years later. He set up as a peddler in Parral, Chihuahua, where his sons Salvador and Elias were born. Doroteo Arango, later known as Pancho Villa, was on his grandfather's peddler's route and in his credit books, Karam said. When the Mexican Revolution broke out in 1911 the Karams moved to Shafter, Texas, and that is where the photograph was taken that morning in 1918. Ramon Karam is the tall man in the middle of the back row, with his wife, Maria, on his right. Salvador is the boy on the far right, wrapped in a bandoller of bullets and holding a rifle. Raymond Karam's father, Elias, is between them, in short pants but also gripping a rifle.

254

Karam told me that after the murder the family moved to McAllen, Texas, at the urging of a relative there who told them that the Lower Rio Grande Valley was "just like the old country, lots of breezes and palm trees." But before they left Shafter Ramon's brother, Daniel, hunted down three of Ramon's murderers and killed all three of them, one of them in a pig sty, according to the family story. "Daniel was a giant of a man," Karam told me. Daniel was evidently something of a wild man, famous in his later years in the Lower Valley for making fortunes and then losing them in all-night card games.

In the Lower Valley, the Karam family resumed peddling and eventually opened a clothing store in McAllen. "There were about 30 Lebanese families in the area, all peddlers," Karam told me. "There was a Jewish wholesale merchant in Mission, Sam Greenfield, who supplied all of the peddlers, and he liked my grandmother. He said she had an honest face, so he helped her start the store, and my father ran it." They had a rough time at first, and they spent the Depression "living on stacks of soda crackers and cans of sardines," as Karam put it, but after World War II they began to prosper. George Karam, the little boy with the lasso in the front row of the photograph, moved to Donna, Texas, and opened his own store, Karam's Department Store, which became such a community fixture that when George retired and closed the store in 1979 the mayor of Donna declared June 23 "Karam Day" and George was honored with a parade. Elias continued to manage the McAllen store.

Prosperity enabled Grandmother Karam to do two things that she had been putting off for years. In 1950 she sent Elias, now in his mid-forties, off to Lebanon to find a wife and continue the family, and she ordered a tombstone for her husband's and Salvador's grave. A cousin, Monseigneur John Trad, long-time pastor of St. George Marionite Catholic Church in San Antonio, was involved in both enterprises. He went with Elias to the family's home town of Barhalioun in Lebanon to help him choose a wife, and he wrote out the Arabic inscription that is on the tombstone. Raymond Karam thinks that the tombstone was made in McAllen. When it was finished, Monseigneur Trad journeyed with the family from McAllen to set it in place at El Indio.

And that is how the Arabic tombstone got to El Indio, where it remains as a monument not only to two murdered peddlers but to the tenacity and endurance of an immigrant Lebanese family in Texas.

February 9, 2012

HOW RAY AND CLARICE GOT BY

SELF-PUBLISHED BOOKS, made possible by the computer and by an increasing number of companies who bind and distribute authors' works, have been a boon to grassroots historians, that is, historians who write about the lives of ordinary people. Self-published books often contain a wealth of detail about everyday life that cannot be found in ordinary sources: how peaches were put up, how horses were shod, how the wash was done in kettles. A case in point is Betty Ray Ogle Baker's *Fun and Games Through Depression and War*, published in 2009 by the author, who lives in Fort Davis. It is the story of Baker's parents' lives in the Big Bend during the 1930s and 40s, and it is a grassroots historian's dream.

Ray Ogle, cowboy, and Clarice Selman, schoolteacher, were married in Alpine in the fall of 1928. Almost exactly a year later the bottom dropped out of the stock market and the Great Depression hit. Jobs became as scarce as hen's teeth. In 1929 there was no unemployment insurance, no Social Security, no Medicare, no safety net. It was the America that Ron Paul would have us go back to. The story that Baker tells of how her parents got through the Depression is a classic.

In 1929 Ray Ogle had a good job, earning 10 dollars a day in Alpine, hauling water to construction sites for the State Highway Department, but when his mother died he had to take time off to bury her, and when he got back he found that his job had been given to someone else. Ray and Clarice used Ray's last pay check to stock up on groceries and then took their infant daughter and moved to Ray's father's farm on the Rio Grande, about three miles from Langford Hot Springs. They lived in a half-finished adobe house, where Clarice cooked in the fireplace and fed their baby milk from a borrowed cow, which they fed on Spanish dagger blossoms.

At one point Clarice learned that her stepfather, a Baptist preacher had lost his church and that her mother was literally starving. She persuaded Ray to go across the river and buy a gallon of sotol for five dollars, on credit, which she put in their car and drove to a ranch near Marathon, brazening her way through a Texas Ranger checkpoint with a baby blanket thrown over the jug of sotol. She sold the sotol to the rancher for $15 and was able to send $10 to her mother, which kept her in groceries for a month.

Eventually Ray got a job shearing sheep for a rancher who could not afford to pay a shearing crew but who had credit at a wholesale grocer in Alpine and was able to pay Ray in flour, sugar, beans, and coffee. A good shearer could shear 200 sheep a day at 10 cents a head; Ray could shear about 100 a day, so the job kept them in staple groceries for quite a while. When he finished with the sheep he was hired as a cook for the Gage Ranch's fall round-up at three dollars a day, three times an ordinary cowboy's wages. This carried them through the winter.

When their savings from the cook's job ran out, Ray heard of a deal that just might sustain them until better times came. Banks all over West Texas had foreclosed on herds of livestock and were desperate to find people to look after them. Ray agreed to take over a herd of 800 Angora goats, with the understanding that he could have the income from the hair. He and his brother Lorimer, who had a job driving a road-grader for the county, went into partnership and leased 16 sections on Nine Point Mesa. Ray and Clarice moved two 12' x 14' cabins from the Ogle farm to Nine Point Mesa, joined them with a breezeway, and built a brush arbor in front of them which they slept under. They called their new home Pluto Valley, a reference to the effects of the water in the creek that ran by their new house. There was a popular patent laxative in the 1930s called Pluto Water. It was compounded with water from a mineral spring at French Lick, Indiana and the label said, "If nature won't, Pluto will." The mineral-laden creek water on Nine Point Mesa had the same qualities.

When their nanny goats dropped their kids they had a flock of 2,000 goats to tend. They supplemented their mohair income by shooting javelinas and selling the hides for $1.00 each, and Ray continued to hunt deer all year round even though hunting was only legal six weeks out of the year. Betty Ray Baker quotes her mother as saying that, "Since we furnished their pasturage, we felt that we had a perfect right to eat them." They always referred to their illegal venison as "wild nanny" to prevent their children from inadvertently spilling the beans about it.

Ray Ogle finally worked his way out of poverty by selling horses that he bred on the ranch to the army at Fort D.A. Russell at $30 a head. He accumulated enough for a down payment on the leased land, and then when the war started he opened a construction company. He and Clarice had made it through.

Baker has one unforgettable vignette in her book. In the late 1920s, Ray Ogle's mother, Minnie Ogle, would walk from the family farm on the Rio Grande to the Langford Hot Springs post office to pick up the mail, which was delivered twice a week from Marathon. There was a piano in the post office, and Minnie Ogle would play it while the neighbors who had gathered to wait for the mail truck to arrive sang hymns with her. It must have been the most musical post office in Texas.

Betty Ray Ogle Baker is just a tad over 80. She is currently living with her daughter in Midland while recovering from injuries sustained in an automobile accident, but when she comes home in May I plan to have a long visit with her. She told me on the phone that "writing keeps me out of meanness and off the streets." She is clearly a crackerjack.

February 23, 2012

THOROUGHLY MODERN MOJELLA

MOJELLA MOORE OF Alpine is a cosmopolitan, sophisticated, and beautiful woman of 81 who lives in a 10-room, ranch style house north of town. Her living room has wall-to-wall carpeting and is furnished with comfortable easy chairs, couches, and a flat-screen television set. Her ample kitchen is equipped with an icebox, a dishwasher, and an electric stove. She is firmly planted in the 21ST century. She was wearing slacks and a chic top the day I visited with her. She is a modern woman.

But Mojella (she was named after a character in Helen Hunt Jackson's novel *Ramona*) Moore spent her childhood in the 19TH century, even though she was born in 1929. Her first home was a one-room adobe house on the O Ranch, northwest of Candelaria and below the Candelaria Rim, where her parents, Joe Bailey and Edith Rogers, raised goats. Her father added an adobe screen porch to the front of the house, with canvas flaps that could be lowered, and that porch served as a bedroom for Moore, her two broth-ers, her parents, the schoolteacher that occasionally boarded with them, and "whatever strays came along," she said. The other room was furnished with a wood cook stove, a table and some chairs, and some cabinets. There was no electricity. A fireplace provided heat and kerosene lamps gave light after dark. Moore told me that once, during the Depression, her family went for a year without going into town. She said during that time she asked her mother if they were poor and her mother said, "No, we're not poor at all. We just don't have any money."

However, they had goats, which were kept "under herd," meaning that goat herders with dogs tended the goats from camps on the ranch. The herders were usually from Mexico, and would spend six months or so in their camp and then go home for a month, to be replaced by a friend or relative. The goats were Angoras. They were hair goats, not meat goats, and were raised for their fleece. "As far as I know we never ate a goat," Moore told me. The goats were driven to the ranch corral and sheared twice a year by a traveling gang of shearers, and that was about the only out-of-the-ordinary event in the young Mojella Moore's life. "It was an occasion I really looked forward to," she told me. The half-dozen shearers, their boss, a cook, and a swamper—a man-of-all-work—brought a gasoline-powered shearing machine, to which mechanical clippers were hooked up. It took about 10 minutes to shear each goat, and the shearers were paid by the goat. Moore recalled that the boss handed each man a lead token when he had sheared a goat, and the tokens were redeemed for cash when the shearing was finished. There was work for Moore and her brothers, too; they combed the burrs out of the goats' fleece before the shearers got to them.

Moore's family eventually moved from the O Ranch to the nearby Dow Ranch, and she remembers riding horseback to drive herds of goats up the Candelaria Rim to the Brite Ranch, where they were loaded into trucks. She told me that she rode horseback as a baby, sitting on the saddle in front of her mother, and by the time she was five she could ride by herself. "I learned to ride on a horse named Dunny," she said. "Dunny taught several aunts and uncles and my brothers to ride, and he taught me, too."

In 1948 Moore married Ed Moore, who was a river rider for the Department of Agriculture, trying to prevent Mexican cattle infected with hoof-and-mouth disease from crossing the Rio Grande into Texas. The river riders worked in pairs, each man patrolling an 11-mile stretch of river each day. One went upstream from their camp, one went downstream, and the next day they switched. The Moores' first married home was a tent at Porvenir, up the river from Candelaria. "It was a government tent," Moore said, "but it was better than the adobe house the other rider lived in."

Ed and Mojella Moore eventually built a store on the Juan Prieto Ranch between Candelaria and Ruidosa, and Mojella ran the store. "We sold everything—groceries, candy, clothes, everything," she told me. "90 percent of our customers came from across the river. We had a beer joint in the back room—that was a prerequisite in those days—and that was where the river riders gathered." There was no electricity at the store, but they kept the beer cold in a butane refrigerator.

The Moores bought candelilla wax at the store. Because the Mexican government had a monopoly on the purchase of the wax in Mexico and set an artificially low price on it, much of the wax gathered in Chihuahua was smuggled across the river and sold on the American side. "Many a time I took a bobtail truck down the river to meet my wax men," Moore told me. "I would take the wax to the U.S. Customs station at Presidio to declare it and then go to the bank in Ojinaga to get pesos to pay the wax men. They would lay out in the brush on the Texas side until I got back." The bank in Ojinaga, she recalled, was a one-room affair with a counter across the middle, entered through an unmarked door in a wall near the plaza.

While Moore was running the store, her widowed mother managed Kingston Hot Springs, now Chinati Hot Springs. There was no electricity there, either. Visitors paid 25 cents for a bath in the springs, and they could rent a cabin for $10 a week. The cabins were furnished with kerosene stoves.

In 1956 Moore moved completely into the 20TH century. She and her husband opened a feed store in Alpine, Moore's General Store, and she worked behind the counter while her husband hauled cattle in an International semi-trailer truck with removable sides. She recalled that the local ranchers all gathered in the coffee shop at the Holland Hotel at 5:00 AM and that was where cattle deals, including hauling contracts, were made. If you weren't there you just missed out. The Moores closed the feed store in 1981 and opened a self-storage business, which Mojella Moore, now a widow, still manages. She is a thoroughly modern lady.

January 13, 2011

APACHE ADAMS, THE COWBOY OF LAST RESORT

APACHE ADAMS IS not a typical Big Bend cowboy but he is the quintessential Big Bend Cowboy, having an excess of the qualities that turn a good cowboy into a superlative one. He is a fine horseman, a superb roper, and he has no back-down, to use his own phrase (which he employs about someone else, not himself). He has broken fingers, arms, legs, a collarbone, a hip, and a pelvis trying to get a job done, and has worked with those bones broken until he accomplished what he set out to do, whether it was roping a bull or trying to get a trailer off high center. Adams is a man who is completely devoid of quitting sense. As Don Cadden, who has just written a book about Adams called *Tied Hard and Fast: Apache Adams, Big Bend Cowboy* (Denver: Outskirts Press, 2011), told me, "People say Apache's done crazy things but when all else fails they call him."

Don Cadden's book about Adams should be required reading for any young person who thinks they might want to be a cowboy. There is no romance in it, but there is a lot of hard and danger-ous work. The book could have been titled *Wrecks I Have Been*

In, because many of Adam's stories end in situations that either involve personal injury or miss it by a lasso's breadth. But some of them are hilarious. Here is a sample: Adams is working cattle with his son and a friend. The friend is using Adams's good saddle. The friend ropes a big bull, but he has forgotten to tighten the saddle's cinch and so when his horse puts on the brakes he and the saddle go right over the horses's head, "like you'd squirt a seed out of a prune," Adams says. The friend has tied his lasso hard and fast to the saddle horn, so Adams's good saddle is now bouncing along behind the bull. Adams tries to rope the bull, but every time he gets close enough to throw, the saddle bounces up and his horse shies off. Finally he gives up on the bull and ropes the saddle, so now he has the bull on two ropes with the saddle in between. His son gets another rope on the bull, but then his cinch breaks, and he and his saddle part company with his horse. Adams now has the bull, three ropes, and two saddles flopping around him. You have to buy the book to find out what happens next.

Adams was born in 1937. His parents named him Ernest Paul, but his abundant coal-black hair earned him the nickname "Apache" as a child. Apache fits in with the other somewhat peculiar Adams family names. Apache's father was Ulice Adams, and he had an uncle named Elba and a great-uncle named Harmon. All three were ranching in the Big Bend when Apache was born. He was on a horse before he could walk, and he grew up speaking Spanish as well as English. He was definitely a child of the border. Over the years he became not only a well-respected cowboy but a well-known raconteur. He polished an inherent talent for storytelling by performing at the Alpine Cowboy Poetry Gathering.

Several years ago Adams was doing some cow work for Jeff

Fort on Fort's Pinto Canyon Ranch, and Fort's wife, Marion Barthelme, gave him a tape recorder and asked him to tell his stories into it as he was driving around. She turned the tapes over to Don Cadden, and, with Adams's help, Cadden organized the material on the recordings into a book in Adams's voice. One of the best parts of the narrative is Adams's western idiom. He speaks of a corpse as being "graveyard dead." Nervous cattle are "trotty." Horses that clamp down on the bit and fail to respond to it are "cold jawing." Bulls that are "brushed up" are not especially well-groomed but are hiding in the brush. Cadden has footnoted some of these terms for Eastern readers.

Adams makes a specialty of finding cattle that are brushed up. When a ranch has been sold or the lease is up and the rancher needs to move his herd elsewhere, he will hold a roundup or two and even scour the place with a helicopter, but there will always be a few wild cows that will hide out in the brush, and that is where Adams comes in. He is the cowboy of last resort. He will bring a couple of his men in and they will clear the place out. A number of the stories in Cadden's book revolve around these cow hunts. On one occasion he was called to the 02 Ranch to find what the lessee thought were about 30 cows, which Adams agreed to gather on halves, meaning that he got to keep half of the cattle he found. When he and his men were through they had 178 cows and bulls roped and tied. Some of them had never seen a human being. Cadden says that Adams is so good at this because he is an expert tracker and "he'll rope anything."

Don Cadden is the ideal person to translate Adams's taped narratives into print. He told me that he literally had to get inside of Adams in order to do it, but he has known and worked with

Adams for 21 years and has a way with words himself, as he is a published poet and songwriter. Cadden grew up in a rural suburb of Austin, but he fell in love with the Big Bend and cowboy life when he got a summer job as a brakeman on the Southern Pacific, working the run between Sanderson and Valentine. An Austin friend then helped him get hired for a roundup on the D Ranch in the Guadalupe Mountains one spring. "I knew enough to tell the men I was working with that I didn't know anything, and they helped me along," Cadden told me. Then, he said, he met Apache Adams at an Alpine Cowboy Poetry Gathering. He asked Adams if he could work with him, and Adams took him along on a cow hunt. "It was like going from elementary school to college in one day," Cadden told me. The two men became fast friends, and this fine book is the result of that friendship.

July 14, 2011

FEDERICO VILLALBA IN THE BIG BEND

WE ALL LEARNED from our school text-books that American history began on the Atlantic coast with the settlement of Jamestown and Plymouth and swept westward across the continent as Anglo-American pioneers in covered wagons fulfilled the nation's Manifest Destiny to stretch its boundaries from sea to shining sea. Those of us who grew up in the Southwest knew from childhood that there was something wrong with this story because there was physical evidence of an earlier Spanish presence all around us: the missions in California and Texas, the plaza and the Governor's Palace in Santa Fe, the presidios in Arizona, all built long before Anglo-Americans arrived in these places.

These buildings are part of the legacy of the Spanish push from Mexico into *el norte*, the northern frontier of New Spain, as the Spanish called Mexico. While the Anglo-American western frontier lasted only about 150 years, from say 1740 to 1890, the Spanish and their descendants in Mexico pushed their northern frontier forward for nearly 300 years, from Juan de Oñate's settlement of New Mexico in 1598 down through the 1880s, when ranchers from Chihuahua crossed the Rio Grande and established themselves in the Big Bend. Oñate started it all; his colony's thousand-mile trek from Zacatecas to Santa Fe is one of the great epics of American history. It was immortalized by the poet Gaspar Pérez de Villagrá, who accompanied Oñate to New Mexico and wrote a 34-canto poem, *Historia de la Nuevo Mexico*, describing his fellow-colonists' exploits. The poem has been translated into English several times and is well-known to Southwestern history buffs; later documents describing the Spanish settlement of *el norte* remain the exclusive province of scholars, which is a shame.

But now a book has appeared which is a neat chronological bookend to Villagrá. Juan Manuel Casas's *Federico Villalba's Texas: A Mexican Pioneer's Life in the Big Bend*, published last month by the Iron Mountain Press in Houston, is a collection of family stories about one of the last pioneers of *el norte*, Federico Villalba. Villalba was a native of Aldama, Chihuahua, who as a young man was drawn north by the offer of a land grant on the Apache frontier by the Mexican government. In 1882 he established a small ranch at San Carlos, on the south bank of the Rio Grande. A few years later he joined several other San Carlos ranchers in moving their herds across the river and laying claim to grazing land that is now within the boundaries of Big Bend National Park. Villalba's ranch prospered. He opened the store that is now the Study Butte store and acquired a part interest in several cinnabar mines. In 1889 he married Maria Cortez of Fort Davis; they had six children together. Federico Villalba lived and ranched in the Big Bend until his death at the age of 75 in 1933.

There would be nothing exceptional about Villalba's life

except his status as a pioneer were it not for two tragedies that were the direct result of the clash between the northward-moving *el norte* frontier and the westward-moving Anglo-American frontier. In 1923 Villalba's son Jorge shot and killed the brothers Jack and Winslow Coffman, who had come to his house drunk, shouted racial epithets, fired pistols at him, and threatened to kill him. Jorge was indicted for murder in Alpine, was ably defended by attorney Charles E. Mead, and was acquitted, but the legal fees cost his father his beloved Las Barras ranch. In 1931 another Villalba son, Jacobo, was murdered, probably by an Anglo named Det Walker, with whom Jacobo had quarreled repeatedly over the years. Casas's retelling of these two incidents, which he places in the larger context of conflict between Anglo and Mexican residents of the Big Bend during the years of the Mexican Revolution, take up about a third of the book.

There is absolutely no question that this conflict was real and that it is well-documented. Historian Kenneth Ragsdale, in his *Big Bend Country* (Texas A&M University Press, 1998), put it up front. "Traditionally," he wrote, "one of the distinguishing features of the Big Bend country has been its divided society.... Some of the region's less responsible citizens found in Anglo ethnocentrism the license to dominate and sometimes abuse the less fortunate, specifically the Mexicans." The story that Casas tells about the Villalbas bears this out.

It is important to realize that Casas's book is not history, nor is it intended to be. Casas is a great-grandson of Federico Villalba, and *Federico Villalba's Texas* is a collection of family tales, originally compiled to satisfy Casas's mother's desire to see something about her grandfather's experiences as a Big Bend pioneer in print.

Casas, who is a retired para-legal and social worker, told me that, where possible, he had checked the stories against courthouse records and other archival and published sources, but he has also invented dialogue and offered conjecture where sources could not be found. The result is what folklorist Mody Boatright called a family saga, "a cluster of lore, transmitted and modified by oral transmission, which is believed to be true." This does not mean that it is any less valuable than footnoted history based entirely on documents, nor perhaps any less true. It is just different, and it cannot be judged by the standards of historians. Casas is a lively writer, and he entwines the story of the Villalba family with references to other Big Bend characters and topics—Sheriff Everett Townsend, sotol smuggling, Robert Cartledge, the Terlingua school, Candelario and Pablo Baiz, Howard Perry and the Chisos Mining Company. What is important is that he tells these tales from a different point of view than that of most of the Anglo-Americans who have recorded them. It is enlightening, for instance, to know that most of the Mexicans in the Big Bend regarded Everett Townsend as a thoroughly fair and honest man, and that Howard Perry, in a play on his last name, was known to them as *el perro*—the dog.

Reading Casas's book is like listening to old men telling stories by the stove on a winter day, and, like listening to old men, it is well worth doing.

August 14, 2008

DOWN ALAMITO CREEK WITH ARMANDO VASQUEZ

 IF THE TEXAS Historical Commission gave out medallions for historic significance to people as well as buildings they would surely present one to Armando Vasquez. Vasquez, a tall, sinewy man of 85 with silver hair, a beautiful smile, and a measured, courtly manner, has lived in Marfa for 60 years, but he was born in Casa Piedra, south of Marfa on Alamito Creek, and he makes weekly trips to the family ranch there just to keep things in order. Over the years, he has absorbed the landscape and the folklore of the Alamito Creek Valley until it has become as much a part of him as his heart or his liver. His knowledge of the land and people along that creek goes back to his grandfather's time and beyond.

Vasquez's grandfather was Natividad Vasquez, who settled at Casa Piedra in 1889; his great-grandfather was William Russell, a Kentuckian who came to Ojinaga before the Civil War and married into the Rodriguez family there. Armando Vasquez is part of an extended network of intermarried Presidio and Alamito Creek families that include the Herreras, the Russells, the Hernandezes, the Kleinmans, the Rodriguezes, and the Nietos, an extraordinary group with roots that stretch back into the American South, Austria-Hungary, and Mexico. Vasquez is the repository of tales from all of these relatives.

I recently made a hot, dusty trip down the Casa Piedra road to Presidio with Vasquez, stopping at various points along the way so that he could show me his personal landmarks, each of which triggered a story. Our first stop was at Perdiz Creek, which Vasquez told me in his childhood was known to local people as Jap Camp Creek because a rancher named Jasper Bishop, nicknamed Jap, had a hunting camp on it. Bishop, Vasquez said, was a bachelor who loved to hunt and loved children. He was killed when he was in his mid-50's; he was climbing a windmill when a rung in the ladder broke and he fell 30 feet to the ground.

A few miles further south we stopped at Matanoso Creek, which Vasquez explained was named after the clumps of feathery grass that grew along its banks, *mata* in Spanish. Nearby, Vasquez said, there was once a spring that was a stopping place for travelers on the old road to Chihuahua. It was called Pielagos Spring. *Pielago* is the Spanish word for the open sea, the deepest part of the ocean. It was a very abundant spring.

At Plata, where the pavement ends, we stopped to look at the ruins of John G. Davis's adobe ranch house, now protected from the weather by a metal canopy. Davis was a North Carolinian who settled on Alamito Creek about 1870 and married a sister of Vasquez's maternal grandfather Carlos Herrera. His ranch, which he called Alamito, was fortified against attack by the Apaches. Vasquez told me how, after Davis's wife died in 1894, when Davis was nearly 70, he sold the ranch, moved back to North Carolina and married the widow who had been his childhood sweetheart. Vasquez said that a cousin had told him that the name Plata, which is Spanish for silver, was given to the place after some workmen building the roadbed for the Kansas City, Mexico, and Orient Railroad in 1930 dug up a cache of silver bars there (a less romantic explanation is that Plata was the shipping point for the silver mine at Shafter).

A few miles south of Plata, we pulled over again so Vasquez could tell me about a spring west of the road called Ojos del Alcaria. It was there, he said, that a ranch cook named Rodriguez had set up his chuck wagon during a roundup about 1900. One of the cowboys came in early for lunch and asked Rodriguez for one of the hot biscuits he had just laid out. "No," Rodriguez said, "everyone eats at the same time." The man took a biscuit anyway, and Rodriguez shot him. "A man killed over a biscuit," Vasquez mused. He went on to say that Rodriguez had two sons who had ended up on the losing side after one of the battles of Ojinaga during the Mexican revolution. "They were both dragged to death behind horses in Ojinaga," Vasquez said, suggesting just retribution for the cowboy's death.

After a stop at Casa Piedra to unload some sacks of feed into Vasquez's barn, we pushed on over the dirt road, now winding up out of the creek bottom and over some bare hills, toward Presidio. At the top of a ridge we pulled off the road, dust swirling up around us, so that Vasquez could show me a grove of cottonwoods on Alamito Creek that he said marked the location of the Alamo Ranch. That was where, he said, a man named Victoriano Hernandez built a fortified adobe ranch house about 1870. According to Vasquez, Hernandez became a wealthy man, and a group of nine bandits decided to raid his ranch and carry off his silver. They picked a time when they thought that Hernandez and his men were all away from home and they charged the house on horseback, firing pistols. The women and children all gathered in corners of the rooms but one of Hernandez's grandsons, a 12-year old boy named Oscar Duke, passed in front of a window and was hit by a bullet and killed. One old man who had been left behind at the ranch routed the bandits with a flintlock musket by shooting one of them in the wrist. When Hernandez returned to the ranch he tracked the bandits to Mexico and killed all but one of them.

When we got to Presidio, Vasquez and I went to the new Las Palapas restaurant for a delicious catfish lunch with two of his cousins. Sitting at a formica table in that gleaming air-conditioned restaurant, I felt that I had suddenly emerged into the 21st century. The stories that Armando Vasquez had told me belong to the 19th century, but they are as much a part of the landscape to him as the creeks and mesas that they are associated with. Thank you, Armando, for taking me back in time for a few hours. And thank you for the lunch, too.

July 1, 2010

THE BRIDGE AT CANDELARIA

CANDELARIA, TEXAS IS literally at the end of the road. It is 48 miles northwest of Presidio, where the pavement of FM 170 ends. In 2010 it had a population of 75. I was down there last month, visiting with Rosa Madrid and her son Reynaldo Pantoja. Rosa is a retired schoolteacher. She was born in Mexico, in the town of San Antonio del Bravo, which is directly across the Rio Grande from Candelaria, but she was brought across the river when she was an infant and grew up in Candelaria. "The seed came from San Antonio del Bravo but the tree was planted here and here is where my roots are," she told me as we talked at her kitchen table. Her life is a metaphor for the two towns. They are separated by an international border but linked by kinship, language, and common interest.

Rosa's house, a commodious bright yellow adobe, is directly across the street from a compound that houses several large adobe buildings and a corrugated metal cotton gin, abandoned for many years ("I am 65 years old and I have never seen cotton here," Rosa told me). But in 1920, when there were 500 people living in Candelaria, that compound was the home of the Kilpatrick family, who owned Candelaria. James (J.J.) and his sons Dawkins Darwin

(D.D.) and James Judson, Jr. (J.J., Jr.) owned 800 acres of irrigated cotton land along the river and the cotton gin; his daughter, Mary Kilpatrick Howard, ran a mercantile store that was part of the compound. During the border troubles of 1911–1920 a detachment of the 8TH Cavalry was encamped on the hill behind the store. Reynaldo Pantoja took me to a point in the cemetery where we could look down on that hill and pointed out the stone cistern built by the troops and the concrete slab floors of the buildings they had occupied. But the Kilpatricks did not trust the army; they kept their own .30 caliber machine gun mounted on the roof of the store to discourage bandit raids from across the river

By the early 1980s the troops and the machine gun were gone, the cotton gin was defunct, and the population had shrunk to fewer than 100, but the store was still there, run by Mary Howard's two daughters, Marian Walker and Frances Howard. The store drew the two towns across the river from each other together. "It was the only store within 50 miles," Johnnie Chambers, who was teaching in the two-room school in Candelaria then, told me. People from San Antonio del Bravo, many of whom had relatives in Candelaria, waded across the Rio Grande to do their shopping.

No one remembers exactly when the footbridge across the Rio Grande connecting the two towns was built, or how many people were involved in building it. Johnnie Chambers thinks it was in the late 1970s, and that the builders were a group of young men who were her former students. Rosa Madrid remembers that two brothers, Cruz and Sixto Flores, were among the builders. I tracked Sixto Flores down in Odessa, where, at 60, he still works as a welder in the oil fields, and he said that he and his brother and some friends built it in 1982 or '83 because "families needed to come to the store." Flores himself was born in San Antonio del Bravo but was living in Candelaria when he built the bridge. It was a suspension bridge, with a plank floor about two feet wide. The piers that supported it were fashioned from old automobile bodies. But it was technically an international bridge, and since no one went through the rigmarole that is required to build an international bridge, it was totally illegal.

The bridge had unintended consequences. Families in San Antonio del Bravo used it to do their shopping, but families in Candelaria used it to visit the Mexican government health care clinic in San Antonio. "We could visit the doctor there free," Rosa Madrid said, "and we could get free medicine." She also said that people in San Antonio crossed on it to use telephones in Candelaria, and that it became a bridge between generations: elderly people in San Antonio used it to visit children and grandchildren in Candelaria. Johnnie Chambers said children in San Antonio used it to attend school in Candelaria.

At first the customs and immigration authorities in Presidio ignored it; it was one of a hundred places along the river where people crossed back and forth informally every day. But after 9/11 the bridge was suddenly seen as a national security threat. "The Border Patrol came here and said terrorists might use it. They told us not to use it. They said we could cross to Mexico but could not come back." Reynaldo Pantoja said, "but people kept on crossing when they were not around. Then they came and tore out the boards on the American side, but people crossed by walking on the stringers. People needed it."

Finally, on July 8, 2008, a small army of Border Patrol agents arrived in Candelaria in trucks and dismantled the bridge, with the help of Mexican Federal Police agents working from the other side of the river. The Border Patrol agents loaded the pieces into their trucks and hauled them to Marfa, where they can still be seen in the back parking lot of the border patrol headquarters. And in Candelaria and San Antonio del Bravo people still cross the river every day, but now they wade across.

The fact is that the border is not a line down the center of the Rio Grande but a zone that extends about 100 miles on each side of the river, a country that is neither Texas nor Mexico and is inhabited by people with a common history, a common language, and common family relationships. If the incoming presidential administration is determined to build a wall between our two countries, perhaps they should build it along Interstate 10. There are places there where it might even improve the view to the south.

January 12, 2017

ACKNOWLEDGMENTS

So many people have helped in the making of this book that I am reluctant to thank anyone by name for fear of leaving someone unnamed. I owe a very special debt to Gene and Aurie West, May Quick, Armando Vasquez, and Mike O'Connor of Marfa; Ted Gray and Liz Rogers of Alpine; and Wid McCutcheon of Fort Davis for introducing me to the Big Bend and patiently answering my questions about the country and its people over the years. Melleta Bell and Lisa Zakharova of the Archives of the Big Bend at Sul Ross State University have been unfailingly helpful in locating documents and photographs for me. I am grateful to Avram Dumitrescu of Alpine not only for his marvelous drawings which illustrate each chapter but for his cheerful friendship.

Avram and I would both like to thank the people who provided access to the objects and places in the drawings: Matt Walter at the Museum of the Big Bend, Gary Dunshee at Big Bend Saddlery, Burt Compton at Marfa Gliders, Adam Bork at Food Shark, Daniel Chamberlin at Ballroom Marfa, Bill Manhart at Fort Davis National Historic Site, Zack Baughman at the Experimental Aircraft Association Aviation Museum, Sara Melancon Bingham at Marfa Public Radio, Andy Cloud at the Center for Big Bend Studies, Vanya Scott at the Denver Police Museum, Lisa Zakharova at the Archives of the Big Bend, Raymond Skiles at Big Bend National Park, Lauren Stedman at Menagerie Press, Karen Little and Tony Snyder at Sul Ross State University, Camp Bosworth and Buck Johnston, Lisa Copeland, Megan Wilde, Tony Cano, Howdy Fowler, Nicholas Westerlink, Scott Hawkins and Mette Carlsen, Carlos Nieto, Emily Verla Bovino, Raymond Karam, Petei Guth, and Don Cadden.

Finally, I would like to thank Robert and Rosario Halpern, publishers of the Big Bend Sentinel, in whose pages the "Rambling Boy" columns on which most of these essays are based have appeared, for their constant encouragement and friendship; Tim Johnson of the Marfa Book Company, who agreed with me that the time had come for a book about the real Marfa and then made it happen; Kyle Schlesinger of Cuneiform Press, whose talent as a designer created a beautiful book; and my wife, Dedie, for her love and support, her tolerance of my writing habits, and her superb editorial skills.

NOTES

P. 18. Carne asada burritos are flour tortillas wrapped around chunks of grilled beef, *carne asada* in Spanish. Calf ropings are timed contests in which two mounted cowboys attempt to rope and tie a calf. One roper, called the header, throws his lariat at the calf's head; the other, called the heeler, aims for the calf's hind feet. Seven seconds is considered an excellent time.

P. 22. Mutualista societies were community-based mutual aid societies created by immigrants from Mexico in the United States in the late 19TH and early 20TH centuries. They provided cultural activities, educational programs, medical and burial insurance, loans, and legal aid for their members. The Marfa Sociedad Mutualista was organized in 1922. It is no longer active.

The Marfa Violeta Club was a Hispanic women's organization founded in 1939. The Violetas met monthly and took annual train trips to places such as El Paso and Carlsbad, New Mexico. In 1940 the group had 27 members.

The League of United Latin American Citizens (LULAC) is a political advocacy group founded in Corpus Christi, Texas in 1929 to resist discrimination against Hispanics in the United States. A Marfa chapter was organized in 1932 with E. Segura as president. LULAC is still in existence, with 115,000 members across the United States, but there is no longer a Marfa chapter.

P. 26. Lucas Charles Brite II (1860–1941) was a pioneer Presidio County rancher who trailed a small herd of cattle from Frio County, Texas to Capote Peak, south of Marfa, in 1885. He built up a 125,000 acre ranch south and west of Marfa, was one of the organizers of the Highland Hereford Breeders Association, and was the town's most prominent citizen in the 1920s and 30s.

P. 27. The Russells, Leatons, Favers, Burgesses, Spencers, and Landrums are all Presidio County families descended from Anglos who came here in the late 1840s and early 1850s and married Hispanic women. Their children were raised as Roman Catholics and generally married into Hispanic Roman Catholic families. By the third generation the descendants considered themselves Hispanic. In some cases, the original Anglo settlers became Hispanicized. Milton Faver, a Virginian who married Francisca Ramirez and settled in the Chinati Mountains in 1857, had to employ an interpreter when his sister came from Kansas to visit him in the 1880s. He had forgotten how to speak English.

P. 32. *Narcotraficantes.* Drug smugglers.

P. 108. "The clop of horses' hooves." Actually, horses briefly returned to Fort D.A. Russell during World War II. During the winter of 1943–1944 elements of the 124TH cavalry, a mounted federalized Texas National Guard unit, were stationed at Fort D.A. Russell before being shipped to Burma, where they became part of the mule-mounted Mars Task Force.

P. 113. "separate elementary schools for Mexican-Americans." In 1942–1943 122 districts in 59 Texas counties operated segregated schools for Mexican-American children.

P. 132. "a Spanish verb that cannot be translated in a family newspaper." The verb is *chingar,* and it is the equivalent of the four-letter English word that means to have sexual intercourse.

P. 137. The names of the mules may be translated as follows: La Zorrera, the slow or lagging one; La Naranja, the orange one; La Maja, the dunce; La Sota, the knave, as in a deck of cards; La Nica, probably a nickname for Veronica; La Pola, a nickname for Apolinaria; La Nene, the little girl; La Tane, probably a nickname for gitana, gypsy; El Zarco, the blue-eyed one; La Concha, a nickname for Concepción; El Tórtolo, the turtledove; El Venado, the deer; El Negro, the black one; La Palomina, the beige or cream-colored one.

P.141. *Norteamericano* is the word used in Mexico to refer to people from the United States, even though Mexico is in North America.

P. 198. Sotol is a plant native to southwest Texas and Mexico, a member of the agave family. It produces a long stalk which can be used as roofing material. Its juice can be distilled into an alcoholic beverage, also known as sotol.

P. 202. An *alcalde* is a Mexican municipal official roughly equivalent to a mayor but with some judicial powers.

P. 208. *Rasquachismo,* from *rasquache,* a word that in Mexico originally meant lower-class or impoverished. The Chicano art movement adopted the term and gave it a new meaning. *Rasquachismo* is an attitude that encompasses adaptation, makeshift solutions, and the re-use of objects and materials.